MY
HUSBAND'S
MISTRESS

BOOKS BY WILLOW ROSE

MY HUSBAND'S MISTRESS

WILLOW ROSE

bookouture

Published by Bookouture in 2025

An imprint of Storyfire Ltd.
Carmelite House
50 Victoria Embankment
London EC4Y 0DZ

www.bookouture.com

The authorised representative in the EEA is Hachette Ireland
8 Castlecourt Centre
Dublin 15 D15 XTP3
Ireland
(email: info@hbgi.ie)

ISBN: 978-1-83618-598-7
eBook ISBN: 978-1-83618-599-4

PROLOGUE

The nicotine tugs at my conscience like a naughty secret, the smoke curling up into the darkness. I shouldn't be here, shrouded in shadows with this cigarette between my fingers, its ember glowing like a warning light. Bradley thinks I've quit. He's wrong about a lot of things.

I take another drag, welcoming the familiar burn in my lungs. As a detective I'm the biggest hypocrite of them all. I'm supposed to keep everyone safe, yet here I am puffing away on a cigarette like it's not going to kill me one day. I wonder if anyone at St. Augustine PD knows about this secret habit of mine. Has anyone seen me sneaking off behind the maple tree by the fire escape? Spotted the smell I cover with jasmine perfume? I've only just been promoted, and I'm pretty sure I'm respected by my colleagues—that they all believe I deserve it after ten years of hard work. It makes me feel like a fraud every time I light up.

I'm gunning for a promotion to senior detective, which means there's even more pressure to maintain a spotless image. As one of the few female detectives around, I'm determined not to give anyone the slightest reason to doubt or criticize me. Yet here I am, a lit cigarette dangling between my fingers. I chuckle wryly to myself—so much for breaking the mold. I guess now that I'm a detective, I fit right in with the classic chain-smoking, hard-boiled cop stereotype.

A car pulls up beside the restaurant.

I take a deep breath.

There he is—Bradley—stepping out of his sleek black Mercedes, straightening his tie as if he's about to charm the judge and jury. He's got that look, you know? Like he owns every inch of the sidewalk. His hair is immaculate, that dark shade I used to run my fingers through before we became a cliché.

He flashes that million-dollar smile, and even from this distance, I feel it—a flutter, a stupid, stubborn little skip of my heart. Damn him for still having that effect after all this time, after everything. But then, Bradley has always been good with illusions, making you see what he wants you to see—a perfect reflection in a stained mirror. We've been together eleven years now, I should know.

He pushes open the café door. The bell above chimes his arrival like a herald announcing royalty. That's Bradley for you, always center stage, even in the mundane act of stepping into a café. He scans the room, his piercing blue eyes sweeping over the clientele like he's searching for someone.

"Who are you looking for, Brad?" My grip tightens on the cigarette, my nails digging into the filter. I should put it out, stomp on it, bury it under my heel like the lies I've stomped out over the years.

This isn't just a casual coffee run; I can tell by the way he holds himself, the anticipation in his step. There's more at stake here than caffeine. I saw the text on his phone this morning while he was in the shower. Now I wait to see who this mystery person is.

The French café's enchanting façade taunts me with its alluring twinkle of lights, reminiscent of a picture-perfect

Parisian setting. The windows are adorned with intricate wrought-iron designs and colorful flower boxes, while the aroma of freshly baked croissants and coffee wafts through the air. I can almost feel the bustling energy inside, as if the entire city were contained within those walls. My heart aches with longing for what could have been as Bradley is enveloped in the warmth and charm of the host.

I'm on the outside peering in, like some dime-store detective from one of those old black and white films. Except this is my life unraveling before my eyes. I fix my gaze on the woman seated alone at a table by the window, her silhouette outlined against the soft glow of the interior lights. I haven't worn a figure-hugging black dress like that in years. Her dark hair flows over her shoulders, much thicker and lusher than my own, in need of a cut.

I lean closer to the glass, my forehead nearly touching the surface as Bradley strides toward her. There's no hesitation, no flicker of doubt—it's as if he's done this a thousand times. For all I know, he has.

"Why are you doing this, Bradley?"

He reaches out, his hand landing on the woman's arm with such familiarity it sends a shock through me.

I let out a long, slow breath.

Time slows, narrows to this one moment. His lips meet hers, and I can almost hear the click of pieces falling into place—a puzzle I never wanted to complete. Missed calls. Late nights. Moments he avoided looking at me. Bradley and this woman kiss with a hunger I can't compete with.

The cigarette between my fingers is a small anchor to reality, its warmth contrasting sharply with the sudden chill wrapping around me. I notice how my hand trembles, a leaf in an unforgiving wind, and I clench tighter, the filter bending beneath the pressure.

"Damn you, Bradley." The anger curls within me like

smoke from a fire about to rage out of control. He's always been a man of appetites, but I fooled myself into thinking I was the only one who could satisfy his hunger.

The click of my heels on the cobblestones punctuates my departure, but I can hardly hear the sharp noise above my own racing thoughts, which I know I have to push aside. I can't afford to be lost in them—not now. There's a clarity in movement, a momentum I need to keep if I'm going to make it through tonight without shattering.

I don't look back at the café window. I always knew deep down that Bradley had secrets, but the weight of seeing them unfold is something else entirely.

"Just keep moving, Darcey," I command myself. It's a refrain that has gotten me through countless crime scenes, through nights when the darkness felt too thick to penetrate. Tonight, it's a lifeline I cling to as I move farther from the lie of us. Knowing I will have to return home and figure out what we do next. I wish I could just leave him. But there's children involved, and that complicates things.

I reassure myself everything happens for a reason.

ONE YEAR LATER

ONE

DARCEY

My footsteps echo against the gravel as I approach the grand estate. The yellow crime scene tape flutters lazily in the gentle afternoon breeze, standing out against the immaculate white picket fence that encircles the property like a defensive shield. The mansion towers before me as a testament to lavish wealth and opulence. Its high walls obscure any glimpse of what lies inside. The windows are covered with heavy curtains, effectively concealing the interior from prying eyes. The gardens are immaculately manicured, bursting with extravagant flowers and perfectly trimmed hedges. Neighboring houses seem miles away behind tall trees, and luxurious cars line the driveway. The mansion is like a fortress, untouchable and mysterious.

"Detective White." A uniformed officer nods as I duck under the tape.

"Afternoon." I barely throw him a glance. I'm too busy taking in the house. Very rich people live here. It stands in contrast to the home I just left. There are very few people with homes this large in Florida.

"Victim is Edward Kane, forty-five years old," the officer

rattles off as we step through the grand front door. "He's a well-known businessman."

"Show me," I command.

As we walk toward a sweeping staircase, Officer Denton tells me there are seventeen rooms in the house. All of them have been searched including the library, guest room, family room, kitchen and four separate bathrooms. I've never spent time in a house so impressive. Most of my cases involve normal working-class folks in Florida. Domestic disputes, suspected burglaries. This is my first murder as detective in charge.

"Detective?" He's looking at me, waiting for me to follow him to the master bedroom.

"Right." I focus on the job. My job. To find justice, no matter how big the house or the bank account. There will be parents who have just lost a son. There could be grieving children, loved ones who will need to find the strength to identify a body, plan a funeral and say goodbye.

I stride down the hallway, my gaze fixed on the closed door at the end. The walls are a gallery of opulence; paintings in gilt frames that I'm sure cost more than my annual salary smirk down at me. Each step on the plush carpet feels like treading on a cloud, or maybe it's just the air of superiority this place reeks of. Wealth whispers from every corner—priceless vases, sculptures that seem to move with an almost lifelike grace, and furniture that looks too immaculate to ever have been touched.

"Can you believe this place?"

I reach for the ornate doorknob, its cool metal intricate with designs that someone probably agonized over. A waste, if you ask me. Twisting it, I push open the door into the scent of old money and fresh blood. It's a dizzying combination.

The room is beautiful—the king-sized bed boasts a headboard carved with scenes that belong in a museum. The sheets look like silk. On the walls, masterpieces are spaced with deliberate precision, each light fixture positioned to worship them.

My attention snaps back to the immediate reality as I see him—Edward Kane—or what's left of him. His lifeless body sprawls on the floor, his skin pale against the darkening crimson pool that's seeping into the fibers of what I assume is a Persian rug.

"Blunt force trauma to the back of the head," I say aloud, mostly for my own benefit since no one else is here except Denton. A statement to connect myself to the scene before me. My heart beat slows. This is where I thrive, among the clues and questions. I've never had the chance to investigate a murder before.

I can do this.

The sight of the dead body punches me in the gut. No time for weakness.

I start with the perimeter, letting my eyes glide over every inch. There's a Monet, or at least a damn good imitation, turned askew on the wall—a silent witness peering out from its gilt frame. Expensive taste, but what does that tell me? People buy art to hide dirty walls and emptier souls, don't they?

A toppled vase lies shattered, porcelain shards scattered across the hardwood floor like a broken promise. Roses, barely wilted, strewn amidst the debris. A sign of struggle.

My gloved hands hover inches away, tracing the invisible lines of an unseen battle. A scuff on the varnished surface catches my eye—someone slipped here, maybe? Was it Edward, grappling with his killer? Or the murderer, rushing to escape? So many questions, curling up in my mind like smoke.

"White, you got anything?" another officer calls from the door. It sounds like Miles Durrant, one of the junior officers I met last week. I wonder if he's as surprised as I am that our first case together is a murder.

"Still looking."

I stand and move toward the body. They say money can't

buy happiness, but I bet Edward Kane thought it could buy safety. Guess he was wrong.

I take in the gruesome sight. His head rests at a sickening angle, the wound a dark cavern in the lush landscape of his silver-flecked hair. No dignity in death, especially when it's laid out on your own bedroom floor. Whatever hit him in the back of the head did so several times, no doubt about it.

"Where's the weapon?" I scan the floor for anything that could have dealt that crushing blow. Nothing stands out—no bloody lamp, no stray pipe. There's a distinct pattern in the wounds, and I realize what it is.

"I believe we're searching for a meat mallet," I call out, my voice bouncing off the marble and mahogany surfaces.

Durrant glances up from his notes, eyebrows raised. "A meat mallet? Are you sure about that?" he asks, flipping through the pages of his notebook.

I nod, feeling the heavy gaze of the deceased lingering on me. "Yeah, that's what it looks like," I reply, attempting to shake off the unease that's settled in my bones.

Durrant moves closer, adjusting his glasses to get a better view of the scene. "It's our first case together, so let's make sure we're thorough," he says, his tone steady but with an underlying excitement.

I appreciate his attention to detail. "Agreed," I say, turning back to the work at hand, eager to piece together the story behind the evidence. I crouch beside the body, my gaze darting from the wound to the surrounding chaos. His arms are flung wide, one hand reaching toward the nightstand as if he tried to grab something or someone. Maybe a last-ditch effort to survive?

I take out my official PD camera, preferring to capture the images myself. The camera automatically timestamps each photo to officially document the scene.

My hands are steady, despite the adrenaline coursing through me. I start with wide shots, capturing the entire scene, before moving in close. The curve of his limp fingers, the splatter radius—every detail is a silent witness waiting to speak. Click. A moment frozen in time. Click. Another piece for the evidence board back at the station. I work methodically, ensuring nothing escapes my lens.

I focus on capturing the tiny specks of blood spatter on the wall.

There's a mahogany dresser, its surface pristine except for a single drawer slightly ajar. It doesn't take much imagination to picture hands grappling, desperately searching for something, anything, to use as leverage in a struggle that only ended one way. The heavy curtains are drawn shut; not even a sliver of Florida sun dares to intrude. Large lamps are strategically placed around the room, casting a bright, artificial glow. They stand tall on tripods, their light illuminating the space with a stark intensity, reminiscent of a professional photoshoot.

I move around the bed, noting the rumpled sheets, the indentation on the pillow where his head should be resting, not... like this.

It was my boss, Lieutenant James "Jim" Mitchell, who called me and told me to attend to the scene. A body was found by the wife earlier today. On a Sunday of all days. She had been out, and came home to find him in the bedroom like this. So far they told me there is no sign of forced entry. The nakedness, the crumpled sheets. My guess is that our friend here let death waltz right through the door—invited it in, maybe, over a glass of fifty-year-old scotch. I look at the whiskey glass fallen to the ground, its contents spilled out. Only one glass though. No lipstick smeared on a flute anywhere.

I step carefully, avoiding the blood. But there's more than just blood; there's a story here. The rug bears the marks of a struggle.

"He definitely knew the killer..." I murmur, my mind clicking pieces into place. "Had to."

My gaze falls upon the body again, on Edward's exposed vulnerability. The absence of clothes speaks louder than any confession. A crime of passion? A setup? Maybe both. It's all too easy, isn't it? Wealthy man, lovers' spat, a moment of rage...

"All right, Eddie," I whisper to the stillness, "it's over now."

I stand up and take a step back from the body, giving myself a moment to observe the scene from a different perspective.

"All that money didn't do you much good, did it?" I murmur quietly, a wry smile playing on my lips despite the grim scene before me. Bradley would accuse me of being bitter. And maybe I am. No, I definitely am—but not about this, not about the wealth wasted on cold marble and empty luxury. It's the pretense of it all, the façade people like these put up while the rest of us face the harsh reality beneath. Growing up with so little taught me to see through their charades, and even with Bradley, life isn't as glamorous as it seems.

With a final glance at the scene, I feel the weight of responsibility settle across my shoulders. I've always been good at puzzles, but this one? This one's going to take every ounce of what I've got. And God help me, I won't let some silver-spoon murderer get away with it—not on my watch.

I encounter Denton in the dimly lit hallway, the echo of my footsteps accompanying my presence. I slide off my gloves with a practiced ease, attempting to divert his attention by speaking before he can bombard me with more inquiries. As I converse with him, I can't help but let my eyes wander, taking in the grandeur of the mansion around me. The ornate chandeliers hang like crystal rain, casting shimmering patterns across the walls. I make mental notes of the layout, the lavish decor, and the peculiarities that might serve as clues in our investigation. My fingers brush against the polished banister of the grand staircase, searching for any signs of disturbance. I pause at a series of portraits lining the corridor, each face captured in stark detail, as if they could whisper secrets of the past. Denton's questions fade into the background as I immerse myself in the scene, piecing together the narrative of this opulent yet enigmatic estate.

The lieutenant told me one thing on the phone when calling me earlier: they're treating Mrs. Kane as a suspect.

"Take me to his wife."

He walks down the hallway ahead of me and pushes open a set of double doors.

TWO

DARCEY

I step into the study. My eyes lock on to her—the woman sitting on the leather couch. She's draped in a sapphire dress that probably costs more than my entire wardrobe, with hair so perfectly styled it looks like a sculpture. The glint of her jewelry catches the light, throwing little rainbows across the walls.

"This is Charlotte Kane," Denton says beside me, "the wife of the deceased."

Charlotte Kane. Even her name sounds like something out of a glossy magazine, the kind that would never feature someone like me unless they were writing a piece on the gritty life of a detective.

There's this sour taste at the back of my throat as I take her in. How can she sit there so... calmly? So... beautifully? When her husband is dead next door.

"Mrs. Kane," I begin, my voice steady. "I'm sorry for your loss."

She turns her head to face me, those hazel eyes locking onto mine with an intensity that almost makes me step back. But I hold my ground, watching as she tries to still her hands, laid bare on the leather surface between us. The slight tremor betrays her, and there's something dark staining her skin—blood, smeared across her knuckles like a gruesome accessory no amount of money can buy.

That will be why the lieutenant thinks she's a suspect.

I lean in closer, pretending to scrutinize her expression, but really, it's her hands that fascinate me—the hands of a woman who could very well have crushed the life out of someone, maybe even the man she claimed to love in her twisted ways.

"Is that blood?" Blood clings to her fingers, too red against the pale skin, and for a moment, the room seems to hold its breath.

"Charlotte?" I soften my voice. "Can you tell me where this blood came from?"

I signal for Denton to come closer and tell him to take a sample of the blood on her hands, for DNA. I'm pretty sure it's her husband's but we need the evidence. Her lips part, but no sound comes forth, and those eyes, they're ice, giving nothing away as she stares into mine. The officer does as he is told and secures the evidence.

"Charlotte? Is this your husband's blood?"

I don't know whether to feel sorry for her or not. Is she completely in shock? Is this her response to finding out her husband has been murdered, or is she tight-lipped on purpose, waiting for her chance to ask for a lawyer? Why hasn't she said anything yet?

"Mrs. Kane, where were you in the past twelve hours?"

I'm met with nothing but silence.

"Did you kill him?" The words are out before I can coat them with any semblance of softness. Denton looks at me. He shrugs. Perhaps he thinks I should hold back my questions for the interrogation room, but I can't help myself.

Silence still hangs between us, thick, oppressive. She just stares, those hazel eyes like fortress walls. There's no flicker of fear, no twitch of guilt. Just cold, hard stillness.

"Fine. If you're not going to talk, we'll have to take you in. Do you have any children that need to be taken care of? I saw a young girl in a photo downstairs?"

She shakes her head, then finally speaks. The sound of her voice almost startles me. "Georgina is with my parents this weekend."

I signal to the other officers lingering by the door. "She's done here. You can book her."

The metallic snap of the handcuffs locks into place around Charlotte's slim wrists, and it jolts me more than I care to admit. The officers recite her rights with a rhythm born of repetition, their voices steady and impersonal. "You have the right to remain silent..." The words bounce off the high ceilings of the study, off the rows of leather-bound books that seem to mock us with their silence.

"Anything you say can and will be used against you in a court of law."

"You have no rights to arrest me," she suddenly says.

"Actually, we do," I say.

She turns her face with a snort and looks down at me. "I didn't kill my husband."

"We'll talk about that at the station," I say.

"I'm innocent."

"They all say that, don't they?"

"Listen to me, woman," she says, and my eyes grow wide.

"Excuse me? It's Detective to you."

"Listen to me, *Detective*," she says, spitting the word out.

I give her one second, and show that I'm listening. "What?"

"I didn't kill my husband, but I know who did."

My heart drops but they lead her away before she has a chance to continue talking, handcuffs clasped around those delicate wrists, a stark contrast to the ornate bangles that slide down her forearm. She doesn't resist, doesn't plead; there's only the dignified tilt of her chin as she steps over the threshold, her heels clicking a morbid rhythm on the hardwood floor.

"Darcey White, what have you gotten yourself into?" I whisper to myself once the door clicks shut behind them, sealing off the rest of the world. The mansion breathes around me, walls echoing with secrets I'm yet to uncover. It's just me now, alone in the lioness's den, surrounded by shadows and the specter of a murder that clings to the air like a second skin.

"Damn it." The oath is a puff of air in the stillness. A detective shouldn't let emotions cloud judgment. But I know this woman, I've seen her before.

Does she know who *I* am?

No. I don't think so... If there's one thing I've learned, it's that gut instincts have a place alongside cold, hard facts.

I remember her black dress. Her thick, beautifully styled hair.

She was Bradley's mistress.

She doesn't know me, and doesn't seem to recognize me at all. And right now, the advantage lies with me. She sees Detective Darcey White, not the jilted wife, not yet. And I intend to keep it that way.

THREE
DARCEY

I step through the front door of my home, and the scent of garlic and rosemary wraps around me like a warm blanket. There's something else, too—red wine, perhaps? Bradley is working his magic; turning simple ingredients into promises of comfort. For a moment, I let myself be lulled by the illusion of domestic bliss.

"Hey," Bradley's voice slides into my ears as he closes the distance between us. That smile of his—so practiced, so perfect —flashes across his face. It's the kind that wins cases and hearts with equal ease. He leans in and presses his lips to mine, soft and sure. For a heartbeat, I wonder what it would be like if he had never broken my trust. How good this would feel.

He told me he wasn't seeing Charlotte any more after I confronted him. He said that it was a fling and he would end it now. He promised me he would never see her again. He began to take on more responsibilities at home, picking up the kids from school, running errands without complaint. It was as if he had transformed into the perfect husband and father overnight. He urged me to take on more at work. He would take care of the children and the home. I found myself staying late more often, focusing on my cases and finally managing to secure that long-awaited promotion. Bradley's sudden change in behavior made me question whether I had misjudged him all along. He would whisk me away on surprise weekend getaways, painting a picture of domestic bliss that seemed too good to be true. In those moments, he appeared genuinely caring and attentive, erasing any doubts I had about our marriage. It was as if he was making up for lost time, showering me with gifts and attention. At first, I questioned his sudden change of heart, but he appeared so sincere, so caring. It felt like I was finally getting the husband—and my children the father—I had always longed for. His charm seemed genuine, his words reassuring. Maybe, just maybe, things could really be different this time. Maybe he really had changed and wasn't seeing her any more. He made that promise a year ago. I chose to believe him. At least most of the time, 'cause that feeling, it's always there, isn't it? The doubt, the questioning. Is he still lying to me? Sneaking behind my back? It is always there no matter how hard I try to get rid of it.

"Welcome home," he murmurs against my mouth.

"Smells amazing," I manage to say.

"Only the best for you," he replies, putting his arm inside my coat and around my waist, his thumb tracing small circles over the fabric of my blouse. It's a caress that might have made me shiver in pleasure once upon a time.

I peel off my coat, a ripple of unease slinking down my spine despite the warmth of our home. Bradley steps back, a proud tilt to his head as he sweeps an arm toward the kitchen.

"Ta-da! Beef Wellington tonight," he announces, eyes gleaming with self-satisfaction. "I've outdone myself, if I may say so."

I can't help but smile. Bradley has always been ambitious in the kitchen. I remember the lasagna he lovingly prepared for our second date, the batch cooking he did when I was in the hospital giving birth to the twins, the delight on his face when I bought him that bottle of port last Christmas.

Before I can offer a carefully measured compliment, a blur of youthful energy barrels into my legs, nearly upending me. Laughter bubbles up from the tiny culprits—our five-year-old children, the twins, Jacob and Emma, their faces flushed with delight.

"Mommy, Daddy made the biggest meat ever!" Jacob, the younger of the twins by seven minutes, grasps Bradley's hand and tugs at it, eager to show off the feast.

"Did he now?" I reply, my voice light, though it feels like I'm swallowing sandpaper.

"Who's hungry for dinner?"

The kids respond to their father with a resounding cheer. "Me, me, me!" Emma chants, her voice piercing the fraught silence that had settled between Bradley and me.

"All right, little monsters," Bradley says with feigned exasperation. "Let's wash up."

I observe as they leave, three companions caught up in their own world of naivety and cluelessness. Before I know it, both children are shouting from another room, sharing excitedly with me about their day while washing their hands for dinner. Their innocent chatter is music to my ears as I listen with a smile on my face.

"And then we saw this really cool bug outside!" Jacob exclaims. "Yeah, and then we played hide-and-seek in the backyard!" Emma adds. Their cheerful voices fill the house with warmth and joy, reminding me of the simplicity of childhood and how precious these moments truly are. The laughter echoes. It's moments like these that threaten to unravel me—the picture-perfect family, a snapshot where everyone plays their part.

But snapshots don't capture the whole story, do they?

I turn away from the domestic tableau and catch sight of Chloe, my oldest, lounging on the couch. She's the product of a former relationship of mine that didn't last, that I barely remember. Her dad, Martin, and I share her fifty-fifty, even if these days, she comes and goes how she wishes. He lives near the hubbub of town, working in a little diner, so she's often with him to be closer to her friends. Her thumbs are flying over her phone screen, her brow furrowed in that teenage scowl that speaks volumes without a word uttered. I cross the room, the worn carpet muffling my steps, and lean down to press a kiss on to her forehead, still warm from the Florida sun.

"Hey, sweetie," I say, brushing a stray lock behind her ear.

She looks up, her expression softening for a moment before the mask of adolescence slips back into place.

"Hi, Mom."

Her voice is a blend of boredom and affection that only a sixteen-year-old can muster. Chloe's presence is still a balm to the anxiety I've been feeling ever since I left the crime scene.

"How was your day?" I ask, sinking onto the armrest beside her, my detective's eyes scanning her face for clues to her mood. A part of me craves the normalcy of this conversation, a respite from the darker inquiries that are consuming my head. I'd told Denton to hold Charlotte overnight, that I'd interview her in the morning. He thinks it's an open and shut case.

"Usual stuff," she replies, locking her phone and setting it aside—a gesture of truce. "I forgot to tell you on Friday, I got an A on my history paper."

"An A? That's fantastic, Chloe!" Pride swells within me. "You worked really hard on that. We should celebrate."

"Maybe," she says, but her smile doesn't quite reach her eyes. It's like looking into a mirror at times; she's inherited my skepticism along with my smile. I wonder if she senses the currents beneath the surface, if she feels the tension that vibrates through the walls of our house?

"Mom," Chloe begins, her voice a soft whisper, "I need to tell you something." She hesitates, her fingers twisting nervously. "I'm flunking math. I wanted to tell you earlier, but I was scared you'd be mad."

I reach out, gently placing my hand over hers. "Oh, Chloe," I say, my voice warm and reassuring. "Thank you for telling me. I'm not mad at all. I'm proud of you for being brave enough to share this with me."

Her smile still wavers, but there's a new light in her eyes. We sit there, hand in hand, feeling the tension ease away, replaced by a comforting bond that feels stronger than ever.

"Any plans tonight?" I probe gently, hoping to keep her talking, to keep her close while I can.

"Um, just homework," Chloe answers, shrugging one shoulder. "And maybe a movie later. With Sarah. I hope it's okay?"

"Sounds good," I reply, trying to mask the emptiness in my voice. I'm physically here, but my mind drifts elsewhere, constantly worried that Bradley might betray me again or that Chloe might discover the truth. For now, though, my attention is on my daughter—the sole reason I strive to keep everything from falling apart.

"Mom, can we bake cookies later?" she asks, her eyes filled with excitement.

"Of course, sweetheart," I smile, feeling a warmth that only she can bring. Bradley has always been kind to her, especially when her own father wasn't around. Her heart would shatter if she ever learned the truth. I could never do that to her, so I kept Bradley's infidelity a secret.

"You're the best, Mom," she says, wrapping her arms around me. "I love you."

Stepping back, I watch Chloe with pride and overwhelming emotion. She's here, in front of me, instead of just a brief hello or goodbye during tense custody exchanges like when she was younger. It's a rare moment of pure happiness, a stark contrast to the usual dread that lingers beneath the surface. Despite our rocky relationship with my ex, Chloe is thriving and excelling in her studies at sixteen. It would be easy for her to use our situation as an excuse to go off the rails, but she hasn't let it stop her from achieving academic success. Till now. The fact that she is failing her math class is news to me, and a slight disappointment. I need to be careful not to make too big of a deal about it, as she doesn't need any added pressure. She's hard enough on herself as it is.

"Mom? You okay?" Chloe's voice cuts through the fog of my thoughts, her gaze sharp and inquisitive, like she's trying to read my mind.

"Better than okay," I respond, my smile stretching across my face. It feels genuine, though such expressions are a rarity for me these days.

"You're disappointed, huh?" she asks, her eyes narrowing slightly as if she can see straight through the layers of my thoughts, just as she always does. "That I'm failing."

"No, sweetie. Just wondering how to get you back on track," I reply, trying to keep my tone light and supportive.

"Bradley said he'd help me," she offers, her voice steady. "He's good with numbers."

I wrinkle my forehead, a habit I've never been able to kick. "Brad said that?"

"Yes," she confirms, nodding with certainty.

"You told him you were failing math before you told me?" I ask, surprise coloring my voice as I try to mask the sting of being the second to know.

Chloe's cheeks flush a soft pink, and she looks sheepish. "Yeah... well... I was worried you'd get mad, and he was there... so I told him."

"So you trust him more than me?" My question hangs in the air, tinged with a mix of puzzlement and a hint of hurt.

She makes a face, scrunching up her nose. "Mo-om! Don't make this about you, please."

I throw my hands up in mock surrender. "Okay. I won't then."

"Good, 'cause it's not. I will fix it, and Brad will help me. You don't have to worry about anything," she insists with a confidence that both reassures and worries me.

I stare at her, my eyes lingering on her determined expression, and a small sigh slips from between my lips, carrying with it a deep lingering concern.

From the kitchen, the clink of glass against countertop announces Bradley's presence before he rounds the corner, flashing that practiced, charming smile—the one that masks more than it reveals. He extends a glass of wine toward me, the crimson liquid catching the light.

"Thought you could use this," he says, and his tone is warm, caring even. But there's something else there, always something else.

"Thanks." I accept the glass. The rich aroma of the Merlot teases my senses, an invitation to relax, to let down my guard. I remind myself that I need to try.

"How was your day?" he asks, those piercing blue eyes scanning my face for clues, for weaknesses.

"Oh, nothing too eventful," I reply, swirling the wine, watching it hug the curves of the glass. My voice is steady, betraying none of the chaos churning inside. I want to scream at him, tell him what happened, that I came face to face with the woman he promised I'd never have to worry about again... That she's a murderer.

Yet I don't.

"Well, that's good," Bradley says, his smile widening. There's an edge to it, though—an eagerness that suggests he's playing at something far deeper than casual conversation. Does he already know? Did she call him from jail? Is he going to be her lawyer?

"I guess so," I answer.

"Now drink your wine," he says. "You look like you need it."

I take a sip, the taste settling me, and reminding me to tread carefully. He watches me, smiling.

"There you go, good girl."

My children's laughter punctuates the moment, a needed reminder of innocence in a room where shadows loom too close for comfort.

Bradley leans in, and the warmth of his breath precedes the soft pressure of his lips. My eyes close reflexively, yielding to the momentary sweetness that belies the tumult beneath. How I wish his kisses didn't melt me. But for years they made me feel at home.

I've never quite felt enough for Bradley, and I had to push down my thoughts of inadequacy, even before Charlotte. He came from a wealthy family. *Is* a wealth lawyer. While my own childhood was somewhat less picture-perfect, my career not exactly one that pays the bills.

I pull back slightly, opening my eyes to find his gaze still locked on mine. His smile holds a trace of victory, as if he's just won another round in a game I never agreed to play. It's the kind of look that could fool anyone into believing in the earnestness of Bradley Cavendish.

"Darcey," he whispers, voice threaded with a charm that used to unravel me. "I heard that Chloe told you about her math class. Don't sweat it. I will help her."

"I'm just a little upset that she told you before me," I say.

"Hey, what can I say? The kid trusts me."

"That's not helping."

He sighs and his eyes grow serious. "You should be glad she feels comfortable enough to talk to me about these types of things. You know I'm here for you, right? It's all about you. Whatever you need."

I nod, because what else is there to do? I need to believe him.

"Everything's just perfect, isn't it?" I remark, blending sarcasm with a hint of longing. He misses the sarcasm and hears only what pleases him.

"Absolutely perfect," he echoes, pouring himself more wine and raising his glass. Our glasses meet with a clink, and he observes me as I take another sip.

"So, how was your day? Busy?" he inquires, as if he already knows the answer, his tone layered with a subtle edge.

"Quite busy," I reply, eyeing him cautiously. "And you? Any new clients lately?" I ask, probing for a hint of what's really on his mind.

"Come on, everybody! Dinner's ready!" Bradley's voice booms through the sound of my youngest fighting over a toy in the living room. The twins barrel past me. I watch them cling to Bradley's legs, their faces alight with the kind of innocent excitement only children seem to possess. He laughs, a rich sound that doesn't quite reach his eyes, but it's convincing enough for them.

"Careful, you two," I chide gently, but my heart swells at the sight. This is what they need—for him to be a father figure.

We shuffle into the dining room, drawn by the aroma of the food. The table is set meticulously: plates aligned just so, napkins folded into neat triangles, glasses filled halfway, never more. It's Bradley's order within the chaos of our family life, and tonight, it feels almost comforting.

"Looks amazing, honey," I say, sliding into my seat. The words are simple, but they don't come easy. How do you compliment the chef when you're also dissecting his every move?

"Thank you, Darcey." His smile is all charm, the practiced grin of a man who knows his role. "I hope it tastes as good as it looks."

We settle into a rhythm of silverware and soft chatter. Jacob looks at me with big eyes. "Mommy, know what? The other day a frog got into our classroom."

"A frog?" I ask. "A real frog?"

"Yes. And then, it just hopped right onto my desk!" he exclaims, waving his arms with excitement.

"No way!" Bradley chimes in, wide-eyed. "Did you touch it?" He leans forward, eager to hear more.

"I wanted to, but Mrs. Thompson caught it first," Jacob continues, mimicking their teacher's stern expression. Laughter ripples around the table.

"Was Mrs. Thompson mad?" Bradley asks, grinning.

"She looked like she was going to turn into a frog herself!" Jacob jokes, making everyone giggle.

"Did she know where it came from?" I inquire, curious. "Did someone bring it in with them?"

"No, we don't know. She just said, 'Next time, let's leave the frogs in their natural habitat,'" Emma quotes with an exaggerated tone, causing another round of laughter.

"And then she told us a story about the time a snake got into her classroom!" Jacob adds, eyes wide with drama.

"Whoa, a snake? That's way cooler than a frog!" Bradley exclaims, leaning back in his chair. He's good at that, listening. Bradley listens, nods, interjects with the occasional question. He then encourages them to eat the food he's lovingly prepared, when we both know they'd have been happy with chicken nuggets. To anyone peering through our window, we must look like the epitome of familial harmony.

But I cannot get my husband's mistress out of my mind.

FOUR

DARCEY

The glass doors of the police station swing open with a hushed swish, admitting me into the sterile chill that always seems to cling to these walls. All I can hear is the click-clack of my heels across the linoleum. Ever since I got promoted, I've been wearing heels. They make me feel more assertive. More in control. But I've yet to get used to the noise. I head straight to the meeting room. Bradley's face flashes before my eyes. Dinner was wonderful. He put the twins to bed while I cleaned up, and for a moment I had been able to forget about Charlotte. We'd cuddled on the couch watching an old show for an hour, until he'd been called by a partner at work. He'd spent the rest of the night in his office after that.

"Morning, Darcey," someone calls out—a voice meant to be friendly that just drills into my temples. I've had a headache since I woke up this morning.

"Morning," I reply, summoning a smile.

I sidestep into the ladies' room, the only place where prying eyes don't follow. The mirror reflects a woman who holds her secrets close, auburn hair pulled tight enough to armor her scalp, green eyes that should have seen betrayal coming. I fish the Advil bottle from my purse—two pills, my tiny white flag against the hangover.

"Damn you, Merlot," I whisper, tossing them back and chasing the bitterness with cold tap water.

"Darcey?"

I turn to see Brittney, my colleague, standing behind me with a concerned look in her eyes. Without words, she asks if I'm okay. Our bond goes way back, back to the days when we both started as rookies on the force. I remember the day when a dangerous criminal pulled a gun on Brittney during a routine patrol, and how I was able to save her life.

"I have such a terrible headache today," I reply, trying to keep it simple as I slide the bottle of painkillers back into my bag. She accepts my answer with a nod and a forced smile, and I am grateful that she doesn't press for more information. Her gaze shifts away from me, perhaps sensing that it's better not to ask.

"Rough night?" she attempts to lighten the mood.

"I get migraines," is all I can offer.

"Yeah, my sister gets those too," she says. "Can ruin her entire day. It sucks that you have to deal with that."

"I'll live, I'm used to it," I reply, shrugging it off as best I can.

Brittney tilts her head slightly, a thoughtful expression on her face. "Hey, how are the twins doing? Must be a handful with both of them, huh?"

"Oh, they're a riot," I laugh. "Always keeping me on my toes. Just this morning, they decided the kitchen floor was their canvas."

Brittney chuckles. "Sounds like quite the adventure. Do you need any help with them? I can babysit anytime."

"That would be great, actually," I admit. "It's always nice to have an extra set of hands. Plus, they adore you."

"Well, the feeling's mutual," she smiles warmly.

"Thanks, Brittney. You're a lifesaver," I say, grateful for her support, then push past her toward the meeting room where the real show begins. The last thing I want to do is spill the broken pieces of my life onto the pristine floor of this office building. It's easier to keep up appearances and pretend everything is fine. Maybe it would be nice to have a friend like Brittney who genuinely cares, but I don't want to burden anyone else with my problems. So I continue on toward the meeting, leaving Brittney behind in the safety of small talk and polite smiles.

The door to the meeting room swings open with a sigh and I step into the familiar beige world of corkboards and stale coffee. Lieutenant James Mitchell—Jim—is already at the helm, his back to us as he scribbles something on the whiteboard. I can see the photos I took yesterday beside his scrawled handwriting. The team shuffles in behind me, a parade of wrinkled suits and half-awake expressions.

"Morning," Jim grunts without turning, the word more cough than greeting.

"Morning," the room echoes, a disjointed chorus.

He spins around, sharp eyes sweeping over us like we're pieces on a chessboard. "We got a lot to cover today. Let's start with the Kane case," he begins and all casual banter dies. "We've been holding Mrs. Kane since we found her at the scene. We have confirmed that it was Edward Kane's blood on her hands. He was definitely murdered. Autopsy has confirmed he suffered a blow to the head. After hours of meticulous searching, we have found no significant clues in their home that could lead us to the killer. Forensics are still working the place, but it's time for us to turn our attention to potential suspects. The wife is our primary person of interest and she needs to be interrogated as soon as possible. She has no alibi for the time of death. We will document her statements and continue investigating until we have enough evidence to make an arrest. On a positive note, she has been cooperative thus far which could potentially aid our case."

My heart picks up its pace. Charlotte. Her name isn't mentioned, but it hangs in the air, unspoken yet heavy with implication. I can feel the hangover pulsing just beneath my scalp, an insistent reminder of last night's attempt to drown out her image.

"Any volunteers?" Jim looks around, but it's clear it's a formality. This isn't the kind of assignment you jump at—not when Edward Kane's blood is still cooling.

But I'm on my feet before I realize it, my voice steady despite the tremor I feel. "I'll take that." Heads turn, curiosity painted in stark relief against tired faces. "It was Sunday so I was the only one on call yesterday. I was there all day," I add quickly, "so I know most about the case."

Jim's gaze locks onto mine, a silent exchange passing between us.

"Okay. Take Miles with you."

"Jim, I've got this," I say, a tinge of insistence lacing my words as I gather up the case file, feeling its weight in my hands. I push ahead of everyone as they begin to talk among themselves, certain Miles won't be able to hear me. He's relatively new, and I'd have no problem working with him normally. But I want to see Charlotte alone. "I can take this one. Miles is swamped with the Delaney paperwork, and well, you know how that can bury a person." I am not exaggerating. The Delaney paperwork has been taking its toll on the office lately. The case is a bureaucratic nightmare, a convoluted mess of financial fraud and embezzlement that seems to have no end in sight. I have no doubt Miles is drowning in the overwhelming task of organizing the files. Rumors have started circulating that Bradley's name appears in several suspicious transactions related to the case, among a bunch of other high profile investors and lawyers. It doesn't make me look good. I don't want to add to Miles' workload, but I can't help but worry if there's more to Bradley's involvement than meets the eye.

Jim arches an eyebrow, considering me beneath the furrowed lines. I wonder for a second if I have been too eager, too fast. Does he realize that I know the suspect? Have I given myself away? The last thing I want is to be taken off this case. I need it.

"You sure? Two sets of ears are better than one." His voice is gravel mixed with concern.

I meet his gaze, steadying my own. "Absolutely. Besides," I lean in slightly, dropping my voice to a conspiratorial whisper, "woman to woman, I think I can get her to open up." Anxiety builds in my stomach.

"All right, White." He concedes with a nod, his decision etched into the craggy lines of his face. "If you think you can handle it."

"Trust me, Jim. It's just a simple chat between gals," I quip, the irony like a bitter pill under my tongue. Or between a wife and her husband's mistress—there's a joke in there somewhere, but it's lost on me right now.

"Room 3," Jim continues, and he gestures vaguely toward the corridor. "She's been waiting all night. And Darcey," he adds, locking onto me with those sharp detective's eyes, "the autopsy isn't official yet, but we're pretty sure Edward took a meat mallet to the back of his head. It wasn't exactly subtle at the scene."

"I saw that. It's been noted."

"You'll need a murder weapon." The corner of his mouth quirks up, a ghost of a smile that doesn't quite dispel the gravity of the situation. "Nothing's been found."

"Yes, boss," I reply, a trace of sardonic respect coloring my tone.

"Also, they have cameras all over the property, but all the surveillance footage from the home was mysteriously deleted for the day of the murder. You might want to ask her about that."

"Of course."

Stepping out of the room, I let the mask of confidence settle over my features. This is what I do—what I'm good at—even if today, it feels like wading into uncharted waters. But I've always been a strong swimmer. Even in a storm.

The heavy door of the briefing room swings shut behind me with a dull thud, and I turn to see Jim continue his briefing. No one is watching me, but I can feel my heart ticking up a notch. My mind is already racing ahead, plotting questions, anticipating answers. But I press pause on that mental chatter, telling myself Charlotte Kane can stew just a little bit longer. I need to calm down.

I slip into the break-room, the scent of cheap coffee and sugar acting like a balm to my jangled senses. I pour myself a cup of the bitter brew, letting the warmth seep into my palms. The donut I grab—a guilty pleasure—is glazed and golden, promising a momentary escape from the weight pressing down on my shoulders. I take a bite, relishing the sweetness, an indulgence before facing what's next.

I sit down in my cramped office, surrounded by towering stacks of case files and half-empty coffee cups. I eat the rest of the donut. Normally, I'd avoid the sweet treats. I'm trying to get rid of a few pounds after having the twins. But today, the sugary rush offers a brief respite.

Opening the worn beige file folder that Jim handed me earlier, I spread it open on my cluttered desk, feeling the weight of its grim contents. As I sift through the pages, the faint scent of ink and paper fills the air, mingling with the smell of stale coffee. Each page is filled with meticulous details, typed in a neat, unyielding font, chronicling every aspect of the heinous crime we're investigating. The photographs, carefully attached to the corners of the pages, are vivid and haunting. Each one tells a silent story: the deep, dark stains on the carpet speak of violence and finality. Each photograph invites me to step back into the scene, to recall the chilling events as if I were there, piecing together the fragments of mystery with every scrutinized detail.

As a senior detective now, it's my responsibility to assemble the puzzle, to bring justice to those who deserve it.

Amidst the sea of paperwork, a memory flashes vividly in my mind. It was the day Jim called me into his office, his expression a mix of sternness and warmth.

"You've done exceptional work, you know," he began, handing me the shiny new badge of a senior detective. "Cracking the Anderson case was no small feat. I'm proud of you, and I have full confidence in your abilities."

I remember the pride that swelled in my chest, the sense of accomplishment mixed with a tinge of apprehension.

"Thank you, Jim," I replied, my voice steady despite the whirlwind of emotions. "I won't let you down."

The promotion came with more responsibility, more scrutiny. But I have welcomed all of it.

As I delve deeper into the files, my mind races with the weight of the investigation. The photographs of the crime scene lay bare the brutality of the act, each detail etching itself into my memory. I can't afford to make mistakes, not now.

I make my way to room 3, my steps deliberate.

Outside, I linger, my eyes fixed on the one-way mirror. Charlotte sits there, unaware of my scrutiny. Even now, she's poised, the very picture of elegance in her tailored dress, her legs crossed at the ankles. Her hazel eyes are calm, fixed on some invisible point ahead. She doesn't fidget. Doesn't betray a single hint of nervousness.

Her words are on repeat in my head. "I didn't kill my husband, but I know who did."

"Look at you," I mutter under my breath, my reflection superimposed over hers, a ghostly overlay. "Sitting there like the Queen of Sheba." There's a bitterness twisting inside me as I watch her, this woman who probably sips champagne for breakfast and thinks nothing of tearing families apart.

She's everything I detest—entitled, aloof, and worst of all, was tangled up with Bradley. It's personal, this disdain that simmers just below the surface. I'll need to put this aside if I want to figure this case out.

I take another sip of my coffee. I need to be the detective, not the scorned wife.

"All right, Mrs. Kane, let's see what skeletons are hiding in your designer closet."

Taking one last fortifying breath, I push off from the wall and reach for the interrogation room door, ready to peel back the layers of Charlotte Kane's composure.

FIVE

DARCEY

I push open the door to the interrogation room. The fluorescent lights buzz overhead, casting a harsh glow on the figure in the chair. Now I'm in the room, and a lot closer to Charlotte Kane, I can see that her raven hair is disheveled from her night in the station; the smudged mascara beneath her hazel eyes telling tales of a night spent away from her silk sheets and feather pillows.

"Good morning, Mrs. Kane," I say, setting my cup down with a deliberate thud. "Sleep well?"

She lifts her head slowly, those once-piercing eyes dull, the veneer of wealth now cracked and peeling like old paint. Her blue silk dress, no doubt designer, hangs loose, less figure-hugging after hours on a steel cot. This isn't the polished socialite the world is accustomed to; this is a woman brought low by cold reality. And somehow, I feel a tiny bit better.

"Detective White," she greets, voice hoarse, words wrapped in the remains of her dignity. "I've had better nights."

"Unfortunately, jail's not a five-star hotel." I take a seat across from her, feeling the weight of my own tangled life press against my chest.

I flick the switch on the recorder as I settle into the chair, its creak echoing through the sterile room. "This conversation will be recorded. This is Senior Detective Darcey White, sitting here with Mrs. Charlotte Kane. For the record, it's 8:23 a.m., and we are discussing the murder of Edward Kane. Do you understand, Mrs. Kane?"

"Perfectly," she says, her chin lifting ever so slightly. It's a small gesture, but it speaks volumes of her defiance.

"Let's start with the basics. Where were you yesterday before you found your husband dead?" My tone is crisp, clinical, each syllable sharpened to cut through any lie she might try to hold onto. We don't know the time of death yet, but according to the preliminary results I read in the case file, it suggests it was between 1 p.m. and 3 p.m. The call came in at a little after 4 p.m., and was made by Charlotte Kane herself.

"I wasn't home," she answers— too quickly—a practiced simplicity in her response. "I came home later. He was already dead."

"You weren't at home?" I raise an eyebrow.

"No, I wasn't," she replies, shifting slightly.

"Then where were you?" I ask again.

"I was out," she answers, her voice steady.

"What time did you leave the house?"

"Around 2 p.m.," she says, glancing at the clock on the wall as if to confirm.

"Were you driving your car or did someone drive you?"

"I drove my car."

"Were you alone or with someone?"

"I was alone."

"Which route did you take?"

"I took the usual route down Main Street," she responds with a small nod.

"Where did you go?"

"I was driving around, running errands," she replies, the corner of her mouth twitching upwards in what could almost pass for a smirk. "Alone."

"What kind of errands?" I lean forward, wondering if this is the sort of excuse she gave her husband when she was off seeing Bradley. "If you visited any stores, we could get their surveillance footage to confirm your alibi."

"Well, I was going to go to Publix, but decided I needed some fresh air instead. So, I went down to the beach. I like to drive there and take a stroll. I do that to clear my head, if you must know. I came home at three fifty-five. That's when I found him." She leans back in her chair, crossing her arms in a show of casual indifference.

I pause, scrutinizing her face for any sign of a crack in her façade, any small indication that might betray the truth behind her calm demeanor. I suspect she's not telling the truth.

"So, there's no one who can verify your whereabouts?"

We would have to review CCTV footage along the way. Her license plate could be seen by the LPR system, so parts of her alibi could be verified.

"Probably not. I wouldn't know."

"I'm going to have you write down the route you took, so we can verify your alibi."

"I don't remember exactly where I went. Just that I drove to the beach and went for a walk."

I sigh. "You understand how this looks, right? Wealthy wife, unhappy marriage—"

"Speculation isn't evidence, Detective. I never said my marriage was unhappy," she cuts in sharply. "And let's not pretend this is about justice. You're enjoying this, aren't you? Picking apart someone like me."

"Someone like you?" I echo, letting a hint of disdain color my voice. Her type, they always think they're untouchable.

"No, Mrs. Kane, I don't enjoy it. But I will do my job, regardless of who sits in that chair."

The air between us crackles with unspoken animosity, a silent war waged across the expanse of metal table. She doesn't know who I am, but she's already picked up on my disdain for the elite. We're two women, worlds apart, each nursing wounds deeper than the other can see. And as the caffeine finally begins to take the edge off my weariness, I prepare to dive into the abyss of lies and secrets. Because beneath her crumbling exterior, Charlotte Kane hides something more than just wealth and privilege. And I intend to protect my own secrets and my own marriage at all costs. I'm deeply hurt by what Bradley did to me, and embarrassed, but I want it to stay in the past where it belongs. I'm hoping it's all over, but there's this doubt inside of me that I can't let go of. I'm dying to ask if they are still seeing one another. Yet I know I can't. It would give me away.

My fingers press against my temples, willing the throbbing pain to subside as the pill dissolves in my system.

Charlotte's gaze fixes on me, a smirk pulling at the corner of her lips.

"Are you hungover, Detective White?" she asks, her voice dripping with mock concern. "Or is it the company you keep in this dreary place that gives you such a headache?"

I drop my hands and fix her with a look that could curdle milk. "You know what gives me a headache, Mrs. Kane? Entitled individuals who think their money can wipe away their sins."

Her snort is derisive, a sound that echoes off the cold walls, grating against my last nerve. "You *are* hungover, aren't you? How unprofessional," she says, the word like a slap. "But then, I suppose I shouldn't expect any less from someone of your... caliber." She glances down at my scuffed and worn heels, a stark contrast to her own red-soled heels. The condescension in her tone is palpable.

"Unprofessional would be letting my personal feelings about your kind cloud my judgment," I shoot back. "So rest assured, I'll treat you just like any other suspect, as you probably realized last night."

Charlotte leans forward, eyes narrowed. "And what kind is that, Detective? The kind that doesn't wilt under your glares or jump at your barked questions?"

"Exactly," I confirm with a nod, feeling the edge of the pill take root, dulling the headache enough to focus on her. Is this why Bradley liked her? She's strong-willed, argumentative, she sees through people—she's a little bit like me. "The kind that thinks they're above the law because their bank account has more commas than most people's."

Her laughter is hollow. "Oh, Detective, if money could solve all my problems, do you really think I'd be sitting here indulging your little power play?"

"Money," I say flatly, "doesn't buy innocence. Remember that."

"You're probably wondering why I haven't called a lawyer by now," she says.

I am wondering about that, but I don't tell her.

"Because my husband recently made an investment that caused us to lose all our money, and put us into debt, so I can't afford it. At least not a good one. And since I do hold a law degree from Harvard, I prefer to take care of myself at this point. And I choose to cooperate, since I am innocent."

"Understood," I reply, considering that she might have just given me a motive. Losing all their money could have made her angry enough to do something like this. I'm guessing she never practiced law and got married straight after law school.

I jot down a note to look into Edward's finances, planning to delve deeper into the situation. I also make a mental note to ask about who stands to inherit the house and other assets, ensuring a thorough investigation.

"You have the right to a public defender," I say.

"I know," she says. "I know my rights. But I don't need one. I have nothing to hide."

I slide a photo across the table, the glossy surface reflecting the harsh overhead lights. "Let's talk about Edward," I say, my voice cutting through the tense air between us. "What was he doing yesterday?"

"I don't know."

"How was your morning? Did you have breakfast together?"

"No. I don't eat breakfast usually. I had coffee outside by the pool, alone."

"You didn't have breakfast together on a Sunday?"

"Like I said, I don't eat breakfast. I like to watch my weight."

I nod. "Okay, so when did you see him last?"

"He went for a jog and came back when I was drinking my coffee on the back patio. He jumped in the pool and did a couple of laps, then went back inside. I assumed he went into his office to work. He usually does that on Sundays. To prepare for the week ahead."

"So, what was he doing naked in the bedroom in the afternoon?" I ask. "While you were running errands? Or rather taking a stroll on the beach?"

She sighs. "Who knows?"

"Was he cheating on you?"

Charlotte's gaze flickers to the photograph, her lips tightening ever so slightly. The image reveals Edward's head, grotesquely smashed in by a meat mallet, a crimson pool beneath him.

"Edward had many... distractions, but they were inconsequential." She pushes the picture away with a manicured fingernail, feigning indifference, as though the brutal scene depicted were merely a trivial inconvenience.

"Distractions that led to murder?" My question hangs in the room, the unspoken accusation heavy between us.

Then she does something unexpected.

She leans over and turns off the recorder.

I stare at her, surprised.

She leans back in her chair. The dark circles under her eyes seem more pronounced. "I told you, I didn't kill him. I don't want this to be on record, because I don't trust it won't come back to harm me."

I put down the pen and stare at her.

"I think I know who did it."

"Really?"

She nods. "His name is... Bradley Cavendish."

"Bradley Cavendish?" I repeat, my heart freezing for a split second. I keep my face expressionless, playing dumb. "And who's he? A friend? A colleague? Why would he want your husband dead?"

"Because," she says, her hazel eyes locking onto mine, "he wanted me all to himself."

That's rich, coming from her. A woman swathed in luxury, even now when her world is falling apart. Her words echo in my skull, bouncing around like a warning siren.

"Bradley did it," Charlotte insists again, and I almost want to laugh. And cry at the same time. Definitely cry. The name... Bradley... it's a punch to the gut every time she says it.

"Did Edward cheat?" she asks suddenly, trying to turn the tables, to claw back some control. "Do *you* know if he did?"

"Stick to answering, not asking," I command, ignoring the jab. I'm good at that—ignoring things. Like how Bradley sometimes hasn't been home in two nights or the way this woman seems too calm for someone accused of murder.

"I'm doing the interrogation here. Besides," I prod, as I try to steer my thoughts back, "you seem pretty certain of Mr. Cavendish's guilt. Why is that?"

"Because I know him," she states simply, a smug tilt to her lips.

Oh, I bet she does. Probably in ways I don't even want to imagine.

"Keep talking," I press, my voice steady as ever. Inside, though, it's a hurricane. I'm swirling with questions, doubts, and betrayal, yet here I am, the detective, the one who's supposed to have all the answers.

"Elaborate on your relationship with this Bradley Cavendish," I say, my voice devoid of any telltale inflection that might reveal the cyclone of emotions churning inside me.

She shifts in her chair, a sleek brow arching. "Why? Isn't that irrelevant to my husband's death?"

"Everything is relevant until proven otherwise," I respond mechanically. The choice to keep my maiden name never felt so vindicating. Darcey White, Detective White—it has an honest ring to it, doesn't it? No silver spoons here, no sir. I earned my stripes without the shadow of a Cavendish looming over me. I refused to take his name, just as I refused to be part of his wealthy and entitled family. I made it here on my own. Worked my way up. Without his help. And now it's saving me.

"Charlotte, focus," I assert, snapping back to the present. "What was the nature of your relationship with this Bradley Cavendish?"

"Professional at first," she says, her gaze darting away briefly before locking onto mine again. "But, it evolved."

"Evolved how?" My heart hammers against my ribcage, but I'm cool as winter frost on the outside.

"Personally." She leans back, a challenge in her hazel eyes. "Intimately, if you must know."

Hearing her say the words makes my heart drop. I look down at the files for a few seconds, closing my eyes to compose myself. "Let's not waste time," I press on, feeling the adrenaline pump through my veins, pushing past the personal hurt, the betrayal. This isn't about me; it's about justice. It has to be.

"Bradley Cavendish—" I begin, watching her closely.

"Is a beautiful man," she interjects quickly, too quickly. "Very attractive."

"Is he now?" I muse aloud, tilting my head ever so slightly. "And did this 'beautiful man' have anything to gain from Edward's death?"

Her lips part, ready with an answer, but I see it—the flicker of hesitation, the slightest crack.

"Detective White," she says, emphasizing my name. But it's just a name—mine by birthright, not some borrowed coat of arms.

"Ms. Kane," I reply with equal emphasis, letting the silence stretch between us. The air is thick with unsaid truths, with lies dressed up in half confessions, and somewhere within this tangled web, I will find what I'm looking for.

"Answer the question," I prompt, leaning back in my chair.

I tap my foot against the cold tile floor. The room is small, claustrophobic—a fitting stage for the drama that's about to unfold. I lean forward, elbows on the table, and fix Charlotte with a stare that's meant to unnerve. "So why do you say this Bradley did it?" My voice is steady, but inside, I'm anything but. "You must have a reason to believe so?"

"I was having an affair with him," Charlotte declares, her eyes never leaving mine. She says it like it's the most natural thing in the world, like we're discussing some mundane fact of life, not adultery laced with murder. "I am having an affair with him."

Her words echo in the tiny room, and something inside me snaps. My fingers clench into a fist beneath the table, knuckles bleaching white. I swallow hard, tasting the bitter bile of betrayal.

He told me it was over.

He promised.

"And why would Bradley kill your husband?" I manage to get out, my voice a whisper thin as ice.

"Because he's jealous of him." Charlotte leans back, crossing her arms as she appraises me with those calculating hazel eyes. "He wanted him gone so we could be together. He was going to leave his wife. He is in a bad relationship."

The air in the room seems to grow hotter. I want to scream, to leap across the table and shake her. Instead, I remain seated.

"Is that so?" I ask, the words slicing through the tension. It's a struggle to keep my composure, to maintain neutrality when all I want is to crumble. But crumble I won't; not here, not in front of her.

"Absolutely." Charlotte's confidence is infuriating. Does she think she can just waltz in and steal a life? My life?

"Interesting," I murmur, hiding my hands in my lap. They tremble ever so slightly. No one would notice—unless they were looking as closely as I look at everything. Always watching, always waiting for that slipup that will unravel the whole sordid story. "Were you complicit in this plan?"

Charlotte sits there, the epitome of calm and collected, seemingly untouched by the gravity of her own words.

"Absolutely not."

My grip on reality tightens, just as my fingers clench around the pen. The muscles in my hand contract, each tendon a steel cable coiling into a fist of fury. The cheap plastic splinters with a satisfying crack, mirroring the fracture lines spreading through my carefully constructed calm.

"Leaving his wife..." Charlotte's words echo, a vile mantra. I feel raw, exposed, like she's peeled back my skin to reveal the ugly truth beneath.

"Let's stay focused, Ms. Kane," I say, my voice a thin veil over the storm inside. I discard the broken pen halves with a casual flick, reaching for another from the cup brimming with them. "Tell me more about this affair with Bradley Cavendish. How did it start?"

Charlotte leans back, crossing her arms—a smug sphinx. "Why does that matter? I've told you what you need to know."

"If you want me to help you, I need to believe you," I reply, the sharp edge in my voice piercing her arrogance. "Unless you want me to turn the tape back on."

SIX

CHARLOTTE

I'm seated across from Detective Darcey White, the surface of the metal table cold and unyielding beneath my fingertips. My heart hammers uncontrollably against my ribcage. She's staring at me with those green eyes, so stern, so unforgiving. If you had told me that I'd be here, in this sterile room being interrogated for my husband's murder, I would've laughed. Called you delusional.

But here I am.

"Mrs. Kane," she begins, her voice as cold as her expression, "tell me more about the affair."

I nod, trying to maintain a façade of calm, but inside my mind is racing. I have told Darcey my suspicion about Bradley and I will only tell *her* this, because I believe I can trust her. She might dislike who I am and where I come from, but she seems like someone I can trust. I kind of like her disdain, and her not buying everything I say because I come from money. It makes her feel real. It's refreshing to have someone who doesn't automatically believe every word I say just because of my wealth. Plus, she's a woman. The lack of female presence is evident here, a stark reminder of the male-dominated environment I have found myself in. In fact, aside from the receptionist I passed on my way in, everyone else I have encountered at this station has been male.

"Of course, Detective," I say. My composure is a mask I've perfected over the years, one that hides the fear gnawing at my insides.

I sense her skepticism, the way she leans slightly forward, as if willing me to trip over my own story. But I won't give her that satisfaction. I can't. My life depends on it.

Can she tell how frantically my mind is working, looking for a way out of this web? I have told her how I lost everything. That I can't even afford a good lawyer. I'm lost.

"Bradley gave me what I longed for. What Edward couldn't give me," I say. "I guess it stems from my childhood. Never feeling loved, or that anyone even cared. That's how Edward was. He was just like my parents."

My fingers curl into my palm, nails digging into the flesh as I try to anchor myself amidst Darcey's piercing gaze. It's like she knows—knows that beneath the polish, there's a girl who grew up too fast in a world that never wanted her. I wonder if I should tell her my story, tell her that my life has been rough too. But would she listen?

"Parents are supposed to care, aren't they?" I say. "Mine were more interested in their social standing and the bottom line of their bank account than in their only daughter."

I lean back against the chair, feel its unyielding hardness press against my spine—the same way life has, without the cushion of parental affection or guidance. "I learned young that if I cried, nobody would come. So, I stopped crying."

Darcey's expression doesn't waver, but I plunge ahead, compelled to share snippets of my solitude. "Do you know what it's like, Detective, to celebrate your tenth birthday with a housekeeper who can't even remember your name? Or to have parents who find your high school graduation less important than a business trip to Milan?"

A flicker of something crosses her features—pity?

"By sixteen, I was making decisions that most adults couldn't handle," I continue, the words tumbling out now. "Choosing colleges, managing trust funds that felt more like shackles. Every step of the way, proving to an absent audience that I didn't need them—that I didn't need anyone."

"Sounds lonely," Darcey says, and I'm startled by the hint of softness in her voice. But I shrug it off, letting the bitterness seep into my words.

"Lonely doesn't begin to cover it. It's not just being alone; it's feeling invisible in a crowded room, it's screaming in silence because no one taught you how to ask for help."

The memory of those nights spent in my vast home comes rushing back—the shadows creeping along the walls as if to mock my isolation. The way I'd wrap my arms around myself, rocking gently, trying to mimic the embrace I so craved.

"Charlotte," Darcey prompts, drawing me back to the present, to the reality of these four walls closing in on me. But I've already said too much, revealed the cracks in my armor.

"Let's get back to Bradley," she says, her tone shifting, businesslike once again.

I nod, swallowing down the lump of my past, locking away the vulnerability that has no place here. Ready to face her questions with the same tenacity that got me through those solitary years. Because that's what survivors do—we endure. Yet I can't seem to snap out of it. The past is hitting me, dragging me down.

I'm tracing lines in the table, its surface icy and impersonal, when a memory seizes me. I'm eight again, hugging my knees in the corner of a room that's too big, too empty—just like the hollow feeling inside me. My parents' voices rise and fall downstairs, oblivious to my existence.

"Mommy?" I whisper into the void of our house, voice barely a ripple in the vastness. "Daddy?" But there's no answer; there never is. The grandeur of our home is like a mausoleum.

Jump ahead, I'm twelve, wrestling with textbooks as heavy as the silence at dinner. Every A on my report card a silent scream for attention. For recognition. Yet, their eyes skim over the grades like they're nothing but figures in a business report. "That's expected," they say, before returning to their world of socialites and galas, leaving me to navigate mine alone.

High school graduation—I stand on the stage, a sea of proud families before me, but mine is an ocean away, their absence a gnawing tangle in my chest. I accept my diploma with a plastered-on smile, the applause a bitter reminder of who isn't clapping for me.

It's those very moments, stacked upon each other like precarious building blocks, that forge my resilience. I remember fighting through college applications without a guiding hand, securing valedictorian speeches with nothing but the grit in my belly. Each acceptance letter was a declaration: I can do this on my own.

"Charlotte?"

I blink, the interrogation room snapping back into focus. I can see her studying me, trying to dissect the resolve she sees before her.

I feel my spine straighten, my chin lift. I'm not just telling Darcey; I'm reminding myself of the mettle that courses through my veins. The countless nights burning the midnight oil, the days I spent mastering the art of unwavering confidence, all while navigating a labyrinth of loneliness that would have ensnared someone less tenacious.

"Every challenge," I continue, my voice steady, "was another chance to prove that I didn't need them, or anyone. That's how I got here, Detective. That's how I became the woman who doesn't flinch in the face of adversity."

Darcey nods, almost imperceptibly, and I wonder if she understands what my life has been like. But it doesn't matter if she does. Because I know. And that's enough to keep me standing, unbroken, undeterred.

"I've worked hard for everything I have. I wouldn't sacrifice it all for a little bit of revenge."

Darcey is sharp, insistent. "Charlotte," she says, and I steel myself for the onslaught. "Just tell me about Bradley."

It's like walking onto a stage, the spotlight burning down on me. My mind races, flipping through memories like pages in a book I wish I could rewrite.

"He loved me. He was kind to me. He had a way of making the world seem... malleable, as if everything could bend to his will. Unlike Edward." My voice is steady, but inside, even the mention of his name makes me panic.

"Charming," Darcey muses, jotting something down in her notes that I can't see.

"Charm is an understatement," I reply. "He is magnetic. People just gravitate toward him—you know, the kind of person that lights up a room when he walks in."

"But there's always a flip side to that coin, isn't there?" she presses, and I swallow hard. The air feels thick, like I'm trying to breathe through a blanket.

"Of course," I concede, my eyes darting to her face, searching for any hint of where this is going. "No one is just one thing. He... he could be complicated."

"Complicated how?" Her pen pauses, and those cold eyes fix on mine, unblinking. "Did you feel trapped by Bradley?" she asks, leaning forward slightly.

"Trapped? No, the only person I've felt trapped by is Edward," I admit, choosing my words carefully. "There's a thin line between devotion and possession, Detective. And Edward... he often blurred those lines."

"Give me an example," she says, her voice soft now, coaxing

secrets from the vault of my memory like a locksmith finessing a lock.

I hesitate, my mind flashing back to whispered arguments, to nights spent staring at the ceiling while Edward's shadow loomed over me. To promises that felt more like threats, to love that left bruises no one else could see.

"Sometimes," I begin, feeling the weight of the past pressing down on me, "love can feel like a cage. And Edward—"

"Edward what?" Darcey prods when I falter.

"Edward knew exactly how to build them," I finish, meeting her gaze with a defiance born of years spent hiding in plain sight. "I worked hard to finish law school, and yet I was never allowed to practice. Because women in Edward's family didn't work."

Darcey leans back in her chair, the creak of the faux leather loud in the sterile room. She steeples her fingers, gaze fixed on me like a hawk eyeing its prey. "We're all over the place here, why don't you start from the beginning? Forget Bradley for a moment. How did you meet Edward?"

A tight smile tugs at the corners of my mouth despite the chill that question sends down my spine. I take a deep breath, trying to steady the tremor in my voice. "It was at a charity ball—"

"Which one?" she interrupts, pen poised above her notepad.

"The Children's Heart Foundation Gala," I clarify, remembering how the opulent chandeliers had cast everything in a soft golden hue that night. "I was there alone, just trying to lend support, and he... he gravitated toward me."

"He liked you?" Darcey asks.

"A lot." I let out a half laugh, thinking back. "He approached me with such confidence. We talked for hours about everything and nothing."

"Sounds enchanting," she says dryly. I'm losing her...

"Enchanting, yes, for a time." I clench my fists under the table, hidden from view. "But when someone shines that brightly, you sometimes miss the shadows they cast until you're standing right in them."

"Go on," she prompts, leaning forward slightly, her ponytail shifting over one shoulder.

"Edward could be intense. What began as attentive quickly turned... all-consuming. Calls, texts, surprise visits to my apartment." I pause, recalling how thrilling his attention once felt. "At first, it was flattering. But then it became clear he needed control."

"Control?" There's a flicker of something in Darcey's demeanor now, a crack in her professionalism. Curiosity? No, recognition. She's looking for a motive, so she can pin this on me.

"Of everything," I continue, my heart racing. "He wanted to dictate what I wore, who I saw. It was like being under a spell that I couldn't break. The man knew how to pull strings, always saying the right thing, twisting reality so subtly that I questioned my own judgment. And he'd be cold. Unloving. Once he had me hooked in, he changed."

"Did you ever confront him about it?" Her voice is almost sympathetic.

"Confronting Edward..." I trail off, a cold sweat breaking out on my forehead as I remember the last time I tried. "Let's just say, it didn't make things better. I found my own ways to survive."

Darcey nods slowly, scribbling notes that I can't see. "And yet you stayed with him."

"Sometimes we stay in situations that hurt us," I say, meeting her gaze unflinchingly. "Because the pain becomes familiar, and there's comfort in familiarity, isn't there?"

The question lingers in the air, carrying a heavy weight of meaning. Darcey remains quiet, but her silence speaks volumes.

She seems to understand more than she lets on. Maybe it's because we're both women; I hope that my story will resonate with her in a way it may not with others.

"Edward had this way of knowing things he shouldn't—like he had eyes on me even when he wasn't there. He would ignore me for days if I did something wrong, like once when I tried to leave the house and leave my phone at home, so he wouldn't be able to track me."

My hands are shaking now, and I clasp them together to still them. "Edward knew things about me that I'd never told him, my movements, conversations I'd had. It felt like being watched by an invisible audience. He told me who I could hang out with and then they reported back to him the things I said. I had to cut off many of our friends and only hang out with one that I have known since university. I even got a new maid, one I made sure I could trust and was loyal to only me."

"Sounds suffocating."

"It was suffocating," I correct her, a bitter taste on my tongue. "I felt like I was going to die in my marriage. Until Bradley came into the picture."

SEVEN

CHARLOTTE

I tap my fingers on the smooth surface of my chair, and swallow hard against the lump forming in my throat. There's an itch under my skin, a crawling anticipation as I prepare to peel back layers of myself. It's not just nerves; there's a thrill too, the kind that comes from standing at the edge of a precipice.

"Charlotte?" Darcey's voice pulls me back to reality, her gaze searching mine.

"Sorry," I reply, brushing away the remnants of my memories. "I was just reflecting on how things were back then."

"It sounds a bit lonely," she comments thoughtfully. "What was it like during those times? You talked about the controlling behavior, the coldness from him. Is it safe to say you were very unhappy in your marriage?"

"Excruciatingly. But I guess I should've known. Marrying a guy straight out of Harvard. They're all the same. By the way, Bradley and Edward knew each other from college."

"They were friends?"

"They moved in the same social circles, let's just say that."

"Interesting to start an affair with someone your husband is friends with?" she says.

"I guess I thrive on the danger, right? That's what you want me to say?" I ask. "That I'm so bored out of my mind being a stay-at-home mom, in my big mansion, that I need the rush? To feel alive?"

I straighten up, tapping my fingers against the table. As the vivid memory of one particularly harrowing night—one among many—floods my mind, I am transported back to my living room as Edward comes through the front door.

I recoil as he turns his black eyes toward me, his face contorted with anger. But this time, instead of shrinking away in fear, I stand tall and meet his glare with a steely determination.

He hurls insults and accusations at me, telling me how worthless I am, and that no one will ever love me. He is trying to provoke a reaction like he always does. But I refuse to give him the satisfaction. So many times I have pleaded with him for the love and affection that he can never give me. For him to hold me, to kiss me, but he never does. But not this time. Not tonight. And for a brief moment, I see confusion flicker in his eyes before they harden once again in disgust.

Lying alone in bed that night, I can't stop the tears from streaming down my face. But amidst my pain and heartache, I silently make a promise to myself—a promise to stand up and fight back against him, and never let him break me again. But then, I wonder why I even married him in the first place. Was it because my parents pressured me as soon as I graduated? And now, if I were to divorce him, they would just try to set me up with someone else, possibly even worse? He wasn't always like this, I tell myself. When I met him he was different. I wonder when he changed. It was so gradual, I barely noticed till it was too late and I was stuck.

"Starting an affair seems risky," she says, but I can tell she's hooked on every word.

"Life is risk, Darcey," I retort. "Especially mine." I pause as once again I am transported back in time.

The clink of ice in my glass punctuates the murmur of conversation around me. Perched on a barstool, I scan the room through half-lidded eyes, my gaze landing on a man nursing a whiskey neat at the end of the bar.

"See that one?" I whisper, leaning toward my friend, who looks at me with an intensity that's almost palpable. "Watch this."

I slide off my seat with a graceful ease, the black fabric of my dress clinging to every curve like a second skin. I saunter over to the man, each step measured, hips swaying with a confidence that's taken years to perfect. His eyes meet mine, and there's a spark—a recognition of the dance we're about to engage in.

"Is this seat taken?" My voice is a velvety purr, subtle yet commanding.

"By you, it is now," he replies, pulling out the stool next to him.

We talk. Small talk at first, trivialities that serve as mere vehicles for the electricity building between us. I laugh, toss my hair back, touch his arm fleetingly. The air thickens with tension, with unspoken possibilities.

"Flirting's an art form," I tell Darcey after recounting the incident with a sense of pride. "I've mastered it. It's not just about looking good—it's about making them feel seen. Desired. I started going out when Edward was working late. I wanted someone to notice me."

"And then what?" Her voice is flat, but there's a flicker in her eyes, a curiosity that betrays her feigned indifference.

"Then I go home," I say, my tone almost nonchalant. "I never had much time until Edward got back."

My fingers are twisted together in my lap to stop their trembling. Darcey's green eyes narrow as they always do when she's about to slice through the silence with a question designed to cut to the bone. I feel the weight of her gaze like a physical force.

"Charlotte," she says, her voice is cool and detached, "you said that Edward keeps an eye on everything you do. How were you able to have an affair, then? It doesn't seem to make much sense?"

I nod, trying to appear calm, though my heart races—a trapped bird against my ribs. Each word I utter can tip the scale toward my freedom or seal my fate behind bars. The detective's perception of me feels like a vise, tightening with every glance she sends my way.

"Of course, Detective White," I manage, my words measured, deliberate. But inside, it's chaos, a whirlwind of anxiety. What if she doesn't believe me? What if my explanations aren't enough?

The room is claustrophobic, the air thick with suspicion. A single bead of sweat trails down the back of my neck, and I fight the urge to wipe it away, to show any sign of weakness. She watches me, her expression unreadable, but I sense her mind working, piecing together the puzzle I'm a part of, whether I like it or not.

"Edward goes on a lot of business trips," I answer, watching her reaction closely. "And I met Bradley so innocently. He was at the bar a few times when I was there flirting with men. And the first time we spoke, it was like he had planned it. He gave me a phone."

"Right." She scribbles something onto her notepad, her movements sharp, her focus intense.

"Bradley was very persuasive," I say next, choosing my words with care. "He told me he needed me. He was lonely, he said. He painted a picture of a marriage long devoid of love, and I finally had someone I could talk to. He said he'd been watching me, listening in on my flirtatious exchanges for weeks. He said he was what I needed. That he could make sure our affair never got out."

Darcey's expression doesn't change, but I sense the shift in energy. There's more at stake here than just an interrogation. Her skepticism is a tangible thing, wrapping around my throat, threatening to choke out the truth I'm so carefully curating. I need her to understand, to see past the mistakes I've made. My future, my chance at redemption—it all depends on the results of this investigation.

Darcey continues, her tone deceptively mild, "Your daughter... she's with your parents still, correct?"

The mention of my child causes my heart to stutter. I've fought tooth and nail to ensure she doesn't endure the shadows of my past. "Yes, Detective. Luckily, she was spending the weekend with my parents. I extended her stay there till this is all over."

I glance down, a pang of regret gnawing at me. "I sent my nanny to help her."

"Great." There's a bite to Darcey's words, a subtle jab at all the help I have. I wonder, does she have children? A nanny to help her? Can detectives afford that?

"How can you afford the help and to live in your house still if your husband lost everything?" she asks.

"I can't. Not for long."

"So you sent your daughter away from her own mother? To be taken care of by a nanny?"

"Just for now. I'm trying to do what's best for my daughter, keep her away from all this."

"From all this or from becoming like her mother?" Darcey leans forward, elbows resting on the table, eyes fixed on mine. It's clear she's not just asking about my current predicament but digging deeper, into the murkiness of my history, the roots I've tried so desperately to sever.

"Every day, I strive to give her a better life than I had," I say quietly, the admission costing me more than I want to reveal. "One with love and care, without deceit and fear."

"Bradley," she cuts in sharply, as if uninterested in my

daughter, "was lonely, you said. And you, what? Fell for his sob story?"

I hesitate. The room seems to close in on me, the walls whispering judgment. "It's never black and white, Detective. People make mistakes."

"Mistakes can cost you, Charlotte. They can cost you everything." Her warning hangs in the air between us, heavy and foreboding.

I swallow hard, my defenses crumbling under the weight of her condemnation. Darcey White may not have the whole story, but she has enough to make me question every decision that led me to this cold, unforgiving chair. Maybe I shouldn't have told her a thing?

"Bradley," I say his name on a sharp exhale of breath. "He knew how to weave words into a net, one I found myself ensnared in." I recall that evening, the amber glow of the chandelier casting shadows on our table, making it feel like we were the only two people in the world. "He took me out to dinner once, after an argument with Edward. Said his marriage was over in all but paper."

Detective White's eyes narrow, her lips pressing into a thin line. "And you believed him?" There's a hint of mockery in her voice, a disbelief that I could be so naïve.

I nod slowly, feeling my pulse quicken as though I'm back in that moment, surrounded by the hum of conversation and the clink of cutlery against fine china. "I saw the sadness in his eyes, Darcey. It mirrored my own." My fingers curl into fists in my lap, nails digging into my palm. "We were two lost souls finding comfort in each other."

"So why did you do it?" she asks, leaning forward. "Didn't you think about the fact that this man was married?"

Her question is a blade, one that cuts to the heart of my dilemma. I lean back, trying to put space between us, as if the distance could shield me from her probing gaze. "I did," I admit, the words heavy with remorse. "Every single day." My throat tightens, and I have to force the next words out. "But the heart isn't always ruled by logic, Detective. Bradley was persistent, and I... I was lonely.

"He sent flowers, at first. Gorgeous bouquets that would arrive at my doorstep with notes as soon as Edward walked out the door. I tossed them in the bin, telling myself it was nothing but an infatuation that would pass. Then came the texts, each one carefully crafted to chip away at my resolve. 'I can't stop thinking about you' he'd write, or 'You deserve someone who sees you.' They were relentless, a constant buzz at the edge of my consciousness, eroding my willpower like waves upon rocks. He made me feel like I was the only one who could save him from his loneliness."

"Save him?" Darcey's eyebrow arches, skepticism etched into every feature. "Or save yourself?"

My knuckles whiten. "I didn't need saving," I insist, though my voice trembles with the strain of keeping it steady. "I just... I didn't want to be alone any more."

"Nobody wants to be alone, Charlotte," Darcey says, her tone softening by degrees. "But desperation can make us vulnerable. It can make us overlook the consequences of our actions."

The air feels thick with my desperation as I lean forward, pleading for her to understand, to see the truth beyond the mess I've gotten myself into. "You have to believe me, Detective White. I never intended for anyone to get hurt. I thought I could handle it, that it was just a harmless affair. But I was wrong."

"Affairs are never harmless, Charlotte. They leave casualties in their wake." Darcey's voice is a low murmur, almost drowned out by the roaring in my ears.

"I'm not a home wrecker. He said he would leave his wife.

And he knew that the only way I could be with him is if Edward was gone forever."

Detective Darcey White's face is unreadable, her green eyes giving nothing away. But she looks down at her notes like she doesn't believe me.

"He said he would do anything to have me all to himself. Maybe he is planning on killing his own wife too."

EIGHT

DARCEY

Is my husband going to be convicted of murder? Am I in danger?

These questions race through my mind as I drive home. The steering wheel feels slippery in my hands as the intense Florida sun pours through the windows. My vision becomes hazy, not from the harsh sunlight, but from the tears that have been welling up since I abruptly left Charlotte's interview. I try to blink them away.

My whole life, for the past year, has been a sham.

I told my colleagues that I believe Charlotte is responsible for Edward's death, and I asked them to reach out to his friends and family to gather more information. The rest of the day I had spent buried in paperwork, and writing the report from the interview, trying to keep myself together, and not break down.

"Get a grip." My voice is both reassuring and pitiable against the hum of the car engine. The road stretches ahead, monotonous and unfeeling; it doesn't care about my crumbling marriage or the shards of trust Bradley left scattered on Charlotte's silk sheets.

I reach a red light, and use this chance to yank a tissue from the console and dab at the traitorous streaks marring my face. I can't let the kids see me like this—can't afford to crumble when they need their rock to be steady, unbreakable. So I fix the smudged mascara, pinching my cheeks for color. It's all smoke and mirrors, just like the life I portray.

"Detective White, ready for your next case?" I sneer at my reflection in the rearview mirror. It's a pathetic attempt at humor, but I need to distract myself.

He bought her a phone. The affair was his idea. He promised to leave me. To get rid of Edward...

The light flicks green, and I press the accelerator with more force than necessary. The suburban houses blur past, each one holding its own secrets behind meticulously manicured lawns and freshly painted façades. Mine is just another in the lineup —a perfect little lie.

"Home sweet home," I say through gritted teeth as I turn into the driveway, the rehearsed smile already plastered on my face. I had to let Charlotte go—since I don't have enough to hold her. I feel the worry grow inside of me. What am I even doing? I need to figure out how far I can take this before I put my job at risk. If I do nothing more, and come clean to Jim, I'll be fine. But if I continue with the case, and anyone finds out how I am connected to Charlotte or that Bradley has been accused, my life will be over. I'll have no career to fall back on, no way to support my kids. If my marriage falls apart, and Bradley is innocent, he will most likely get custody of our children. There's a lot at stake.

I push the worry away for now, and smile. I can't let Bradley know what I know. Not yet. Let the performance begin.

The door swings open and I'm instantly swallowed by the cacophony of childhood glee. "Mommy!" The twins barrel into me, their small arms banding around my waist like life preservers tossed in stormy seas. For a fleeting second, their laughter is a salve to the raw wound inside my chest.

"Hey, my little detectives," I muster up enthusiasm. My hands smooth over their hair, the static from their excitement zapping against my palms. They look up at me, all wide-eyed innocence.

"Did you catch the bad guys today?" Emma's question is earnest, her belief in me untainted.

"Every day, sweetie." The lie slips out as easily as my badge clips onto my belt. But the truth? The truth is, I couldn't even detect the betrayal nesting in my own bed.

I disentangle myself from the embrace with the gentlest tug and glance around the familiar chaos of our living room—blocks strewn across the floor, crayon masterpieces adorning the walls. Bradley only collected them from aftercare at the school an hour ago. But their toys are everywhere. All over our home. A home brimming with life.

"Where's Daddy?" I ask nonchalantly, my voice masking the pounding of my heart.

"Upstairs!" Jacob exclaims eagerly, already captivated by the new Legos I am holding in my hand, that I picked up from the store on my way home. It's a bribe, and I don't feel good about it, but I need them quiet for a while.

"Great, go and enjoy those new Lego sets I got for you guys. Mommy needs to talk to Daddy for a minute."

Their eyes light up as I hand them the new toys, and they dash off to play with them. As they are occupied and distracted, I take a deep breath and prepare myself for a difficult conversation with their father.

"Bradley?" My call goes unanswered, the word hanging limp in the air between us. Or rather, between me and his ghost. My heart clenches—a vise tightening with each step I take up the stairs.

"Bradley?" Anxiety laces my words now, a frayed thread ready to snap. He's not upstairs. Not in the kitchen, nursing a beer and pretending today was just another day at the office. He's missing, and for a moment, so is my breath.

I slip through the sliding door and step onto the back porch, the click of the latch behind me sounding like a verdict. There he is, Bradley, my dear husband, perched on the edge of the wicker chair, a plume of smoke swirling above him. It's one of my menthol cigarettes pinched between his fingers, the very ones I promised I had sworn off.

"What's going on?" I ask, voice steadier than I feel, but it's not about the cigarette, not really.

He looks up at me through the haze, eyes narrowing just so. "You tell me," he says, the corner of his mouth twisted around irony and nicotine. "I found these underneath the cushion. You told me you quit."

Guilt nibbles at the fringes of my resolve, like moths to a flame, but then anger, hot and swift, chases it away. He's the liar here. Still, I can't let him see that he's gotten to me, that his duplicity has torn something inside me that might never mend.

He grimaces. "And what are these anyways? Menthol cigarettes? They taste disgusting. Did you switch to these just so I wouldn't notice the smell? That's some devious move there, little missy. You really went out of your way for me not to know."

"Little lies, Bradley," I say, my laugh sharp as shattered glass. "They're like the throw pillows of marriage, aren't they? Decorative. Harmless." My words hang between us, barbed and glinting in the twilight.

Bradley takes a long drag, eyes locked on mine, searching for cracks in my armor. But I've learned from the best; my shield is as impeccable as his tailored suits.

Breathing in the briny tang of sea air, I lean against the doorframe, watching Bradley with an intensity that matches the Florida heat. The children's laughter is a distant symphony.

"Bradley," I begin, my voice threaded with forced casualness, "where were you yesterday afternoon?" My fingers drum nervously on the wood. I remember dialing his number, the ring echoing unanswered while I stood amidst crime scene chaos.

He doesn't look at me, just blows out another stream of smoke that curls up into the fading light. "What are you asking, Darcey?"

"Nothing." I shrug, but it's heavy, like wearing a winter coat in July. "Just wondering. I couldn't get ahold of you all afternoon. You left in the morning without telling me why. I get called in on a case, and have to get Chloe to look after the little ones. I don't hear a word from you all day, and then come home and to my surprise you're cooking me dinner? Where were you?"

There's a shift in the air, almost imperceptible, like the moment before a storm unleashes its fury. "What? What are you accusing me of?" His words puncture the humidity, sharp and sudden.

I watch the cigarette drop from his hand, a smoldering comet crashing to the ground. He grinds it underfoot, the ember dying with a hiss against the damp wood.

"Maybe you should go get drunk as usual," he spits out, the accusation a tangible thing between us. "At least you're nicer when you're passed out."

The words hang, poison-tipped darts, and he turns on his heel—leaving. His footsteps resonate, a countdown to something inevitable, something broken. Inside, the kids' joyous ignorance has turned into screaming and probably fighting.

I'm left standing in the silence, the ghost of menthol and accusation clinging to the air.

The porch seems to shrink around me, the wooden planks a raft adrift in an ocean of turmoil. My fingers trace the railing, rough under my touch, splinters flirting with tender skin—just another discomfort I'll ignore. I collapse into the wicker chair.

The sky bleeds orange and pink above, beautiful and indifferent.

Get it together, Darcey, I think, though the thought floats away like the smoke from Bradley's discarded cigarette. Our marriage, a house of cards trembling in a breeze of lies and half-truths, feels like a weight pressing down on my lungs. I gasp for air, for clarity, for anything solid in this quicksand life.

The screaming turned back to laughter from the twins filters through the window, innocent and untainted. They know nothing of the charade, of the secrets that lurk behind closed doors and whispered phone calls. I stand up, brushing off the invisible dirt of my unraveling life, and brace myself. For them, I can be an actress worthy of an Oscar; for them, I can smile.

I step inside, the transition from shadowed solitude to the warm glow of home jarring. My children's faces are alight with the simple joy of seeing Mommy, and it's like a balm on the raw edges of my frayed nerves. "Thank you, Mommy!" they chorus, waving their toys, their small arms winding around my waist with a force that anchors me, if only for a moment.

Their giggles are the sweetest melody, a counterpoint to the discordant notes of my heartache. The mask is secure, my eyes reflecting only love and contentment as I guide them back to their game of make-believe, where monsters are easily slain and happy endings are guaranteed.

And for a fleeting second, with their heads bent together in whispered conspiracy, I let myself live in their world—a world where the biggest concern is who gets to be the hero today. But even heroes have their demons, and mine are just a room away, lurking in the shadows of doubt and betrayal.

"Mommy will be right back," I say.

The kitchen is quiet as I move toward it and grab a wine glass from the shelf. The bottle of chardonnay is cool in my grasp, the golden liquid swirling as I pour slowly, watching as the glass fills.

With a trembling hand, I bring the rim to my lips, the crisp taste bringing me back to reality—back to the world where villains aren't just part of children's games, and heroes are flawed and bruised. A sigh escapes me, mingling with the scent of fermented grapes, as I brace for the battles yet to come.

The wine warms me, false courage trickling through my veins as I stand at the threshold between sanctuary and battle-field. My eyes flit across the room, landing on a photo of Bradley and me, smiles too wide to be true. The glass feels heavy in my hand.

"Mommy, are you okay?" Jacob's voice is a lifeline, but it tugs at the edges of my guilt.

"Of course, sweetheart," I lie with a smile that feels fake, setting the glass aside. I kneel to their level, pulling both into an embrace that's more for me than them. Their small arms around me are a bandage over a wound that won't close.

Before bedtime, we spend some playful moments together. The twins and I gather around a pile of Lego pieces, embarking on a creative endeavor.

"Let's build a castle!" Emma suggests excitedly, already reaching for the blue blocks. "With a princess in it."

"Nah, I want to make a spaceship," Jacob counters, grabbing the gray pieces.

I laugh. "How about a castle that can fly? And the astronaut being a woman wearing a crown? That way, everyone wins."

As they assemble their whimsical creation, the room fills with laughter and chatter, each child's preferences subtly shining through. The twins' distinct personalities become apparent—one with a penchant for adventure and the other with a flair for fantasy. Once the Lego masterpiece is complete, I finally guide them to their beds, their earlier protests now forgotten.

I tuck them in, kisses and promises of tomorrow fluttering like moths against the darkness that settles in my chest.

. . .

The house is eerily silent now the twins are in bed, a stillness that amplifies silence. I linger in the hallway outside their room, closing the door softly. My fingers trace the worn wood grain of the banister, each line serving as a map to the uncertainty and confusion inside me. What am I going to do? How can I protect my children from this mess?

As a detective, I'm used to searching for clues and following leads, but so far I haven't found any evidence Bradley and Charlotte's affair is continuing.

But how can I trust anything they tell me at this point?

Stepping out onto the porch, I inhale the crisp night air. There's a discarded cigarette lying on the faded wood.

Do I believe her accusations? I'm not sure. But even if I don't believe her, then I do believe that Bradley continued the affair when he told me it was over. And that leads me to decide that my marriage is over.

"Someone thinks they can get away with murder," I whisper into the darkness, my own words startling me with their truth.

I should be stronger than this. A skilled detective who can solve any case except her own failing marriage. A mother who can protect everyone but herself. It's almost comical.

With a heavy heart, I retreat back inside and lock the door behind me—not just on the night, but on the part of myself that longs to break free from this masquerade. How can I continue with this case while also protecting my children? And most importantly, how can I trust anyone again after all these lies?

NINE

DARCEY

I step out of my modest sedan—a sharp contrast to the luxury vehicles lining the circular drive—and the grandeur of Charlotte's parents' mansion looms over me, an ostentatious display of wealth that's as subtle as a sledgehammer.

I pause, taking in the elaborate fountain at the center of the drive, water dancing gracefully under the afternoon sun. The mansion is a behemoth of classical architecture, with towering white columns guarding the entrance like sentinels. Each window, arched and framed by heavy drapes visible from the outside, hints at secrets held tight within those opulent walls. Gardens meticulously landscaped, not a single petal or blade of grass out of place, stretch out on either side of the walkway. They're probably tended daily by more gardeners than there are plants, I think bitterly. And I thought the Kanes' home was luxurious. At least something Charlotte said in that interview room was accurate; her parents have high standards.

A deep breath does little to steady the tremor in my hands, but I force my legs to move. My footsteps echo over the marble steps leading up to the double doors—rich mahogany set with intricate ironwork. It's all just... too much.

I can almost hear Charlotte's smug voice in my head. I wonder what she thought when she saw Bradley's home. I can't imagine she has ever been to our house, but perhaps she looked it up? Had she looked up our address online and seen our small, unassuming house? Did she see it as a reflection of my worth as a wife and mother?

It is an unsettling thought, knowing that she has some knowledge of my life and my home, while I was completely unaware of her existence until a year ago. She doesn't know who I am, but she knows Bradley has a wife and children. Did she see our little home and immediately decide she is the better match for my husband?

The more I think about it, the more I begin to question my own worth. Does Bradley see me as unremarkable compared to the glamorous and successful Charlotte? Does he feel trapped in our simple life and seek excitement and escape with her? Does he see her as more compatible since they come from nearly the same background? Walk the same social circles?

A sudden anger and bitterness rises up within me. How dare she come into my life and try to steal my husband, my life?

I reach for the doorbell, fingers hesitating for just a moment before pressing the button. The chime that sounds is melodic, resonating through the cavernous space behind the doors and mocking my racing pulse. Waiting here, I feel like an impostor in my own skin, every second stretching into an eternity while I imagine the judgment waiting on the other side of the door. My life might be crumbling, but I can't let it show—not here, not with her.

Get it together, Darcey, I chide myself, *You're not just some jilted wife; you're a damn good detective. Don't forget that.* The door hasn't even opened yet, and already I'm fighting the first battle: keeping my anxiety firmly in check.

The door swings open, revealing a butler whose face is as blank as the pristine walls that flank the grand entrance.

I show him my badge. "Detective White here to see Mrs. Charlotte Kane."

I nod to him—a reflex—my attempt at politeness that feels out of place in this house bloated with wealth. He doesn't return the gesture, simply turning on his heel to lead me inside.

"Ms. White," he intones, and even his voice is polished to a sheen that grates against my nerves.

"Detective," I correct him, though I doubt he cares. The title might command respect on my turf, but here it's just a reminder of the chasm between my world and theirs.

I trail behind him, my gaze roaming over the foyer. The marble floors are a tapestry of opulence, veins of gold threading through the stone like rivers of liquid wealth. Crystal chandeliers hang from the ceiling, each droplet of glass reflecting light, splintering it into a thousand shards of brilliance that dance across the walls. It's beautiful, sure, in an ostentatious kind of way that screams of money spent for the sake of spending.

"Please, this way," the butler says, and I follow him down a corridor bathed in sunlight that spills through expansive windows. The light is almost too pure, too clean, like everything else in this place.

And then we're there, in a sitting room where Charlotte waits, perched like some exotic bird among the plush cushions and elegant drapes. The sun caresses her silhouette, setting her raven hair aglow as if she's part of the decor—another expensive piece in this collection of luxuries.

"Detective White," she greets me, her voice cool as she stands, movements precise and practiced. There's tension in the way she holds herself, a stiffness that belies the calm exterior. I can see it because I know what to look for—the subtle signs of strain that people think they hide so well.

"Charlotte," I reply, keeping my tone neutral. We're not friends, far from it.

Our eyes meet, and in hers, I see something flicker—recognition, maybe, or the reflection of our shared predicament. It's hard to tell with Charlotte. She's mastered the art of concealment, wrapping her true thoughts in layers of ambiguity like one of those Russian nesting dolls.

"Have a seat." She gestures to an armchair opposite her, its upholstery too perfect, too untouched. I take it, the fabric warm beneath my palms, and brace myself for the conversation ahead.

I lean forward. "I believe you," I declare without preamble, the words sharp and clear in the opulent silence of the sitting room. I lean back.

"Believe me?" Her tone is guarded, eyes narrowing ever so slightly as if trying to decipher the angle I'm playing. Trust doesn't come easy in our line of work—or in our personal lives, for that matter.

"Everything you've told me about Bradley Cavendish."

I keep my voice low but insistent. The sunlight paints everything in this room gold, except the truth. It's essential she understands the gravity of what we're discussing. "But we need to keep this between us. Can you do that?"

Charlotte takes a moment, her gaze drifting toward the sprawling gardens visible through the French windows, perhaps contemplating the weight of privacy in a gilded cage like this. There's a flicker of something in her eyes—skepticism maybe, or the edge of fear. She knows the stakes are high; after all, she's not just playing with fire, she's dancing in it. "Why can't I tell anyone else, if you believe me? Aren't you going to help me convince your colleagues?"

"Because I'm your best shot at getting out of this mess without losing everything. Right now you're the one with a motive, because of the affair, the loss of the money. You were found with Edward's blood on your hands. I spent all day at the station today listening to everyone saying how they all believe you killed him, and trying to figure out how to build a case with what we got so far. It doesn't look good for you." I don't bother sugarcoating it. We both know the score—even if part of me resents that she's wrapped up in it. "Bradley's clever, but he's left a trail. They all do. I can find it, piece it together. But only if we're careful. Only if he doesn't suspect a thing."

Her lips press into a thin line. The idea of teaming up with me must churn her stomach, but desperation makes strange bedfellows. And desperation is something I can smell on her like the expensive perfume that fails to mask it.

"I can tell you still have feelings for him." Her face softens. "But one of you will have to go down for this."

"Fine," she concedes with a nod, the carefully sculpted indifference cracking just enough to let me see the real Charlotte—the one who's aware that swimming with sharks means you might get bitten.

"We need to gather evidence. Quietly, methodically. I need you to document everything." I sit back, crossing one leg over the other, trying to emulate some of the nonchalance she wraps around herself like one of her fur stoles. "I'll need access to certain... items. Things that can tie him to his actions beyond a reasonable doubt."

She doesn't say anything for a beat, two beats, three. Then, with a curt nod, she's on board, the unspoken agreement hanging heavy between us like the Florida humidity. "We'll have to be discreet."

"Discretion is my middle name," I lie smoothly. Discretion has never been my game—I'm more of a blunt instrument than a scalpel. But for this? For the chance to expose Bradley for the lying snake he is? I can play the part. Especially when the role I'm stepping into might just be the lead in the story of my life.

"I need you to show me the phone Bradley gave you," I demand. I'm keenly aware of each ticking second as I watch her, the green eyes I keep hidden behind skepticism now dissecting her every micro-expression.

Charlotte stalls, her manicured fingers betraying a slight

tremor before they dive into the abyss of her designer purse. She's playing for time, and it irks me, the way she can't just give a straight answer without a performance. But then, this whole mansion is a stage for the wealthy, isn't it? A place where you can pretend the world outside doesn't exist with its grime and struggle.

She draws out the sleek device, its screen a black mirror reflecting our mutual distrust. As she hands it to me, our fingers brush, and I feel the weight of our unspoken pact. It's heavier than the phone, laden with secrets and lies—a currency that's all too familiar in my line of work.

"Be careful with that," she warns, her hazel gaze locking onto mine for an instant before flitting away, as if she's afraid of what she might find there.

I nod, even though we both know I'm anything but careful. I'm a hurricane dressed up as a detective, something untamed and relentless. But I'll play the part—for now. For this.

I swipe through the phone, each message and image a breadcrumb on the trail of duplicity that Bradley has left behind. The gallery is a testament to his double life, one where promises are as flimsy as the paper-thin walls of our crumbling marriage. My finger hovers over a series of pictures, a narrative in pixels—empty wine bottles lined up like soldiers after battle, silent witnesses to my nightly capitulations.

"What's this?" My voice is steady, betraying nothing.

Charlotte shifts, crossing one leg over the other, her black dress hugging her form. "Bradley," she begins, her tone almost clinical, "he sends those pictures when his wife... well, when she's had too much wine and is passed out."

There's no softness in her words, no cushion for the blow.

"Wife's passed out drunk again," I mimic, reading the text out loud, letting my voice take on a sneer that mirrors Bradley's hidden scorn. "Then he snaps a shot of the aftermath, sends it along with an emoji with a shrug saying, 'What should I do?'"

"Yes."

The picture on the screen is a cruel snapshot of a reality that I can't shake off. I remember that night too well, the tension in the air just before everything fell apart. In the picture, I'm on the couch, asleep after too much wine. You can't see my face. I am wearing my navy blue blouse and black trousers, trying to keep up appearances even as my world crumbles around me. We had a fight. It got ugly. The kids were already tucked into bed, oblivious to the storm brewing between their parents.

As I stare at the image, a surge of anger and helplessness washes over me. I am relieved though that Charlotte can't recognize me.

The photo burns into my retinas, a visual slap that leaves an invisible welt on my psyche. The room feels too small suddenly. Charlotte's gaze is steady, but there's something there, a flicker of satisfaction? It's gone before I can read it fully.

"Must be nice," I say, the sarcasm dripping from my lips like venom, "to be the sober confidante while his wife drowns."

I look away for a second, but I don't let the sting show. I can't. He was embarrassed of me. Making fun of me. But my drinking, it's the only thing that's kept me sane for the last year. A deep feeling of shame builds inside me. I clench my jaw as Charlotte languishes on the chaise longue, her slender leg draped over the side with a casual grace that screams control. Her voice is honeyed poison, each word measured for effect.

"Tomorrow she'll blame me again," she purrs, repeating the words from his text, eyes narrowing in mock concern. "Tell me I'm not a good husband to her. It's the same all the time." My fingers tighten around the phone, knuckles whitening. I can almost hear the smirk in her voice, see it dancing in those hazel depths that don't miss a trick. I'm made of sterner stuff than I realize. My heart hammers against my ribs, but I keep my face impassive.

"Is that so?" I manage to say, words clipped. The effort it

takes to keep my tone even, to not let the hurt bleed through, is monumental. But I manage because that's what I do—I manage. I've been managing my whole damn life.

"Bradley has his... quirks," she says lightly, as if discussing the weather or the price of tea. "I didn't particularly enjoy the way he spoke about his wife. It's one of the reasons I realized he might be capable of killing Edward."

I swallow hard, my throat suddenly dry.

"Everyone has quirks," I reply, forcing a shrug, though it feels like moving mountains. "Some are just more destructive than others."

Her eyes lock onto mine.

"Indeed," she murmurs, a ghost of a smile playing on her lips.

I struggle to keep my composure as I speak, the words feeling like gravel in my mouth. "Let's not lose sight of what's important," I say firmly. "We have to stay ahead of him if we want to gather enough evidence to protect you and incriminate him. Right now, we have nothing, and that's not good."

She meets my gaze for a moment before nodding in understanding, allowing me to continue scrolling through her phone. I notice that the timestamps on the texts are recent and frequent, but there are also other photos on the phone.

As I scroll through the phone, my heart races at the implications of what I might find. The texts between Charlotte and Bradley are like daggers to my already wounded pride. I can feel a surge of anger bubbling beneath the surface as I try to maintain my composure.

Among the texts and pictures lies a series of photos that make my blood run cold. Images of me, passed out drunk on the couch. I'm unrecognizable, yes, at least he had the decency to make sure of that. But I'm still vulnerable and exposed, and they are captured without my consent. Plus, it doesn't end there. There are also intimate and explicit photos of her with

Bradley. The bile rises in my throat, a mix of anger and disgust churning within me.

I force myself to maintain a neutral expression, but inside, I'm seething with rage at the violation of trust laid bare before me.

"This is good," I urge, my voice barely concealing the intensity of my emotions. "But we need more if we're going to nail him to the wall." I look up at Charlotte, her hazel eyes reflecting a mix of fear and determination.

"We have to be strategic about this," I continue, my mind racing with possibilities. "I want you to think back... Is there anything in your house? Something that could tie him to the crime scene without a doubt?"

"I can look," Charlotte says.

I take a deep breath, letting it out slowly.

I tilt my head, eyeing Charlotte with a skeptic's gaze. "Why doesn't he leave his wife?" The question hangs in the air, sharp and heavy. My hands are steady at my sides, but there's a storm brewing within me, threatening to spill out in words and accusations. "If things are so bad?"

"Because she's the mother of his children." The words escape from Charlotte's lips as if they carry a weight, and I realize that she does actually care about my family. "She has threatened to take full custody if he ever left. She told him he'd never see them again."

Ah, no she doesn't. Her eyes drift, perhaps catching a reflection of her own life in the grandeur that surrounds us. "He loves those kids too much." There's an ache in her voice, a tenderness I hadn't expected to hear.

"Darcey, if you didn't kill Edward, and Bradley did, he can hardly love his children that much. He's happy to sacrifice a life to ensure he gets to play with two women."

I swallow down the bitterness, letting it dissolve slowly. For a moment, we're two people caught in the crossfire of someone else's war, understanding more than we should and less than we'd like. The silence stretches between us, thick and suffocating. I tuck a stray strand of my auburn hair behind my ear, feeling my hand tremble with contained emotion. My gaze shifts, trailing from the opulent wallpaper to Charlotte's expectant face. Her story sits between us like an unwanted guest at a dinner party. I almost laugh at the irony—the perfect father in her story is nothing but a ghost in mine. The ghost who haunts the corners of a house too big for its sparse warmth, who whispers empty promises into the night air that only serve to chill my bones.

"He's hardly a hero," I say, sarcasm lacing my words. They float up, hitting the ceiling where the chandelier hangs like a gilded crown, dripping crystals and false light. It mocks us both, for different reasons.

Charlotte's mouth tightens just a fraction. She catches the barb, understands it's more than a jibe—it's an accusation wrapped in velvet.

"Darcey," she starts. Her eyes, those pools of hazel, ignite with the memory, the corners crinkling ever so slightly as if she's reliving every clandestine touch. "We have something real. Had something real."

I watch her, this enigma wrapped in black silk, clenching her hands together like she's holding onto the ghost of his presence. "We love one another..." The words spill from her lips and then hang in the air, trailing off into a dreamy whisper.

I know what it's like to be wrapped up in Bradley's charms.

"And now you worry he's a murderer? That's a twist," I say.

She nods, looking at her perfectly manicured fingers. "He's a good man. He must have just lost it. In a rage of jealousy. He has often told me how he hated Edward and the fact I was with him. He even once said he'd like to see him dead. If he murdered Edward—as I think he did—I understand that he needs to pay the price. No matter how much I love him. They told me the surveillance footage was erased, and besides me, he is the only one who would know how to do that. I have shown him how it works in the app, deleting footage when he came over so Edward wouldn't see it. Plus he told me he has the same brand of cameras at his house, and uses the same app. He's very familiar with it. Do I want him to be innocent? Of course. I care about him. He's been nothing but good to me. But I don't believe he is."

In a brief moment, I truly see her. Not as the mistress, not as the enemy, but as someone who has been fed lies for every meal and believes they are the truth. She's caught up in it all, in him, and I can't help but wonder if she ever finds her way back to reality when he leaves her bed. And then I think about myself, how I too have been betrayed by Bradley. How I struggle with the idea that my husband could be a murderer. Do those moments of love and happiness we shared even count anymore? Or have they been overshadowed by his secrets and actions? I remember defending him to friends who eventually turned their backs on me. I was lost in him, blinded by my love for him. But now, I question everything.

I start shifting gears, because there's no time for pity—real or feigned. "We have to be careful." Each word is deliberate, carrying the weight of our precarious situation. "If the police—my colleagues—find out about any of this, it won't end well for either of us. I risk losing my job, my career. Do you understand that? They want you to take the fall for this. Everything right now points at you. I take a huge risk in believing you."

She folds her arms across her chest, a shield against the gravity of my stern warning. But her posture betrays her; the set of her shoulders is tense, ready to spring or flee. "I know what's at risk, Darcey," she says, but there's a flicker of fear in her eyes, quick and darting like a shadow.

"Good." I lean in, dropping my voice even further, a conspiratorial hush meant for only us. "You will have to be a good actress. Because Bradley can't know we're onto him. No one can."

"I'm not an idiot." A sharp edge returns to her words, the defense mechanism of a cornered animal. But I see the understanding there too—the acknowledgment of shared risk. We're both playing with fire, and neither of us wants to get burned.

I shift in my seat, the plushness of the cushion beneath me a stark contrast to the hardness clenching in my stomach.

I break the lingering silence that's grown thick with unease, "We need to talk about the murder weapon."

Her eyes snap to mine, the hazel irises hardening like marbles. She knows what this means—knows that we're wading into even murkier waters now.

"It could be your protection," I press on, urgency sharpening my voice like a blade. "It has to be somewhere in your house, or in the proximity, maybe tossed somewhere on the property. We haven't been able to locate it, but it has to be there, somewhere. I have a distinct feeling it is. It's crucial you find it before anyone else does. And when you do, don't touch it. Call me, right away. The last thing we need is your fingerprints on it. That would ruin everything and point the finger right back at you." Every word feels like a stone in my mouth, heavy with the weight of consequences yet to unfold.

Charlotte's posture stiffens, but her nod is firm—a gesture that conveys understanding despite the fear that momentarily flickers across her face. "I'll look for it," she whispers, resolve bracing her words as if shaping them into a shield.

The room suddenly feels colder, as if the air itself bears witness to the gravity of our conversation. It hangs between us, an invisible yet palpable force acknowledging the stakes we've just raised.

"Find it quickly, Charlotte," I say, more insistent now. "Before it's too late. And please make sure your parents don't come to the station. I will handle it."

My fingertips graze the cold surface of Charlotte's glass coffee table, a barrier as much as a piece of furniture between us. "Remember," I whisper, leaning closer so only she can hear, in case the house has ears, "Bradley can't know about this—about any of it." I let the words hang in the air, heavy with warning.

Charlotte eyes me with that same composed look she gives everyone, but I see the crack in her armor. It's in the slight tremor of her hand, the way her perfectly painted lips press into a thin line. "I told you, I'm not an idiot," she says coolly, though her voice is a fraction higher than usual.

I straighten up, my gaze locked on hers. "It's not about intelligence. It's about caution." My tone is firm, but it's like I'm speaking more to myself than to her. Can't afford slip-ups. Can't give Bradley—or anyone—the slightest hint.

"Got it," she retorts, her snobbish edge slipping through despite the situation. Classic Charlotte, always needing to have the last word.

I nod once, curt and professional, and rise from the velvet embrace of the antique chair. My legs feel stiff, my movements robotic as I take those final steps toward the door. The tension in my shoulders doesn't ease; it never does these days. A glance back at Charlotte seals our unspoken vow. Her hazel eyes hold mine, and for a fleeting second, they're not the eyes of the woman who's been sleeping with my husband. They're the eyes of an ally in a twisted game that neither of us wanted to play.

"Be careful," I say, the words slipping out softer than intended. It's a strange kind of kinship, born of necessity and desperation, but it's all we've got. Her nod is subtle, almost imperceptible. But it's there—a silent acknowledgment, a shared resolve.

I turn away, the click of the door closing behind me sounding more like the cocking of a gun. With every step, I feel the invisible threads of our alliance pulling taut. There's no going back now.

The moment the door clicks shut, a shiver scuttles down my spine. My steps echo on the marble as I traverse the opulent foyer, each footfall a drumbeat counting down to an unknown finale. The grandeur of this place suffocates me—the towering columns, the ostentatious displays of wealth. For a second, I envy Charlotte her ignorance within her gilded cage.

Outside, the air is a slap of humidity against my skin. I pause at the top of the steps, looking back at the mansion that looms like an elegant fortress. The sun dips low, throwing long shadows across the manicured lawns, splashing the world with oranges and pinks that have no right to look so beautiful given the ugly truths they're concealing.

The keys jingle in my hand, a tiny sound swallowed by the vastness around me. The weight of what's at stake settles in my chest—a leaden reminder that Bradley's deceit is just the tip of the iceberg. That we might be chipping away at something much more dangerous than a simple affair.

As I walk into the driveway I see something, a pickup truck parked by the garages. On the side of it, it says Crystal Clear Pool Cleaning. I remember in this moment having seen that name before. In the Kane files back at my desk, a list made by one of my colleagues who was working for them at the time of Edward Kane's death. Did her parents perhaps use the same pool company? Maybe even the same guy?

I start walking, the gravel crunching under my boots—a soft and steady, unlike the pulse racing in my ears. This could be something. The guy who cleans their pool might have seen things. Heard things. He could be my way in, a crack in the façade of the Kane household.

As the mansion's opulent backend unfolds before me, my

own modest split-level flashes in my mind—no shimmering pools or landscaped gardens there. Just the reality of mortgage payments and making ends meet. I'm hit with this surge of... what? Resentment? No, I can't let that happen.

The pool area assaults my senses next, all azure water and manicured hedges, a postcard of wealth and leisure. For a fleeting moment, I let myself be awed, let myself imagine a life where this is my daily view. But that's not me. It'll never be me.

I edge closer to the pool, my eyes snagging on the pool guy. He's young, probably mid-twenties, with a confidence that radiates from him as he works. His T-shirt and shorts combo are casual against the backdrop of grandeur, yet he fits right in, his easy smile an accessory as much as the skimmer in his hands. It's like he's grown up around money—or at least has become immune to its allure.

"Excuse me," I call out, slipping into my professional persona. "I have a question. Your company... the name... do you by chance work for the Kanes as well?"

"Hey there," he replies without missing a beat, turning off the humming pool vacuum and pulling out earbuds I hadn't noticed before. "Yeah, been taking care of their pool for a good while now." He gestures to the pristine water behind him, where not a single leaf dares to trespass. "It's what I do. You need something?"

He goes back to skimming the surface with precise, practiced sweeps, as if performing a ceremonial rite rather than mundane maintenance. Each motion is fluid, economical, betraying an intimacy with the task that comes from years of repetition.

"Detective Darcey White," I introduce myself, extending a hand that feels suddenly clumsy. "I'm investigating the murder of Edward Kane. I'm sure you have heard about it."

"Yes, yes, I have. Awful what happened."

He gives my hand a firm shake, his grip surprisingly strong for someone whose day job involves balancing pH levels. "Name's Tyler. And yeah, whatever you need to know, I'll try to help out."

"Appreciate it, Tyler." I pocket my hands, keeping my tone light despite the weight of suspicion knotting in my stomach. This guy, Tyler, he's been around. Seen things. Maybe more than he realizes.

I lean against the cool stucco wall, arms crossed as I watch him. Tyler's got one of those grins that says he knows the effect he has on people, especially when he winks at the lady next door who's pretending not to watch him from behind her fluttering curtains. It irks me, this ease he has with himself, like a cat stretching in the sun without a care.

"Tyler, I'm particularly interested in Charlotte Kane," I say, trying to sound casual, as if I'm asking about the weather and not digging for dirt on my husband's mistress. "You've been working for her for a while, right?"

"Sure have." He doesn't miss a beat, his movements never faltering as he skillfully tests the chlorine levels. "Great woman."

"Ever notice anything... odd?" I venture, studying his face for any flicker of a tell. "About her?"

He chuckles lightly, a sound that seems too carefree for the gravity of my question. "Odd's one word for it," he replies, glancing up with a smirk. "Like that time Charlotte decided to sunbathe right next to me." He nods toward a chaise longue by the pool's edge. "Wearing next to nothing. I mean, seriously, man, she was topless."

I feel a prickly heat crawl up my neck, but I keep my voice steady. "That so?"

"Yup. And Edward?" He tilts his head back. "He was watching from the big ol' window above the pool area, face like thunder. Charlotte, though, she just laughed and asked me to rub sunscreen on her back. As if she wanted him to see."

"Sounds like she was playing a dangerous game," I muse aloud, more to myself than to him.

"Or maybe she was just bored." He shrugs, finally setting down his skimmer and looking at me directly. "Rich folks, they get their kicks however they can."

The laughter in his eyes doesn't reach the tightness around his mouth. I file away his words, the image of Charlotte baiting Edward, something dark and twisted coiling beneath the surface of their marriage.

"Interesting," I say, the word tasting bitter on my tongue. But it's another piece of the puzzle, another glimpse into the life of a woman who seems more enigma than flesh and blood. And I can't help thinking, if Charlotte's willing to provoke her husband so openly, what else might she be capable of?

"Is this type of... interaction a regular occurrence for Charlotte?" My words hang between us like the hazy heat above the pool's surface.

He pauses, a shadow flickering across his sun-kissed face. "You know, you see a lot of things when you're just the help."

His hands work the pool net with less certainty now, scooping leaves from the water with mechanical movements. "People forget you're there and..." He trails off, glancing up at the mansion as if he expects someone to be watching us now.

"Go on," I urge, sensing his reluctance.

"It's not just her. It happens." His voice dips lower, and I have to strain to catch his words. "Lonely women, they flirt. They think it'll bring some spark back. As if I'm just another pool toy."

The discomfort in his voice is palpable, and I feel a twinge of sympathy—or is it recognition? I've seen that look before, in the mirror, when I think about the wedding ring that feels heavier every day.

"Must be tough," I say, trying to keep my tone neutral, despite the tightness constricting my chest.

"Part of the job," he replies. I can tell there's more he's not saying, secrets that cling to him like the chlorine scent in the air.

I lean against the cool tile of the poolside, watching him as he kneads his hands together. There's a restlessness to him now, something that wasn't there before. I see it—the way his gaze darts to the mansion, then back to me, as if tethered by some invisible string.

"Edward," I begin, the name tasting like sour grapes on my tongue. "Did you ever have any encounters with him or was it mostly the wife?"

He exhales sharply. "It's not my place, but since you're asking—there was this one time." He pauses, swallows hard. The net in his hand hangs limp, forgotten.

"Tell me," I insist softly, trying to keep my voice from shaking. I need to know.

"Okay." He nods, almost to himself. "I was there, doing the usual rounds. She was there, Charlotte was, flirting with me, touching my shoulder the way she does. Out of nowhere, Edward just bursts out through those French doors leading to the pool area. He was livid, face red and everything. He..."

The pool guy's jaw clenches, his words catching like they're snagged on something sharp.

"He what?" My heart hammers, each beat resonating with the gravity of what he might say.

"Grabbed her. By the arm. Hard." His fingers reflexively curl into a fist. "Dragged her back inside. She was pleading with him, saying it wasn't what he thought, but he didn't listen."

"Did she get hurt?" The question is out before I can stop it, my detective shield slipping just enough to reveal the woman beneath.

"Next day, I saw her. A bruise blooming right here." He

touches his own cheek, tracing an invisible mark. "Like a shadow that wouldn't fade."

The air between us feels charged, heavy with unspoken truths. His eyes are wide, haunted. He knows too much for someone who just skims leaves and checks pH levels.

"Anything else?" I probe, keeping my tone gentle. "Anything at all can help."

He looks torn, caught between the desire to stay out of it and the weight of what he's seen. "No, that's—that's all I got. I wish... Sometimes I think maybe I should've done something, you know?"

"Hey." I reach out, lay a hand on his arm, feeling the muscle tense beneath my touch. "You're doing something now. Sharing this with me."

He nods, uncertainty etched across his face. He's just a kid, really—a kid who's seen too much in a world that's supposed to be all about sunshine and chlorine.

He drops his gaze to the ground, the hose in his hand dripping into a puddle that reflects his conflicted expression. "I know it looks bad," he starts, his words slow and heavy with guilt. "But what could I do? I'm just the pool guy. It's not my place. Plus, I work for my uncle; I can't just... rock the boat."

"Right." I nod, understanding the precariousness of his position yet unable to quell the frustration brewing inside me. He's scared, I remind myself, trying to quash the anger at his inaction. His admission doesn't excuse him, but it explains his silence. Powerless or unwilling to act, the result is the same: Charlotte suffered.

"Thank you for telling me," I manage to say, forcing a tight smile. My brain is already racing, connecting dots, painting a picture I'm not sure I want to see. The pieces are falling into place, and each one makes my job clearer, my resolve firmer.

"Sure," he mumbles, turning back to his work as if our conversation had never happened.

As I walk away, my steps feel lighter, energized by purpose. There's a story here, woven through the chlorine and the luxury, and I'm going to unravel it, thread by thread. Every detail he's given me is another clue, and clues are what I build cases on. This puzzle won't remain unsolved. Not on my watch.

I reach my car, the metal cool and impersonal under my touch. Sliding into the driver's seat, I don't start the engine right away. Instead, I sit, the notepad on the passenger seat staring back at me. The pool guy's words, his hesitations, they dance in my mind.

"Flirtation as a game," I muse, fingers tapping on the steering wheel. "But who was being played—Charlotte or Edward?"

More questions, more doubts. That's all these people seem to give me. And yet, it's fuel, isn't it? It's what keeps me going, the belief that behind every lie there's a sliver of truth.

I turn the rearview mirror slightly—not to look at the road behind me, but to meet my own gaze. Green eyes stare back, weary yet wired with the kind of adrenaline that comes from chasing ghosts and guilt. I see the furrow of my brow, the faint lines etching their doubts across my forehead. They're not just from squinting in the sunlight or frowning at suspects; they're from the nights spent questioning if the truth is worth tearing down walls for. Destroying my marriage for?

"Damn right it is," I say to the woman in the glass.

I flick the air conditioning on full blast, letting the cool air battle the heat that surrounds me. The engine hums, ready and willing.

I pull away, leaving behind the grandeur of the mansion, the scent of chlorine and deceit still lingering in my nostrils. My fingers grip the steering wheel, knuckles whitening. For a second, I let myself imagine driving away, leaving this all behind, just taking off. But then I remember the twins' faces, my daughter's half smile, half plea every time she looks at me. They're the reason I can't turn back, why I have to see this through.

TEN

DARCEY

The station's fluorescent lights feel harsher somehow, buzzing faintly above me, casting everything in stark relief—including my doubts—as I walk in the next morning. I haven't slept much. What am I going to tell Jim, my boss? He will ask for updates soon and I have nothing to give him. He knows Bradley is my husband. If I tell him he's my suspect, and Charlotte my husband's lover, then he will remove me from the case. I can't tell him anything. Not yet.

"Darcey?" The voice breaks into my spiraling thoughts, bringing me back to the here and now.

I turn to see Jim approaching, his salt-and-pepper hair seeming more pronounced under the artificial light. His expression is unreadable, a testament to years of experience, but there's an urgency in his stride that puts me on alert.

"Jim," I acknowledge, slipping back into the role of Detective White. "What's up?"

"The Kanes' housekeeper just walked in," he says, his voice gravelly, the sound oddly comforting. "She's ready to talk. Can you take that one?"

My pulse quickens, a fresh wave of adrenaline washing over

me. The housekeeper. What will she know? Does she know about the affair? Did she see when Bradley sent Charlotte flowers? Will she support Charlotte's story? If she mentions Bradley by name on record, I will be off the case. I have to make sure she doesn't.

"Sure." The word is sharper than I intend, clipped with the edge of my anxiety. "Let's see what she has to say."

As we walk toward the interview room, I run through the possible scenarios in my head. The housekeeper could blow this case wide open, or she could just as easily reinforce the walls closing in on me. I remember what Charlotte said about getting her staff on side. I hope this woman is prepared to keep Charlotte's secrets. My hands clench and unclench, fighting to keep the tremor from showing.

"Thanks, Jim," I add, shooting him a look that I hope conveys confidence. "I've got it from here."

I plaster on a smile, trying to hide the guilt gnawing at my conscience. He nods understandingly and leaves me alone with my thoughts. As I watch him stroll away, I can't help but remember all the times he has supported me, encouraged me, and helped me grow in my career. His unwavering trust in me only intensifies the weight of my betrayal now. My heart aches as I think about how his wife Nancy sent me flowers when I got my promotion, and how Jim has always been my biggest cheerleader. How could I have become this selfish person, taking advantage of someone who has always had my best interests at heart? Tears prick at the corners of my eyes as I realize the damage I have done to our friendship and to myself. What have I become?

The door to the interview room clicks shut behind me, sealing us in a bubble of tense anticipation. I draw in the sterile, recycled air and let my gaze land on a woman whose hands twist and knot like she's trying to wring answers from her own skin. It's a dance of nerves I'm all too familiar with. Before he left, Jim handed me a report that I am now scanning. Intel gathered about the woman I'm about to interview. How much she charged for her services at the Kane household, her hours working there, and most importantly if she had an alibi for the time of the murder, which she did. She is not considered a suspect, I conclude.

"Good morning," I offer, the corners of my mouth lifting in a practiced smile. In this room, pleasantries feel as thin as the veneer of my perfect life. I slide into the chair across from her, the metal legs scraping against the floor as it nudges along an inch, echoing off the bare walls. My index finger rests on the button of the tape recorder in front of me, but I don't record our conversation. I'll take notes instead.

"Could you state your name for the record, please?" My voice is steady, but inside there's an itch of unease, a relentless whisper reminding me how appearances can deceive. Like the calm surface of my marriage, hiding the rip currents swirling beneath.

The housekeeper's voice trembles faintly as she replies, "Rodriguez. Carla Rodriguez."

I lean forward, pen poised over my notepad, etching her identity into the case that might finally distract me from the sham waiting at home.

"Tell me about your duties in the Kane household," I begin, my tone light but eyes sharp, watching her every move. "How would you describe your relationship with Mr. and Mrs. Kane?"

The housekeeper's gaze flicks up, meeting mine for a fleeting second before darting away. She swallows hard, her voice a notch above a whisper. "I've been with them for years. Cleaning, cooking, laundry. You know, keeping everything in order. But I only recently became the head of housekeeping."

"Everything?" I prompt, sensing there's more beneath the surface of her succinct job description. "What exactly does 'in order' mean for Mr. Kane?"

Her laugh is a dry leaf skittering across a pavement. "Mr. Kane... he's particular. Everything has to be just so." She hesitates, then rushes forward as if the words can't be held back. "Like, he measures the space between picture frames. Millimeters matter to him. And the cushions"—she gestures vaguely, mimicking plumping—"if they're not fluffed to precisely the same height, you'll hear about it."

I can't help but make a face at this. I thought Charlotte might have exaggerated Edward slightly, but perhaps everything she has said about him is true. Does he like control? Demand perfection? "Go on," I say, tapping on the notepad.

"Silverware. It has to align with the edge of the table, perfectly parallel. He inspects the shine under the light, looking for smudges that aren't there." A shudder runs through her. "Once, he made me iron his socks because they weren't 'crisp enough.' Socks."

"Sounds exhausting," I comment, but my mind is racing. Perfectionism or control? Obsessive-compulsive behavior or a power play?

"Exhausting doesn't cover it, Detective," she says, her eyes now locked onto mine, a glint of something like defiance—or fear—flickering within their depths. "Working for Mr. Kane... it's like walking on a tightrope strung over a depthless pit. You learn to balance or you fall."

"Thank you," I say, noting down her words. Whether she realizes it or not, the housekeeper has just painted a portrait of a man who might push someone to the brink. And from a great height, even a saint might fall. And suddenly I do feel a tiny bit of sympathy for Charlotte.

"Let's talk about Mrs. Kane," I say, watching her closely.

She hesitates, then the words start to flow, tumbling out with a tremor that belies her calm exterior. "She's nice. She's... nicer than he is. Edward Kane is a very demanding man, everything must be perfect, especially Mrs. Kane."

I nod, scribbling notes while processing her statement. She tells me about Mrs. Kane's beautiful dresses, how much time she spends alone with her daughter, reading books, and dressing up, pretending to be princesses. She swims in the pool every Wednesday, she plays tennis on Thursdays. She always gives Carla a Thanksgiving basket, filled with fresh pumpkin pies for her family, and a bonus at Christmas. She sneaks it into Carla's Christmas card.

My pen pauses mid-sentence, hovering over the notepad like a hawk circling its prey. The housekeeper's words stall in the air. I lean in, elbows on the table, bridging the distance between us. "What else can you tell me?" My voice is soft, almost coaxing, desperate for her to tell me something of consequence.

She glances up, hands clasped tightly in her lap. "Well," she starts, eyes darting down to where her fingers twist and untwist the hem of her white shirt. "There is more."

"Go on," I urge, keeping my tone even, despite the pulse quickening at my temple.

"When Mr. Kane is away..." She hesitates, and I see fear flit across her expression, chased quickly by resolve. "Mrs. Kane... goes out." Her voice is barely above a whisper, as if the walls themselves might betray her confidence.

I nod, encouragingly, scribbling her words onto the paper that holds so many secrets. "Out?"

"A lot," she confirms, and there's an edge in her voice I haven't heard before—an edge of worry that makes my next breath catch. "The neighbors, they see her come home late. What would Mr. Kane think if he knew about it?" There's an unspoken plea in her eyes, begging for understanding, for absolution. "But I don't tell him."

"Thank you," I say. "For sharing this. I know it feels like betrayal for you as I can tell you clearly care about her, but you're doing the right thing."

She nods, though it's clear the confession has taken its toll. "I just... I don't want her daughter to know."

"Of course not," I reply, feeling the weight of her loyalty to Mrs. Kane—a loyalty that now tethers her to this investigation. So Charlotte does live under a strict rule. I feel sorry for her once again.

"Was she at home the day Edward died?" I ask, my voice low, almost hesitant.

The housekeeper's eyes dart up to meet mine, uncertainty etched into the lines of her face. "It's possible," she says, a slight tremor revealing the confidence she tries to muster.

The possibility hangs between us, a specter that neither of us wants to acknowledge fully. But it's there, a dark shape lurking in the corners of this puzzle. I scribble a note, the pen scratching loudly in the quiet.

My voice is soft but insistent as I probe deeper into the labyrinth of the Kane household. "Did Mr. and Mrs. Kane ever fight?"

The housekeeper's fingers knot together, a tangled mess of nerves. She glances down at her lap before meeting my eyes again, a flicker of fear—or is it empathy?—passing over her features. "Oh yes," she exhales, the words tumbling out in a rush. "Mrs. Kane... Charlotte, she loses her temper quite quickly if Edward ignores her. It's not pretty when she feels slighted."

I nod, encouraging her to continue, but I'm shocked that it's Charlotte's anger that comes to Carla's mind. Charlotte and Taylor said Edward lost his temper.

"Can you explain what happens when she gets angry?" I ask, feeling a prickly heat crawl up the back of my neck.

The housekeeper wrings her hands, her voice low and hesitant. "She shouts, throws things sometimes. Then, she'll storm out." Her eyes dart around the room, as though the walls might close in on her for betraying these secrets.

"Go on," I coax, sensing her hesitation.

"I fear that maybe... perhaps she got angry on the day Mr. Kane died and lost control," her voice breaks ever so slightly. "She gets mad a lot with him, you know. When he doesn't show her enough attention. She becomes so... so desperate."

A shiver runs down my spine at the implications, the pieces clicking into place with a chilling clarity. Could her rage have led her to murder?

"And where were you at the time of Mr. Kane's death?" The words slip from my lips effortlessly, but they're laced with a weight that could tip the scales of this investigation.

The housekeeper's gaze meets mine, and for a moment, her nervousness seems to dissipate. "I had the day off," she says, her voice steadying. "I was visiting my grandchildren, as I usually do on Sundays. Went to church in the morning. I didn't hear what happened till later that night. Such an awful... I couldn't believe it, you know? You think you know people, but... really... I can't believe Mr. Kane is no longer here."

"Thank you for coming in," I tell her, and I mean it. Her insights have been a flashlight in the murky waters of the Kane household. "You've been of great help." And as I conclude the interview, the gratitude I express is not just a formality—it's genuine.

I rise from my seat, the metal chair scraping against the floor like a jarring note off-key. My mind churns with the new information, gnawing at the edges of what we know about Charlotte Kane. Could a woman so poised really crumble under the weight of neglect? Was she capable of having done something unthinkable?

I turn away, the door handle cool against my palm, a small click as I open it.

The housekeeper's revelations are ricocheting inside my skull, and I can't shake the image of Charlotte losing control.

Is this woman more dangerous than I realized?

ELEVEN

CHARLOTTE

I slam the door of my BMW shut, the sound ruining the peace of the lush gardens, and march toward the gardener, who's pruning the roses with less care than I'd like. "Those are Jackson & Perkins," I snap, pointing at the maimed blooms. "Do you even know what that means, or should I spell it out for you?"

"Sorry, ma'am," he mumbles, avoiding my gaze as his hands fumble with the shears.

He doesn't know he will be out of a job in a few weeks. He's already been paid for the rest of the month and I expect him to deliver, to give me my money's worth. I need to maintain my image among our neighbors, and keep up appearances. At least for now.

"Sorry won't revive them, will it?" I hiss, feeling my control slip. "Start over. And this time, pretend you actually respect the living things you're handling." His compliant nod does little to quell the tumult in my chest, and I make my way upstairs.

My footsteps echo down the hallway lined with doors—seventeen in total, each one leading to a room I could escape into. But there's only one door that matters now, its frame looming ominously as I approach. The bedroom where everything changed. The police have finally finished their work here and left the property, and I can return to just a little bit of normalcy. I watched the final police officer, that little lad I heard Darcey call Denton, jump into his cruiser, taking his crime scene tape with him. There are still tiny bits of the fluorescent yellow plastic flapping around outside, but the gardener will grab those too.

I push it open and enter the stillness. My eyes are trained to spot any imperfection, at Edward's behest.

I let out a low scoff. Seventeen bedrooms in this house, and I had to sleep at my parents' house last night, as if displaced from my own home.

I think of Georgina's little face when I left this morning. Her sadness. My parents may have the grandest, most beautiful toys, but she's barely allowed to touch them. I think of the doll's house in the corner on a tall table she cannot reach. But, I remind myself that soon we will leave this all behind.

I exhale. No one knows we're leaving. And that's the way it will stay. Darcey can pry and prod all she wants, but she won't find anything substantial—nothing to pin me down, nothing that will stick in court. I've made certain of that. And once this dies down, we'll leave.

"Carla did a decent job," I admit begrudgingly, scanning the space for imperfections. But then I see it—a faint crimson stain on the Persian rug. It's almost imperceptible, but not to me. Carla will have to do better. She'll scrub it again tomorrow, erase every trace of Edward's existence from this room.

Descending to the wine cellar, I'm surrounded by rows of bottles cradled in mahogany racks, the soft lighting casting a golden glow. I slide open the high glass doors, and my fingertips graze something cold and hard tucked behind the vintage collection. A chill runs up my spine as I spot the dried blood—an unwanted souvenir from the night Edward drew his last breath.

Now I know I can relax.

It's still here.

Those detectives failed to find it.

"Out of sight, but hardly out of mind." I glance back once more, but not before selecting a bottle of Veuve Clicquot. "From one widow to another," I say. I deserve a treat. Then I decide to grab two bottles—for good measure.

I take hold of the second bottle, sliding the glass doors closed, sealing away the evidence along with a sliver of my conscience. I step back upstairs, fill the jacuzzi and watch the bubbles rise, the tension beginning to ebb away. The champagne cork pops, the sound a momentary release from the tightrope of suspense that has become my life.

The bubbles caress my skin, and for a fleeting moment, I forget about the day's events. But as I sip my champagne, the effervescence can't quite lift the heaviness in my chest.

I think of Detective White. If only she knew about the little nest egg waiting for me across the sea. But Darcey, who probably grew up in some dingy apartment, chugging cheap beer and making do with thrift-store finds, couldn't possibly comprehend the complexities of my world.

The water laps against the sides of the tub, and I lie back, allowing the heat to envelop me. My mind drifts to the gardener, his hands calloused and dirtied from labor.

I think about Georgina. Tucked up in the crisp new sheets in the bedroom my mother has made her. I cannot bring her home yet. Luckily she loves her grandparents. She didn't have to grow up with them, like I did. She isn't old enough to realize that soon they'll see her as another young woman to marry off for status. I know I have to save her from their claws. Or they'll ruin her life like they did mine.

"Tomorrow," I promise myself. "Tomorrow, Carla will scrub away the last reminders of Edward's existence, and I'll be one step closer to freedom."

I think of Darcey again. Have I convinced her to trust me? I need her to look at Bradley not me. I need to save myself. The question is, have I done enough?

TWELVE

DARCEY

I lean against the railing of the back porch, letting the sound of rain wash over me. It's moments like these—caught between the storm outside and the one in my head—that I find a strange sort of solace. With a flick of my lighter, the end of the cigarette glows to life, and I draw in a long, steadying breath, still thinking about Carla's words, and how I only just managed to avoid Jim as I rushed out of the building after she left, making it to nursery just in time to collect the twins.

My phone vibrates against the wooden tabletop. I hope I see Charlotte's name, that she's found the weapon used to kill Edward, and this can all be wrapped up with one sweep for fingerprints.

But Bradley's name flashes on the screen; just seeing it ignites a familiar twist in my stomach.

"Hey," I answer, struggling to keep my voice even, while my free hand unconsciously taps out a nervous rhythm on the porch rail.

"Darcey, I'm sorry, but it looks like I'll be tied up at the office longer than expected." Bradley's tone is smooth, practiced —too practiced. He doesn't wait for me to respond before he continues, "Something with the Henderson case came up; you know how it goes."

"Sure, I know," I reply, exhaling a stream of smoke into the night. My fingers grip the phone a little tighter. As so often before, I wonder if he is telling me the truth. The Henderson case has been all-consuming these past many months. Bradley is a high-powered lawyer, renowned for taking on tough cases and winning. He could be telling the truth.

He could also be lying.

"It's OK, the kids have seen you plenty this week. I'm sure they'll be asleep soon."

"If they give you any trouble you can FaceTime me," he says, and I can tell he's smiling at the image of either of the twins desperate for him to come home. Ever since I got promoted and am often not home for bedtime, the twins prefer to be tucked in by their father. He is always the fun one.

"It's fine, Bradley. Really." The lie tastes acrid on my tongue, mingling with the flavor of tobacco. "We've been down this road enough times."

"Thank you for being so... accommodating." His gratitude feels as empty as the space beside me on the porch swing. He lets out a sigh, feigning relief or maybe regret—it's hard to tell with him. "I'll make it up to you, Darcey. I promise."

"Sure," I say again, softer this time. What else is there to say? I press the end call button before he can fill the air with more hollow assurances.

As the line goes dead, I take another drag, the sound of the rain a constant drumbeat above me. Here I am, cloaked in shadows and doubt, wondering if every late night at the office is just another lie dressed up in a crisp suit and a convincing smile. I flick the cigarette butt into the darkness, watching it arc through the air before it's swallowed by the night.

"Make it up to me," I whisper to no one, my laugh humorless. "Like hell you will."

The rain's steady rhythm on the porch roof is a lullaby, and for once, the house echoes it with silence, not chaos. I check the monitor; the twins are finally asleep, and their soft breaths make me relax. I lean back in the creaky swing, resting my head against the damp wood, letting this rare moment of tranquility sink into my bones. It feels fragile, fleeting, like a soap bubble ready to pop at the slightest touch.

As I stare into the shroud of night, my mind flickers back to a time when life was less complicated—or at least, when I believed it was. Bradley's face swims into focus, all charm and sharp blue eyes, the kind that could cut through glass and still come out looking clean. I vividly remember handing him a citation for parking in a restricted zone, back when I was just a rookie on the force. But even after I repeatedly warn him, he still keeps coming back to that same spot just to see me. It's an unconventional start to what will eventually become us, a family. One day—after five tickets—he invites me out, and on the day of the date I go and sit at the bar of the restaurant, while waiting for him.

"Beer, please," I say to the bartender, who gives me a look like I'd just asked for a pint at a wine tasting. That's when Bradley slides up beside me, his smile easy and warm. "The ladies here drink wine," he tells me, a playful tease in his tone. "Or champagne."

I remember shrugging, trying to mimic his ease.

"Never really liked wine," I admit. "I'm more of a beer person. Grew up around it, you know?"

"Okay," he replies, his voice smooth as silk, eyes crinkling in amusement. "That's kind of refreshing."

There is something about him that night, a magnetism that pulls me in despite every internal warning bell. He is everything I am not—polished, poised, and from a world where the word "no" is just a suggestion.

"Stick with me, kid," he whispers later, after convincing me to try a sip of his expensive Châteauneuf-du-Pape, which, to my own surprise, I don't hate. It is rich and complex, a flavor that speaks of money and secrets.

"Only the best," he promises, and I laugh—a real laugh, not the hollow sound that fills my throat these days. But behind that laughter, a small voice nags at me, whispering questions I am too caught up in the moment to ask out loud. How far can I wade into his world before I start drowning?

"Only the best," I echo now to the empty night, the irony not lost on me. The best lies, the best acts, the best masks. I snuff out the second cigarette against the porch railing, the embers dying with a hiss. How did I get here, from that woman who took pride in her beer, to one who can't even trust her own memories? Who am I beneath the surface that Bradley polished so well?

Only the best, indeed.

I lean back in the worn chair, the damp wood cool against my skin through the thin fabric of my shirt. Bradley's world has always been the music of clinking crystal and hushed voices— while mine is the hum of neon signs and the crack of pool cues on a Friday night. When he first brings me home, to meet the family that lives in a house you could mistake for a small museum, my stomach knots tighter than the laces on my worn-out sneakers.

"Mother," Bradley says, his voice smooth as aged whiskey, "this is Darcey."

Her gaze sweeps over me like a cold breeze, taking in my thrift-store dress and the freckles I can't hide. The silence stretches out, filled with the weight of her appraisal. Her mouth pinches into something resembling a smile—more a concession than a welcome—as she offers a hand adorned with rings that cost more than my car.

"Darcey, dear, do you play tennis?" It is the sort of casual question that isn't a question at all but a sizing up, a way to place me on the social ladder. I'd only ever swung a racket at a garage sale to see if it made a good whoosh sound.

"Can't say that I do, Mrs. Cavendish," I reply, my voice steadier than I feel. "I'm more familiar with bar sports—darts, billiards." There is a titter from someone at her side—a cousin or an aunt, they blur together—and I know I have landed myself squarely in the "novelty" box.

"Quaint," she murmurs, turning away to discuss something about a garden party fundraiser. Quaint. The word hangs between Bradley and me, a chasm that seems too vast to cross.

But we do, somehow. We find laughter in the differences, how he's never tasted a corn dog and I've never seen a ballet. Our worlds collide, creating sparks that warm us both. The nights spent stargazing in his parents' perfectly manicured backyard, him pointing out constellations while I point out satellites—those moments weave us together in unexpected ways.

"Look, a shooting star," he says one evening, a rare excitement in his voice as he holds my hand.

"Make a wish," I whisper, squeezing his fingers, feeling the soft hands of a man who works with his mind, not his hands like those I'd known before.

We wish for different things, probably—he for something grand and worldly, me for a moment just like this one, quiet and simple. But when I tell him my wish, to have a family with laughter and love, his eyes soften, and he tells me he shares that dream. We are more alike than different in the ways that matter. And then there's Chloe, his gentle touch and playful banter with her filling my heart with joy— showing me just how brilliant and caring he truly is. He patiently listens to her stories and laughs at her jokes, showing off his brilliant sense of humor. It's heartwarming to see how quickly they form a bond, and it only reinforces my desire to build a family based on love and laughter. Even if his family doesn't approve of her, or his relationship with her—and me, for that matter.

When the twins come, their cries echoing through the halls of our home—a blend of his sophistication and my practicality—I see the bond between us strengthen. Late-night feedings and early morning giggles, the way he cradles them with a tenderness that belies his usual composure—it is like discovering a hidden passage in a well-read book, a depth to Bradley I didn't know existed.

"Look at us," he says one night as we watch them sleep, swaddled bundles of potential. His hand finds mine in the dim light, fingers entwining. "We're actually doing this, aren't we?"

"Yeah," I breathe out, a mix of awe and exhaustion. "We are."

And for a time, it feels like enough—like maybe quaint can meld with exquisite, creating a life uniquely ours. But then something changes. I am not sure exactly when it happens. It's all a little blurry. Fact is that I like the red wine he serves me and I don't stop.

I remember still the first night it goes wrong for me. We have hired a babysitter. We are at a restaurant. One of those really nice and expensive ones that Bradley has gotten me used to. I remember that I lean back in the velvet upholstered chair, the kind that's more about looks than comfort, and I watch Bradley as he converses with the waiter. His charm is like a well-oiled machine, effortless and smooth. The soft clinking of cutlery and murmured conversations fills the upscale restaurant, a noise that's both foreign and fascinating to my ears.

"Darcey," Bradley says, turning to me with that confident smile, "I've ordered something special for us tonight."

The waiter pours wine into his glass and he tastes it.

"Ah, perfect." Bradley nods after a ceremonial sip, and then two glasses are filled; one slides across the white linen tablecloth toward me.

"Try it," he urges.

I lift the glass, the aroma richer than any wine I ever nursed back home. The first sip is tentative; the flavors complex, a dance of berries and spices that twirls across my tongue. It's not just grape juice—it's like drinking a piece of art, layered and deep.

"Wow," I admit, surprised by my own enjoyment. "This is... good."

"This is a 1982 Château Lafite Rothschild. It costs almost two grand."

I almost spit out my wine. "Two grand? For how many bottles?"

"Just this one." He laughs.

Laughter rises from my chest, a mix of the wine's effects and his amusing remarks. To me, spending such an extravagant amount on wine seems absurd. I can't wrap my head around the fact that he would do that. He reaches for my hand across the table, and I allow him to take it, feeling the warmth of his touch travel up my arm. Our relationship has its complexities, especially when it comes to finances. As a partner at his law firm he makes way more than me, and his family has money, mine doesn't. He often tries to offer me money, and even had the audacity once to offer me a monthly allowance, but I always decline. I earn my own living, and even though it's significantly less than his, I take pride in my independence.

"Cheers to new experiences," I say, raising my glass.

"Cheers," he echoes, clinking his against mine.

As the evening unfolds, the wine flows freely, and my usual restraint starts to loosen. I find myself laughing louder, sharing stories I've kept to myself for years, but he laughs and nods along.

"Tell me more about growing up in Jacksonville," he prompts, his gaze never leaving mine. "Tell me stuff you have never told me before."

So I do. I tell him about the cramped apartment, the smell of fried food from next door, and how I'd sit on the stoop watching the sun dip below the rooftops. All the while, I'm sipping on that rich red wine, feeling it warm me from the inside out.

But there's a niggling thought, poking through the haze of alcohol-induced giddiness. Is this really me? This woman savoring expensive wine and recounting tales to charm her well-off husband?

"Are you okay?" Bradley interrupts my internal debate, his concern genuine.

"Absolutely," I assure him, pushing aside the doubt. "Just enjoying the night."

And I am, aren't I? Even if a small voice whispers that I might be losing bits of myself in my new life with Bradley. Maybe I'm drinking too much because it's my first evening out in months. Because I've spent every moment since the twins were born trying to show his family how perfect a mom I can be.

* * *

Next thing I remember is the sunlight that filters through half-closed blinds as an unwelcome intruder. My eyes snap open, and I'm greeted by a blurred snapshot of my bedroom—the familiar yet unfamiliar sight of luxury that's never quite felt like mine. I blink hard, trying to clear the haze that has nothing to do with the morning light and everything to do with how much wine must've flowed the night before.

"Good morning," Bradley murmurs from beside me, his voice smooth, his presence an anchor.

"Morning," I manage, my tongue feeling thick and clumsy in my mouth. I try to sit up, but my head spins traitorously, forcing me back onto the pillow. Panic flutters in my chest as hazy fragments of memory collide and collapse before they can form a coherent picture. What happened after that second... or was it third bottle?

"Bradley, I..." The apology sticks in my throat, and shame floods my senses as I struggle to find words for transgressions I can't recall. "I don't remember coming home. Who has the kids?"

His body stiffens slightly, and he turns to face me with those piercing blue eyes that always seem to see too much. There's a hint of annoyance—a shadow crossing his otherwise perfect façade.

"Darcey, I've been with them," he starts, his tone carrying an edge, "you don't remember anything?"

I shake my head, bracing for the impact of his disappointment. A detective who can't piece together her own evening—it's almost laughable. Almost.

"Nothing after dinner," I confess, and there's a vulnerability in admitting that, a crack in my armor he's not used to seeing.

He sighs, and the slight anger ebbs away, replaced by something that might pass for concern if I didn't know better. "You were... pretty out of it. But you had fun—said it was one of the best nights in a while."

"Did I?" My heart races in a mixture of relief and new worry. If I spoke, what truths—or lies—did I let slip? I look to the trash can and my eyes fall on a used condom. I don't even remember having sex. This is bad. There's a bruise on the side of my leg that I try not to look at. I must have fallen down at some point. It's embarrassing.

"Of course." His hand finds mine, and he squeezes gently. "Look, it's okay. You apologized already last night. Let's just forget about it."

"Right. Sorry, again." The word tastes bitter, a stark contrast to the rich wine that I'd found surprisingly palatable. I should be grateful for his forgiveness, but instead, I feel a hollow guilt settling in my stomach, a weight that won't lift with his reassurances.

"Hey," Bradley says, softer now, brushing a lock of hair from my forehead. "It's forgotten, okay?"

"Okay." I nod, but the unease lingers, the doubt that maybe I should remember, that maybe there's something important buried in the blackout.

"Let's get some breakfast, yeah? Get you something greasy —that'll help." He smiles, the practiced charm slipping back into place as if it had never left.

Back then I remember telling myself everything was fine.

Sometimes, I think now, the realization chilling me to the bone, *the most dangerous lies are the ones we tell ourselves.*

THIRTEEN

CHARLOTTE

Carla, bless her, has the kitchen warm and smelling like a bakery in full swing. But today the scent of fresh muffins and sizzling bacon feels like an affront. "Just coffee, please," I tell her, my voice cool and even. The disappointment in her eyes doesn't escape me, but I can't entertain food right now—not with the acid of anxiety churning in my stomach.

"Of course, Miss Kane," she replies, her tone subdued, her eyes lingering on me a moment too long. Does she suspect me? No, I push that thought away. I know Darcey must have interviewed her by now, but Carla has been with us for years. Carla turns back to the stove, sliding the breakfast meant for me onto a plate for someone less fraught. The gardener, or maybe the pool boy. With a porcelain mug cradled between my palms, black liquid gold inside, I take a sip, letting the bitterness ground me.

I glance out the kitchen window, the steam from my coffee hitting my face for a moment. My hand pauses mid-air, the warmth from the mug seeping into my fingers, forgotten. There's a car outside, not just any car—a detective's car. Darcey's car. A thud of unease settles in my stomach as I slowly set the mug down.

"Everything okay, Miss Kane?" Carla's voice breaks through the silence, but I barely register it.

"Fine," I say, too quickly, a little breathless. "Excuse me."

I move toward the front door, each step feeling heavier than the last. My mind races, thoughts tangling like the overgrown ivy on the garden wall I keep meaning to have trimmed. Why is she here?

I grip the cool metal of the doorknob and take a deep breath, letting it out slowly, crafting the perfect hostess smile. The door swings open, and there she stands: Detective Darcey White, the embodiment of my current nightmare, her auburn hair pulled back in that no-nonsense ponytail, green eyes scanning me before I can even speak.

"Detective Darcey," I greet her, keeping my voice steady. "What an unexpected surprise. To what do I owe the pleasure?"

"Charlotte." Her tone is neutral, but those eyes... they're doing that thing where they look right through you. It's unnerving how she does that. "We need to talk."

"Of course." I step aside, my heart a staccato drumbeat against my ribs. "Please, come in." She has that look on her face —the one that says she's not here for pleasantries.

"Do you have any plans for today, Charlotte? Anything... in particular?" Darcey inquires, her eyes lingering on my dress.

"I'm heading to the yacht club," I reply, trying to sound casual despite my nerves. "Just having lunch with a friend. You know, the typical activities of a wealthy housewife." My words are meant to be light, yet they hang in the air, thick with unspoken doubt.

"Oh, the yacht club sounds lovely," Darcey says, her tone slightly envious. "I've been meaning to go there myself. Who's the lucky friend?"

"Just an old acquaintance," I say, waving my hand dismissively. "Nothing too exciting."

We shift the conversation to safer topics, like the weather, which has been unusually sunny for this time of year.

"Isn't it amazing how the sun just lifts everyone's spirits?" Darcey comments, glancing outside. "It's like a little gift in the middle of all this routine."

"Absolutely," I agree. "It makes everything feel so much more vibrant."

Darcey mentions her twins, who have been keeping her busy with their endless energy. "Honestly, I don't know where they get it from," she laughs. "Sometimes I wish I could bottle some of their energy for myself."

I smile and share that my daughter is still enjoying her time with her grandmother, giving me a rare moment of quiet. "It's been so peaceful, almost surreal," I admit. "But I miss her chatter."

"Isn't it funny how we crave the chaos when it's gone?" Darcey muses. "Motherhood is such a balancing act."

"Indeed," I nod. "But I suppose that's what makes it all worthwhile."

Darcey gives a slight nod, clearly not convinced by my nonchalant demeanor. "Any progress in finding the murder weapon? Have you been actively searching?"

I reply confidently, "Of course, but so far, no luck. I would have informed you if I had any news."

Darcey's tone grows urgent, "We need to speed up the process. Right now, you're still the primary suspect and we need to prevent you from ending up behind bars."

My voice trembles slightly as I respond, "Yes, that's understandable. How do we go about clearing my name? Can we perhaps get a confession from the real murderer?"

Darcey lets out a heavy sigh. "Can you cancel your lunch plans today?"

Surprised, I respond, "I can, but why?"

Darcey hesitates before answering, "I want you to meet with him instead."

My eyes widen in shock, "With who? Bradley?"

Darcey confirms my suspicions, "Yes. Ask him about Edward and what he knows."

"Let me get this straight. You want me... to make him confess to murdering my husband?"

Darcey's gaze is unwavering, her green eyes piercing into mine. "I want you to get him to slip up. To reveal something incriminating without realizing it. Maybe get him to repeat that he wanted to see Edward dead, that he has thought about killing him. Record it on your phone. We need to shake him, Charlotte. Make him feel the pressure closing in."

I swallow hard, the weight of her words settling heavily in my chest. "What if he gets suspicious? What if he knows I'm onto him?"

Darcey leans in closer, her voice barely above a whisper. "Then you play along. Act like everything's normal, like you're still under his spell. Gain his trust so he lets something slip."

The thought of facing Bradley, of pretending to be the adoring wife while trying to coax out a confession, sends a shiver down my spine. But Darcey is right; I need to do this for Edward, for myself.

"I'll do it," I say, my voice firm despite the quiver within me. "I'll meet with him and see what I can uncover. But Darcey, if things go south, if he catches on... what then?"

Darcey's gaze softens for a moment, a flicker of sympathy crossing her features. "If that happens, you call me immediately. We'll have a plan in place to keep you safe, Charlotte. You're not in this alone."

I nod, my heart racing as I prepare for the treacherous game ahead. But Darcey's words of support give me a glimmer of hope—she is on my side. As she rises to leave, her hand lingers on my shoulder, offering a surprising warmth that I hadn't expected from her.

"Remember, Charlotte, tread carefully," she says, her eyes filled with concern. "Bradley is a master manipulator, and we can't afford any mistakes."

I take a deep breath and attempt to dispel the doubts and fears creeping into my mind. Darcey is right—I need to be strategic in my approach to Bradley. He won't fall for desperate pleas or direct orders. It will take something clever and calculating to entice him.

"How about sending him a photo of your dress?" Darcey suggests, her lips turning up in a sly smile.

I can't help but chuckle at the idea—it's both ridiculous and brilliant at the same time. "You know what they say, 'a picture is worth a thousand words'," I quip back.

We share a knowing look, confident in our plan to outsmart Bradley and bring justice to Edward. But as Darcey turns to leave, I can't help but notice the dark circles under her eyes and wonder if she's been sleeping at all. "Any updates on the investigation?" I ask quietly. "Have they found anything?"

Darcey shakes her head, her expression growing serious once again. "Not yet. We're still working through all the leads." She pauses before adding, "Have you heard from any of Edward's friends or family? They could provide valuable information."

I shake my head sadly. We've been estranged from them since Edward's death. They seem to think I'm guilty too, that I murdered Edward. But Darcey's reminder only adds fuel to my determination to find answers and bring closure to this never-ending nightmare.

Watching her go, I'm left alone in the opulent sitting room of my mansion, the weight of Darcey's words bearing down on me.

I pull out the "Bradley phone" from my purse, staring at it

with a mix of resentment and determination. This little device holds so much power, so much evidence that could unravel everything. With a deep breath, I begin composing a message to Bradley, feigning casual interest in seeing him for lunch. Each word is calculated. I add a picture of me in my dress, like Darcey suggested.

As I hit send, a wave of nervous anticipation washes over me. The seconds feel like hours as I wait for Bradley's response, my heart pounding in my chest. Finally, the familiar chime of a new message breaks the tense silence of the room.

I hesitate before opening it, steeling myself for whatever manipulative words Bradley has crafted this time. As I read his reply, a sinking feeling settles in the pit of my stomach.

Bradley's message is simple and to the point, agreeing to meet me for lunch at the yacht club. My heart races but I work on masking my unease, knowing that this meeting could be the key to unlocking the truth about my husband's murder.

* * *

Leaving the confines of the mansion, I step out into the bright sunlight, my heels clicking against the polished marble pathway. The breeze offers little relief from the heat of anticipation that grips me tightly. My car waits at the foot of the marble steps, gleaming in the sunlight like a beacon of both freedom and danger.

As I slide into the driver's seat, the leather interior creaks slightly under my weight. My hands grip the steering wheel, knuckles turning white with tension as I sit there, battling conflicting emotions.

The engine purrs to life at my touch, a gentle reminder of the control I have over this situation. Yet, as I navigate through the gates that guard the estate, a sense of unease settles over me like a dark cloud.

The drive to the yacht club feels endless, each passing mile laden with unspoken dread and uncharted territory. I need a plan, a strategy for what to say. But Bradley is charming, clever. He will see right through me. What have I gotten myself into? Am I walking straight into the lion's den?

FOURTEEN

DARCEY

I park the car with precision and the engine's hum dies as I cut the ignition. Outside Charlotte's estate, shadows play across my dashboard, and I watch her emerge an hour after I left, all grace and poise.

She doesn't see me. And I remind myself, why would she? To someone like Charlotte Kane, I must be nothing more than an insignificant thorn in her perfect, privileged world—easily brushed aside with a flick of her manicured hand that she uses to wave at her valet. I thought I liked her for a moment. In her parents' intimidating house. In that second, as we stood in her opulent family home and she regaled me with tales of her luxurious yet lonely life, I briefly allowed myself to feel a tinge of pity toward her. She seemed like a scorned woman, just like me. But then, reality hit me like a ton of bricks. Unlike me, she has wealth and status to fall back on, and parents who can bail her out of any trouble.

I shake my head, trying to quell the bitterness and resentment I feel toward Charlotte. How much I still hate her doesn't take away from Bradley's mistakes and the uncertainty surrounding him as he lies beside me in bed or picks up our chil-

dren from school. And it most certainly doesn't change the fact
that I'm still haunted by the question: is he capable of murder?

I start my car and trail behind Charlotte at a safe distance.

The yacht club looms ahead, painting the marina with an
air of unattainable luxury. Charlotte saunters inside without so
much as a backward glance, and I feel that familiar twinge. Is
this where they always met? I've never been here.

I hand my keys to the valet with a nod, slipping him a
discreet tip to ensure my anonymity. My steps are measured as I
make my way to the bar, where the hushed clinking of ice in
glasses fills the space between murmured conversations and the
distant laughter of the privileged.

I find a seat at the bar that affords me a clear view of Charlotte's table, tucked away just enough to avoid detection. She's a
magnet for the eyes, even mine, despite the acid churning in my
gut. I drum my fingers on the polished wood of the bar, each tap
a reminder of why I'm here—not just to observe, but to disentangle the tapestry of lies my life has become.

"Chardonnay," I tell the bartender. It's a prop, really; something to occupy my hands while I keep vigil over the woman
who's ensnared my husband in her web.

Bradley steps in as if he owns the very air we're all breathing. His tailored suit clings to him. My fingers grip the glass a
little too tightly.

Easy, Darcey, I remind myself, my pulse thudding against
my temples.

Bradley's piercing blue gaze doesn't search; it finds its target
immediately, just like I knew he would. There's no hesitation in
his step, no flicker of guilt when he pulls out a chair and sits
opposite Charlotte. He was the same that night at the café a
year ago. He doesn't seem to focus on anything else when he's
meeting Charlotte. He leans forward, his smile practiced and
all-too-perfect. It's a scene I've witnessed before, each replay a
knife twisting deeper into my chest.

"Damn you, Bradley." The words are a low growl, meant only for me. My hand trembles as I grip the stem of the wine glass, my knuckles turning white. Fury seethes through my veins as I watch Bradley and Charlotte, my husband and his mistress. But I force myself to take a deep breath and remind myself that I am not here for revenge. No, I am here for answers. My marriage is over now anyway, though I can't help but feel a twinge of pain at the sight of them together.

Keep your cool, I coach myself, swallowing down the fury with a sip of wine.

I lean in, elbows on the bar, nursing the wine that's long lost its appeal. My eyes don't dare blink as I watch them, Bradley and Charlotte, their conversation unfolding like a silent movie I can't tear myself away from. She's all gestures, hands weaving through the air, painting pictures only he can see. He's leaning back, smiling a smile he once only had for me.

Charlotte tilts her head just so, hair cascading over one shoulder, and I can almost hear the honeyed laugh she must be offering him. If it were me, I'd go straight in with the truth: my husband is dead. But Charlotte's a different woman. She knows how to charm just as much as Bradley does. She must be trying to ease him in, win him over, make him relax before she mentions anything about Edward's untimely death.

Amidst all their drama, memories flood back to me—memories of Bradley at work, when I went to see him in court doing what he's good at, as a successful lawyer, his calm composure never wavering even under immense pressure. How ironic that now he has lost control in the most personal aspect of his life.

I continue to observe them closely, waiting for a sign or hint of what they may be discussing. Has she said anything yet? Has she asked him if he killed Edward like we agreed she would?

And then I see it... his jaw is set, and there's a furrow creasing his brow now, a shadow creeping over those polished features. The tension between them thickens, tangible as the humid air outside.

I think she just did.

I can't believe it. I didn't think she'd have the guts to actually do it. I was so sure she'd back out.

Not what you expected her to say? I muse, the corner of my mouth lifting in a wry smile.

The waiter drifts by their table, and Charlotte doesn't miss a beat, lifting her empty glass as Bradley sits stunned. She orders another, voice undoubtedly smooth and controlled, the very image of composure. While waiting for the new glass of wine, she gets up and goes to the restroom. Bradley sits in deep thought. Once she gets back, the wine has arrived, and she sips it, almost gulping it.

"Slow down, princess," I whisper, though I know she won't heed a word.

It's not concern for her well-being that tightens my chest; it's the possibility that in her drunkenness she'll forget to press record on her phone or miss his words, the evidence we need. What is he saying?

Bradley's hand slams the table with force but he manages not to make a sound. Only I see the anger at their table; all the other patrons are oblivious to what's going on. I lean in and can just about hear his voice, a weapon sharpened by years in the courtroom, fierce despite him not raising it. "What are you saying? What are you accusing me of, Charlotte?"

Charlotte's chair scrapes back as she recoils, her eyes flashing with a defiance that only seems to fuel Bradley's anger. What started as subtle jabs has escalated into an open wound, raw and bleeding out for all the privileged patrons to see.

"Why won't you answer a simple question? You're the one who—" She bites back the rest, but it's too late. Her words hang unfinished, dangling like bait.

I lean even closer.

Bradley stands abruptly, his chair nearly toppling in the wake of his fury. He runs a hand through his thick hair. I know this gesture all too well. He is trying to compose himself, to stay calm. He does the same while in the courtroom, but this time he loses the battle.

"This is pointless." He mutters to himself. He throws his napkin down—a white flag he never meant to wave—and storms off.

Charlotte sits back, a lone figure amidst the aftermath. She dabs at her eye, and for a moment, her mask slips, revealing a glimmer of vulnerability. It's quickly replaced by the familiar cold veneer as she signals the waiter without so much as a glance around the room.

"Another glass," she orders, her voice steady despite the tremor in her hand. Her speech is getting slurred.

Damn it, Charlotte, my professional detachment is fraying at the edges. *What are you doing to yourself?*

The worry gnaws at me, unbidden and unwelcome. I can't afford to care about Charlotte Kane, not when there's so much at stake. But as I watch her, lost in a sea of wine and whispers, I can't shake the feeling that we're both drowning in different ways.

My eyes narrow as Charlotte's silhouette sways precariously through the restaurant. The clinking of glasses and low murmur of conversations fade into the background, my attention homing in on her erratic movements. She teeters in her stilettos, a hand flailing for balance, and then—she lurches. A waiter, balancing a tray full of drinks, sidesteps just in time, saving both himself and Charlotte from a disastrous collision.

"Watch it," someone hisses, annoyance lacing the air with tension.

"Sorry," she slurs, voice barely carrying over the ambient noise. Her apology is a half-hearted song, sung by someone who's already too far gone to grasp the notes of sincerity.

I push away from the bar, my heart thrumming against my ribs. The detective in me wants to stay detached, observe from a distance, but something pulls at my conscience, tugging me toward action. I can't let her get behind the wheel—not like this.

"Can't believe I'm doing this," I mutter, weaving through the crowd, trying to keep her in sight without drawing attention. My palms feel clammy, and there's a bitterness in my mouth that has nothing to do with the chardonnay I didn't finish.

The warm air hits me as I slip outside, just in time to see Charlotte tottering toward the valet podium. Her elegant dress seems to mock her current state, dark fabric undulating like a shadow come to life.

"Miss Kane!" the valet calls out, uncertainty creasing his young face as he catches her keys mid-air.

"Here you go, James," she responds, each word a clumsy dance partner to the next.

"Are you okay to drive?" His voice is low, meant for her ears only, but I catch it, feel a pang of gratitude for his discretion.

"Perfectly fine," she insists, but her legs betray her, buckling as if the ground beneath her is shifting.

"Damn it, Charlotte." The words are out before I can stop them, an involuntary whisper of concern.

"Darcey?" It's more of a confused murmur than a question, her hazel eyes struggling to focus on me.

"Let me help you," I say, reaching her side in a few quick strides. The scent of wine is heavy on her breath, and she wobbles dangerously close to the edge of the curb.

"Help?" There's a flicker of resistance, a flash of the strong-willed woman she normally is, but it fades fast, washed away by a tide of red wine and wounded pride.

"You've had too much to drink," I tell her, more for my own benefit than hers. "You're not driving today."

"Can't... I need to..." She trails off, her body swaying like a palm in a hurricane.

"Shh, it's okay." I steady her with a firm hand, squashing the embers of anger that Bradley has left smoldering in my chest. I'll deal with him later.

"James," I call to the valet, fumbling for some cash in my pocket and handing it over. "Keep the car here for the night."

"Of course, Mrs. White," he replies, catching the bills deftly.

"I'm too damn nice," I repeat to myself, the words becoming my shield against the storm of emotions threatening to spill over. But right now, it's not about being nice—it's about doing what's right, even if it's for someone who's turned my life into a psychological chess game.

"You're not getting behind the wheel," I say emphatically.

"Home..." she slurs, her voice barely a whisper before her eyelids flutter closed, and her consciousness slips away like sand through fingers.

"Damn it, Charlotte," I mutter under my breath as I prop her up. Her head lolls onto my shoulder, her raven hair spilling over my arm. I swipe the keys from her limp hand—a shiny token of trust, or maybe just luck.

I half carry, half drag her to my car, propping her in the backseat with more gentleness than I feel. The plush leather swallows her slender form, and for a moment, I envy her oblivion.

"Always the Good Samaritan, Darcey," I scoff at myself, slamming the door shut a little too hard. My reflection in the window sneers back at me, green eyes full of allegations and a ponytail that seems to mock my attempt to keep everything tied together neatly.

The car starts with a purr. I grip the steering wheel, the leather cold and unyielding beneath my fingers, much like the choices laid out before me.

. . .

The road unfurls ahead. Charlotte's shallow breaths whisper from the backseat. I glance in the rearview mirror, catching sight of her crumpled form—a broken doll discarded among my leather seats.

"Great," I say, the word laced with a bitterness that tastes like bile at the back of my throat. "Just great, Darcey. What now?"

My knuckles whiten as I grip the steering wheel tighter, memories playing tag in my head from when I first saw them together a year ago. Bradley's laugh, Charlotte's coy smile, the way they leaned into each other, their secrets knitting together. And here I am, ferrying his mistress home, like some kind of twisted chauffeur.

I can feel the tension knotting in my shoulders. The empathy I didn't know I had for her clashes with a resentment so deep it could drown both of us. I should hate her—she's everything I detest. Yet, here I am, saving her from herself. Feeling terrible that I told her to meet him, that she had to deal with him.

Maybe it's not about her, I admit with a reluctant sigh. *Maybe it's about me.* Because if I let her drive, and something happened... No, I can't go down that road; it's dark and winding, and there's no coming back.

Taking care of Charlotte won't be easy, especially when every fiber of my being screams to toss her to the curb. But that's not who I am—or at least, not who I want to be.

The road stretches out as my mind races, navigating the familiar roads, replaying the choices that led me here. The late nights spent poring over case files instead of tucking my kids into bed, the countless lies swallowed to keep up appearances, the sting of betrayal from a man who vowed to love and cherish me. How did my life become this twisted tale where I rescue the other woman, the homewrecker?

I think about his reaction in the club. His anger. He nearly lost control. Was that guilt? Fear? Was there any surprise on his face when he heard Edward is dead?

I should be able to read anyone; that's my job, to tell who's lying, who's innocent and who's guilty. But I've never been able to read my husband.

"I still love him." I hear Charlotte murmur in a soft voice.

"It's not her fault, it's his," I mumble, my voice hollow in the confines of the car. I, of all people, know what it's like to lean on alcohol to deal with Bradley Cavendish. But today, my empathy feels like a weakness, leaving me vulnerable, exposed. I should be raging, screaming, throwing Charlotte out into the street for the vultures to pick over. Instead, I'm her savior, her guardian angel with a detective's badge.

I take a deep breath, trying to suppress the rising tide of anxiety. "Just get her home. Just do what's right." The mantra does little to soothe the disquiet in my soul, yet I cling to it, a lifeline in stormy seas.

The car hums beneath me. I needed Charlotte to come through for me today, yet she couldn't even do that. I wonder about her mental state. She seems to be unraveling.

I feel sorry for her. Is she grieving the loss of the love of her life? Grappling with the idea he's a murderer, just like I am? Or is she still so in love with him that she'll turn on me when she finds out who I am? Can I trust her?

FIFTEEN

CHARLOTTE

My eyes snap open, and I'm staring at the ceiling—a white expanse that feels too close, as if it's pressing down on me. The sheets are tangled around my legs, a restraining net of silk. My heartbeat hammers in my ears like an alarm bell that won't silence.

I force my leaden limbs to move, pushing myself into a sitting position. The room is dim, shadows creeping along the edges where the evening light fails to reach. My gaze flickers to the digital clock perched on the bedside table, its red numbers glaring back at me: 6:00 p.m. Evening? No... It can't be.

I went to the yacht club, I recall, the image of polished decks and the clink of glasses coming to mind. Bradley was there, his piercing blue eyes looking at me intensely. My memory is a jigsaw puzzle with pieces missing—our words blurred, his face contorted in anger.

The words echo through the silent room, bouncing off the walls and returning to me in a hollow whisper.

"We got into a fight," I confess, my voice barely audible as I try to grasp onto any memory of what happened. But it's like trying to hold onto smoke—everything after is just... black. A void where time should be. Panic sets in as I realize that this is the first time we've ever argued and I can barely remember it. Desperately, I run my fingers through my hair, trying to shake loose the cobwebs of confusion that cloud my mind.

But it's no use. The details slip further away with each passing second. As I close my eyes all I can see is him, Bradley Cavendish, the man who I thought would be my way out of this suffocating mausoleum of a life. What happened? I know I asked him about Edward.

Questions swirl in my head, but there are only fragments in there. Along with a deep sense of betrayal and loss. And somewhere in the back of my mind, another question lingers—did I really believe Bradley's surprised reaction when I asked him about Edward? Or did his response only add to the confusion and doubts that have been gnawing at me?

A knock at the door pulls me back from the edge of my unraveling thoughts. It's a soft, rhythmic tapping, familiar and edged with worry.

"Miss Kane? Are you all right?" Carla's voice seeps through the wood, tinged with an anxiety that twists my stomach into tighter knots.

"Fine," I manage to say, although the word tastes like a lie on my tongue. "I'm fine, Carla."

"Would you like something to eat?" There's a pause, her concern palpable even through the barrier between us. "I made dinner. Do you want me to bring you some before I leave for the day?"

The very thought of food sends a wave of nausea crashing over me. My hand flies to my mouth, and the room spins.

"Actually, Carla..." I struggle to keep my voice steady, "could you bring me a bowl?"

"Of course, Miss Kane." Her reply is swift, no hesitation, no questions—a discretion I've come to value in her.

I hear her footsteps retreat, and then return, quicker now.

The door opens, and she stands there, holding a simple white porcelain bowl. Her eyes scan my face, reading the distress that I can't quite camouflage.

"Here you are." She offers it to me, her movements deliberate, careful not to invade the space I guard so fiercely.

"Thank you," I whisper, clutching the bowl like a lifeline as she turns to leave, closing the door with a gentle click.

Alone once more, the roiling in my gut crescendos until I lean over the side of the bed, the contents of my stomach emptying. The act is violent, a purging of more than just physical sickness. With each heave, I feel the remnants of my encounter with Bradley leaving my body, though the taste of betrayal lingers bitter on my lips.

I make it downstairs. As I step out onto the expansive marble terrace, the Florida sun casts a warm glow over the rows of white roses out front. The air is thick with the scent of blooming bougainvillea, and I can hear the distant sound of waves crashing against the shore. I relish these rare moments of solitude in my chaotic life. That sound is the one thing I've enjoyed about living here all these years. And yet, even in this peaceful setting, thoughts of Georgina flood my mind. I desperately need to speak to her before my mother tucks her in for the night. The thought of missing out on bedtime rituals with my daughter weighs heavily on my heart.

The constant buzzing of my phone reminds me of my husband's recent passing. I am bombarded with messages and calls from acquaintances wanting to extend their condolences. Bouquets of flowers are delivered daily, each one a reminder of his absence. Old "friends" have come out of the woodwork, sending texts asking about funeral arrangements and offering their support. But I can't bring myself to respond.

As I inhale the evening air, my eyes catch sight of something that sends a chill down my spine. There, nestled among the fragrant petals, lies the crushed butt of a menthol cigarette. My heart quickens its pace, and a knot forms in the pit of my stomach. I only know one person smoking that type of cigarette.

Darcey White.

Darcey has been here. Watching me. Monitoring my every move.

The realization hits me like a freight train, shattering any lingering trust I had in her. How could she invade my privacy like this? How long has she been keeping tabs on me? I know she didn't smoke out here when she came to the house to arrest me. I watched her through the window, walking up the stairs of the house, and I heard her enter mine and Edward's bedroom. She ensured I was in the police car, and she went straight into hers as mine sped away.

With shaky hands, I grasp the cigarette butt, my fingers tightening around it like a clamp. Anger bubbles up inside me, mingling with a fresh sense of betrayal. Darcey, the detective I once believed was on my side, has now turned into a hidden menace in the background of my life. But how do I know for sure that Darcey was up to something when I was at my parents' house? Maybe I am jumping to conclusions. Yet, the subtle hints and discrepancies in her recent actions fuel my suspicion, making it hard to ignore the possibility.

I can't risk taking the chance on her.

As I stand there, the setting sun feels harsh against my skin, almost mocking in its cheerfulness compared to the turmoil brewing within me. The clinking of silverware and murmur of voices from the kitchen drift out to the terrace, but they feel distant and irrelevant now.

I pace back and forth, the cool marble beneath my feet unable to quell the heat rising in my chest. How could she justify this intrusion into my private life? The trust we had tentatively built shatters like glass around me, leaving only slivers of doubt and suspicion in its wake.

In that moment, a steely resolve settles over me. I will not be manipulated or watched like some pawn in Darcey's twisted game. I did what she wanted: I confronted Bradley. Now I need a plan for myself.

As the sun dips lower in the sky, casting sharp shadows across the terrace, I steel myself for the confrontation that lies ahead. Darcey may have thought she could control me, or even play me, but she has gravely underestimated my resolve.

Gripping the cigarette butt tightly in my hand, I stride back into the opulent mansion, a sense of defiance burning within me. The clatter of cutlery and Carla's whistling in the kitchen as she cleans the dishes fades into the background as I make my way to my room, my steps echoing down the lavish hallways.

Once inside, I lock the door behind me, shutting out the outside world and its prying eyes.

I squeeze my eyes shut, trying to piece together what I know. Bradley's face looms behind my lids—those piercing blue eyes that always seemed to see right through me, the smooth contours of his charming façade.

"Charlotte Kane, you're stronger than this," I whisper into the dimming room. The memory of our confrontation is still too raw, too jagged around the edges. We were at odds, as always, but the details... they escape me, slippery as eels. Just snatches of sentences, the heat of anger, the cold plunge into oblivion.

Darcey made me do this. She was the one who told me to meet with Bradley and ask him about Edward. She's not trying to protect me. She's trying to nail me for murder. Me and Bradley together. She's watching my every move. She wants me to slip up. She's waiting for me to make a mistake. She wants to nail me for this murder so she can get it off her desk. So she can look good.

Determination claws its way up from the depths, lending steel to my spine.

A plan begins to crystallize, fragment by fragment, until the outline is clear and sharp. It will be cunning, it will be precise, and most importantly, it will hit her where she least expects it. I can't help the smirk that tugs at my lips, a grim herald of the storm on the horizon.

My hand is steady, almost unnaturally so, as I reach for the sleek rectangle of my phone. My thumb hovers over the screen, each contact in my list an ally or another pawn in this twisted game Darcey seems to think she's winning.

I swipe through names, faces, lives—each one a story, a secret, a potential weapon. I punch in a name memorized long ago, before betrayal was a familiar aftertaste on my tongue.

"Come on, come on," I whisper, urging them to pick up. Each ring is an eternity, a chasm between conspiracy and execution.

"Pick up," I urge, willing my heartbeat to quiet its frenetic drumming.

"Hello?" The voice on the other end is cautious, wary.

"Hi, it's Charlotte." I pause, letting the name hang in the air —a banner, a declaration, a challenge. "We need to talk."

A bead of sweat trickles down my temple as I clutch the phone tighter, the cool surface a stark contrast to the heat of my skin. "We need to talk" echoes in my ears like a war drum, calling allies to battle.

"Charlotte?" The voice is tinged with suspicion, and I can almost picture the furrow between the speaker's brows. "You sound so serious. What's this about?"

I clear my throat, fighting for composure. "I need your help."

There's a pause, thick with unspoken questions, and I know that behind those words, gears are turning. I'm asking for more than just a conversation; I'm enlisting a co-conspirator.

"Help with what?" The inquiry comes loaded, a test of my resolve.

The conversation that follows is beyond exhilarating. I can picture the gears turning in Darcey's head when she finds out what I'm up to, the realization dawning that I am not someone to be underestimated—not any more.

SIXTEEN
DARCEY

My fingers tap on the cold metal table, mirroring the pulse of anxiety that throbs in my temples. It's almost the end of another long day. Jim has called me into his office. Across from me, Jim's face is all business, as usual, but there's a flicker in his eyes I've learned to read—trouble.

"The housekeeper, Carla's alibi isn't holding up," he says, his voice gravelly with concern. "The pastor at her church swears she wasn't there Sunday morning."

"Pastor Riley?" I ask, knowing full well the man's reputation for honesty is as solid as the ancient oak pews lining his sanctuary.

"Yep, that's the one. He's adamant she wasn't in attendance." Jim leans forward, his hands clasped together, resting on the file splayed open between us. "We talked to the family and they say she was with them. But not him. He says she hasn't been in for months, and he has been wanting to ask them if she was okay. Sounds like the whole family is covering for her."

I lean back in my chair, crossing my arms over my chest. The precinct's hum of activity fades into a dull buzz behind the clamor of thoughts racing through my head.

"Pastor Riley's word carries weight," I muse, the wheels turning. "But why did she lie? She must have lied for a reason."

"Exactly." Jim's nod is slow, deliberate. "Doesn't make sense unless she had something else to hide."

"Something more personal, perhaps?" The suggestion hangs in the air, undecided whether to solidify or dissipate.

"Could be," Jim concedes, rubbing his chin thoughtfully. "Or maybe she's protecting someone."

"Maybe." But my gut coils tight, whispering a different story —one where the lies stack up like dominoes waiting for a push. Something about this doesn't sit right with me, and the itch to dig deeper is relentless.

"I need you to look into this."

"Of course, Jim," I say, standing up, my mind already sprinting ahead.

I slip out of the precinct with a single purpose sharpening my focus. The Florida sun is setting in the distance, but it's Carla's secrets that scorch my thoughts. I stake out near the mansion, where palm trees sway with more freedom than I currently possess. I'm parked just out of view, my eyes glued to the grand façade, waiting for any sign of movement. I know she usually leaves the house around 6:30 p.m., when she is done making dinner ready. At least that's what she told us when we went over her workday for the Kanes'.

Time crawls. Finally, the gates creak open and there she is— Carla slipping into the street driving her old, rusty car that groans in protest. It stands out against the luxury around it, a testament to some untold narrative.

I wait for the perfect gap before igniting my engine, rolling into the stream of traffic like another drop in the ocean. My fingers grip the steering wheel, each knuckle a pale beacon of tension. Cars zoom past, their colors a blur against the canvas of city life.

Keeping a safe distance, I follow the familiar red tail of

Carla's vehicle, my gaze locked onto it with the intensity of a hawk. Every lane change she makes, I echo moments later; every turn she takes, I note with a mental click. I notice fast that she's not heading towards her home address which is outside of town. She's actually going in the opposite direction. She's heading towards downtown.

The streets are brimming with life—tourists meandering aimlessly, locals navigating the chaos with practiced indifference. It's all so vibrant, so normal, but beneath it lies the undercurrent of something else. Secrets. Lies. They lurk in the alleys, behind the smiles, within every quick glance over one's shoulder.

My instincts, honed from years of dissecting half-truths and catching subtle tells, keep me vigilant. I watch as Carla maneuvers through traffic, her movements deliberate, almost cautious. Oblivious to the detective in her wake, she is just another citizen in this bustling metropolis, yet I can't shake off the feeling that we're both players in a game where the rules are yet to be revealed.

"Keep your friends close and suspects closer," I mutter under my breath, a wry smile tugging at my lips. Irony, always a bitter companion, doesn't fail to highlight the stark contrast between my pursuit and the everyday hustle around us. But my humor is short-lived, suffocated by the growing anticipation for what might lie at the end of this chase.

What are you hiding, Carla?

The deeper we drive into the heart of the city, the more acute the juxtaposition becomes—sunlight glinting off skyscrapers, casting long shadows that seem to reach for us, as if trying to drag the truth into the light. And there I am, trailing behind Carla, caught between the glaring brightness of the world outside and the murky depths of uncertainty within.

Carla's car takes a sudden left, and I'm jolted from my thoughts. The charming façades of St. Augustine's historic district fade, replaced by the cracked sidewalks and graffiti-tagged walls of a neighborhood that doesn't feature in glossy brochures. My fingers tighten around the steering wheel, guiding my unmarked sedan with practiced ease.

"Where are you off to, Carla?" I whisper to myself as her taillights flicker, signaling another turn. She's driving like she knows where she wants to go—no hesitation, no second-guessing. That certainty prickles at me; doubt has become my default setting, and seeing someone so sure-footed stirs a curious envy within me.

The buildings here stand closer together, shoulders hunched, as if sharing whispered secrets. A bar with neon signs buzzes on one corner; a pawn shop squats on another, its windows cluttered with objects heavy with stories I don't have time to unravel. Carla's car is an old model, rust creeping along the edges like a slow infection, but it maneuvers through these streets with familiarity.

She parks in front of a nondescript building, sandwiched between a laundromat exhaling steam and a convenience store flaunting an explosion of colorful produce. Nothing about this place screams significance, yet the tension in my chest disagrees. It tightens further when Carla glances over her shoulder—a quick, furtive sweep.

I slip out, using parked cars as cover, feeling the familiar adrenaline surge of a hunt reaching its climax. Carla's cautious steps towards the entrance seem to reverberate in my own chest, each one synced with the pounding of my heart. I crouch behind a beat-up Honda, peering over its hood. The door swings shut behind Carla, swallowing her whole. I'm left with the echo of that door, a soft thud that seems to mock the anticlimactic end to our little parade. But there's something else—an energy that thrums through the air, charging it with the promise of uncovered secrets.

"Alright, Darcey," I coach myself, "time to see what lies behind door number one."

I push off from the Honda, my legs stiff from crouching. The moment calls for caution, but my feet betray a different story—they're itching to cross the threshold Carla just passed through. Inside, secrets wait, their siren call nearly impossible to ignore.

It's not fear that gnaws at me; it's the possibility of diving headfirst into a dead end. My badge feels heavy against my chest, a reminder of what's at stake. A murder case with more turns than the labyrinthine streets of St. Augustine and every lead could be the one that unravels the knot—or tightens it.

With a deep breath, I command my feet forward. There's a click as the door yields to my touch, less an invitation and more a reluctant acceptance of my presence. The dim corridor swallows the daylight behind me, replacing it with shadows that cling to the walls like cobwebs.

The air is stale, scented with the mustiness of old buildings and the ghost of cleaning products trying to fight a losing battle. It's quiet, almost too quiet—the kind of hush that makes your ears strain for any sound that can cut through the silence.

Are you involved in something, Carla? Drugs, perhaps?

A low, rhythmic thumping filters through the silence, muffled and distant, yet insistent. It grows louder with each step I take, urging me on like the pulse of the city outside. My own heartbeat seems to sync with it, a duet of anticipation and nervous energy.

My hands are clammy as they brush against the wall, seeking guidance in the poorly lit space. Eyes adjusting to the gloom, I notice the hallway isn't completely deserted—doors line the passage, promising or threatening revelation.

There's no turning back now. The truth lies ahead, perhaps behind one of these doors, hidden in plain sight. And I'm about to find it.

I press my ear to the door, the thumping now a rhythmic pounding that vibrates through my body. My fingers curl into a fist, hesitating only a moment before I knock twice and push the door open.

"Really?" The word slips out before I can catch it, half amusement, half disbelief.

Carla is there in the center of a makeshift dance studio, her body swaying with an enthusiasm I can't help but find contagious. She's decked out in neon spandex, the kind that was last in style when my sixteen-year-old was still in diapers. Her arms flail to the beat of a Latin-infused track, commanding a motley crew of sweat-drenched followers.

"Shake it, ladies—and gents! Move those hips!" Carla shouts over the music, her voice as vibrant as her clothing.

My mouth curves into a smile despite myself. This is the secret Carla's been guarding? A secret Zumba class?

"Zumba Queen!" I shout, catching Carla's attention mid-salsa step. She grabs her phone. The music dies down, and all eyes are on us.

"Detective White," she pants, cheeks flushed from exertion. "What are you doing here?"

"I... I want to ask you the same question. Was this where you were at the time of Edward Kane's murder? Doing a Zumba class?"

She swallows, then nods, her eyes looking guilty. She pulls me aside, where no one can hear us, then whispers. "I...I can explain. I lied. I had to. I...I don't pay taxes of my income from this. It's...extra, you know? And it keeps me fit. It's a win-win. But yes, I am guilty of this."

"Tax evasion, Carla? Really?" There's no accusation in my voice, just a playful rise of my brows as I lean against the doorframe.

She hangs her head for a moment, then lifts it with a

sheepish grin. "It started as a small side gig—cash only, you know? And then... Well, I didn't expect to be this good at it."

"Clearly, you've missed your calling." I shake my head, still struggling to match this image with the somber figure from earlier.

"Please don't tell," she pleads, her eyes wide and earnest. "This is just something for me, something that gives me extra money, and I get all of my aggressions out, you know..."

Her voice trails off, and I nod, more understanding than I want to admit.

"Your secret Zumba empire is safe with me," I assure her, already turning to leave. "Just stick to dancing away from crime scenes, okay?"

"Deal!" Carla grins, relief lighting up her features, and the music starts again.

As I slip out the door, the beats chase after me, a reminder that sometimes, life's darkest corners can lead to the most unexpected of revelations.

The last echoes of Latin beats fade into the muffled hum of the city as I push through the heavy door, stepping back into the daylight. My feet find the rhythm of the sidewalk, each step a soft thud against concrete, a beat far removed from the Zumba drum. This whole detour—Carla's secret life of dance and evasion—has nothing to do with blood spatter patterns and alibis.

"Back to square one," I mutter under my breath, hitching my purse higher up on my shoulder. There's relief, sure—an exhalation of tension that had been coiling inside me since Jim's revelation about the shaky alibi. But it's not enough to unclench the knot in my stomach, the one that tightens with every dead-end lead and unanswered question.

SEVENTEEN

DARCEY

I slide the last plate onto the table, the steam curling in the dim kitchen light. Mac and cheese, cut-up hot dogs—comfort on a dish for my twins who giggle and kick under the table. Bradley should've been here hours ago. Where is he? I push the thought aside as I scoop portions onto their plates, drawing on the smile that doesn't match how I feel.

"Blow on it. It's hot," I caution, watching as they puff out their little cheeks, making a delightful show of it. Their laughter, so pure and untroubled, makes something clench inside me. They're too young to see the cracks in our picture-perfect family portrait. And I'll do anything to keep it that way.

"Mommy, look!" Emma exclaims, holding up a noodle with her fork. It dances precariously, almost slipping off. "It's like a worm!"

I chuckle, leaning back in my chair. "A very tasty worm, I hope."

"Yuck!" shouts Jacob, scrunching up his nose. "I don't want to eat worms."

"Don't worry. They're just noodles," I reassure him,

reaching over to ruffle his hair. "No worms on the menu tonight. I promise."

After dinner, the children scamper off to the living room, leaving a trail of giggles behind them. I follow, carrying a plate of cookies.

"Okay, who wants to build a fort?" I ask, placing the treats on the coffee table.

"Me! Me!" they chant in unison, their eyes sparkling with excitement.

I help them drape blankets over the couches, creating a cozy hideaway. "This is the strongest fort in the kingdom," I declare, crawling inside with them. "And the most delicious one, too," I add, passing out cookies and they dig in with their tiny hands.

As the evening rolls on, the children's energy fades, and soon it's time for bed. I gently guide them upstairs, my voice soft and soothing. "Did you brush your teeth?" I inquire, holding open the bathroom door.

Emma nods, her toothbrush in hand, while Jacob makes a silly face in the mirror. "I'm a monster!" he growls, toothpaste foam dribbling down his chin.

I laugh, pretending to cower. "Oh no, not the toothpaste monster! Quick, wash him away!"

Once their teeth are clean, I tuck them in, sitting on the edge of Emma's bed. "What story shall it be tonight?" I ask, picking up a book from the nightstand.

"The one with the dragon!" Emma insists, her eyes wide with anticipation.

"And the knight!" Jacob adds, snuggling deeper under his blanket.

Happy that they for once agree, I open the book, my voice weaving the tale of adventure and bravery. As I read, I glance at their sleepy faces, a warmth spreading in my chest. These moments, these quiet, tender evenings, are what I'm fighting for.

The laughter, the stories, the small joys that light up their world.

When the story concludes, I kiss each child goodnight, whispering, "Sweet dreams, my loves."

As I tiptoe out of the room, I pause at the door, watching their peaceful slumber. This is my reminder, my silent vow to keep their world intact.

But soon my mind wanders, dances around the edge of a question I'm too afraid to ask myself:

What is Bradley up to now? I can't even be certain Charlotte told him about Edward's death. Everything feels out of control.

"Night, night," I whisper. The room is filled with the soft glow of nightlights and the steady rhythm of their breathing. The calm before the storm. Or maybe I'm already in the eye of it, pretending the winds have died down.

The old wooden door groans in protest as I slip out onto the porch, my skin already sticky from the thick, humid air. My fingers fumble between the worn cushions of the lawn chair until I find my pack of cigarettes. With shaky hands, I pull one out and light it, the flame casting eerie shadows on my wrist. As I exhale a cloud of smoke into the darkness, I can't help but feel like I'm releasing all of my doubts and fears with each breath. But then reality hits me like a punch to the gut—I remember the missed calls from work, Jim's urgent expectations for an update. The quiet of the night suddenly feels suffocating.

What am I doing? The end of the cigarette glows bright as I take a drag. Bradley's face flashes in my mind, that charming grin concealing whatever he's up to next. I exhale slowly, watching the smoke dissipate into nothingness. He has made so many promises that turned into even more lies.

"Damn him," I say softly, the words dissolving into the cool air. I lean against the railing, the wood rough beneath my palms. I kill the cigarette and walk back inside, making myself a cup of scalding coffee.

I take a sip, the bitter liquid burning my tongue, and I contemplate Charlotte's next move. I know she holds the key to incriminating Bradley, but the pieces of this twisted puzzle are scattered, waiting to be put together. My hands tremble slightly with a mix of anticipation and fear as I log into my work laptop, determined to unearth any hidden truths.

The soft glow of the screen casts an eerie light in the dim room, illuminating interviews conducted by my colleagues, saved on the system. Words dance across the monitor, painting a picture of Charlotte that is both captivating and concerning. The nanny's account portrays her as a caring mother, fiercely protective of her child, but a subtle mention of an incident hints at a simmering anger hidden behind Charlotte's polished mask.

My heart sinks at the realization that Charlotte may not be as innocent as she appears. A knot forms in my stomach as I read about the incident where she allegedly lost her temper and lashed out at the gardener.

I shake my head in disbelief, unable to reconcile this side of Charlotte with the woman I have come to know. But then again, people are capable of hiding their true selves behind a mask of perfection.

I click on another link and find myself reading an interview with Charlotte's parents. Someone must have reached them before Charlotte had a chance to warn them not to talk to the police. They speak highly of their daughter, praising her intelligence and loving nature. However, there is a hint of hesitation in their words when they are asked about her hot temper. They carefully choose their words, but I can sense an underlying concern in their tone.

I take another sip of my now cold coffee. And as much as it pains me to admit it, Charlotte's past will play a crucial role in determining her future. I have no idea what evidence, if any, she got on her phone. Did Bradley say anything incriminating when they met? I'd tried to get into her phone, but if she recorded their conversation it was on her "Bradley phone".

As I delve deeper into the interview with Charlotte's affluent parents, a wave of unease washes over me. I furrow my brow, absorbing the intricacies of their accounts while grappling with the implications. Could Charlotte's privileged upbringing have shaped her into the enigmatic figure she is today? Demanding? Entitled? Afflicted by mental health issues? Is there more lurking beneath the surface, waiting to be uncovered? I saw her unravel before my eyes earlier today.

With a deep breath, I close the laptop.

A flicker of guilt twinges inside me as I think of Charlotte, sprawled on her plush bed this afternoon, breath heavy with that sickly sweet scent of too much wine.

Too many ghosts in your glass, Charlotte. The image of her, helpless and oblivious to the world, lingers uncomfortably. It's like staring into a distorted mirror, glimpses of my own past reflected in her glazed-over eyes.

My mind unwillingly travels back to those nights that ended blank, wiped clean by alcohol's cruel hand. The first time it happened, I woke up with my head pounding and my pride bruised, swearing never again. But promises are fragile things, especially when Bradley is pouring the wine. Just weeks later, there we were at another dinner, his hand steady as he filled my glass once more. "Live a little," he urged, his voice smooth like the Merlot he so loved to watch me drink.

"Bradley, I—" I started, my protest weak, still haunted by the last blackout.

"It's all in the past, right?" His blue eyes locked onto mine, a challenge and a reassurance all in one. And like a fool, I believed him. I believed the lie that the past could be buried, that the wine wouldn't unbury it. So what if I drank too much once? It won't happen again. Right?

"Stupid," I chastise myself. "Never again," I vow, but the words taste hollow on my tongue. Bradley will be home soon, his grin wide, his intentions hidden. And I'll be left wondering which Darcey he sees—the detective who uncovers secrets or the wife who hides them.

"Darcey?" A voice trails through the hallway, smooth as silk, yet it sends a ripple of tension through me.

"In here," I call back.

Bradley rounds the corner onto the living room, his presence immediately commanding the space. Even in the dim light, I can make out that familiar, self-assured smile on his face. And I'm floored. After everything that's happened today, how can he walk in like normal?

"There you are," he says, stepping toward me. "You look... tense." His brow furrows. "Rough day?"

"Something like that." I force a nonchalant shrug. I don't know what I expected, after all of these years of lying, but it's not this. A crumpled shirt, a tired face... I thought I'd notice something.

"Perhaps a glass of wine might help?" Bradley suggests, already moving inside the kitchen to pour two glasses with practiced charm. I follow him in.

"Maybe just one," I hear myself say, even as alarm bells chime in my mind. It's never just one, is it?

The crystal stem of the wine glass feels cool, too cool, against my fingertips. Bradley's already sipping from his own, eyes never leaving me, blue like the ocean on a stormy day—beautiful but dangerous. I think of him with Charlotte, arguing in the yacht club earlier.

"Darcey?" His voice carries a gentle warmth. He leans against the doorframe with an easy grace, his eyes catching the light just right to reveal a playful spark.

I pause, the rim of the glass hovering near my lips, my fingers tapping a nervous rhythm against the cool surface. An internal struggle rages within me, two armies clashing—one urging me toward him, drawn by the promise in his gaze when I indulge his whims; the other shouting warnings, haunted by echoes of nights spiraled out of control.

He steps forward, settling into the plush armchair opposite me, his movements smooth and unhurried. "Darcey, I've got this great idea," he says, a mischievous grin curling his lips. "Why don't we make tonight different? No TV tonight. Just you and me, listening to some good music, maybe a dance or two? Like the old days? What do you say?"

I shift in my seat, trying to find comfort in the cushions but feeling their embrace tighten like a net. His charm is intoxicating, a heady mix of charisma and allure that keeps pulling me back. "I'm just... not sure," I admit, my voice barely above a whisper.

He darts me a reassuring smile, leaning forward, elbows resting on his knees. "Hey, there's no rush, no pressure," he says, sincerity lacing his words. "Whatever you decide, Darcey, I'm here. But, I promise, tonight's just about enjoying ourselves and each other. We deserve it."

His easy manner, the way he captures the room with a mere glance, it's a magnetic pull I can't quite resist. Yet, I know why I'm trapped in this dance, why I linger in his orbit. It's the hope that this time, perhaps, things might be different.

"I'm just... not sure if I should."

"Should?" He feigns innocence, tilting his head slightly, knowing full well what he's doing to me. It's a dance we've perfected over the years, except I never seem to lead.

"Bradley, I..." The words tangle up with the fear, the wish to be the wife he wants, the detective I am, the mother I need to be. Every role demanding something different, something more.

"Come on," he coaxes, stepping closer, close enough for me

to catch the scent of his cologne—a mix of spice and promises. "You know you want to."

It feels as though the kitchen has shrunk, the walls inching inwards with every breath I take. His hand finds mine, warmth seeping into my cold fingers, guiding the glass upward. My throat tightens, not from thirst, but from dread. Because deep down, in that place where truths are kept locked away, I know— I don't want the wine, I want the peace it promises, a peace I haven't felt in far too long.

"Maybe just a sip," I whisper, betraying myself, because a sip is all it takes. A sip, and I'm adrift on a sea where Bradley sets the course, and I follow, clinging to the wreckage of my will.

"Thatta girl." His grin is victory and sin all at once.

EIGHTEEN

CHARLOTTE

The instant my stiletto heel meets the smooth pavement, a wave of confidence surges through me. With a graceful motion, I emerge from the driver's seat of my sleek black car—my modern-day chariot. Today, I am adorned in an elegant dress that hugs every curve, exuding power and strength. This is my armor—a lesson passed down from my mother that I have embraced wholeheartedly throughout my life. The deep shade of scarlet red against my skin radiates strength and authority, a visual representation of the confidence that courses through my veins.

As I enter the lobby of the TV station, the scent of polished wood fills my nose. The lighting fixtures give off a warm, golden glow, but it does little to calm my nerves. Sweat beads on my forehead and trickles down my spine. I rummage through my bag for some powder and quickly check my makeup in the tiny mirror inside. Thank goodness it's still intact; I can't afford any mishaps today.

"Mrs. Kane?" A young man in a crisp suit greets me with a smile that could disarm the most guarded heart. He seems genuine, but in this industry, who can tell? "We're so glad you're here. This way, please."

"Thank you." I try to control my voice; I want to play the parting of a grieving widow. We walk together, him chatting about the studio's recent renovations, me nodding where appropriate yet barely absorbing a word. Edward's death has hardly been front-page news, but I need this man to think back and remember that he liked me. Tell his friends he met me, but that he didn't think I could have murdered my husband. My mind whirls with the interview ahead, the need to be impeccable.

The stairs loom before us, leading upward to the stage. His presence is oddly comforting, a beacon of friendliness in the midst of my storming thoughts. But companionship, no matter how fleeting, cannot still the anxious energy coursing through me.

"Right up these stairs, Mrs. Kane," he says, gesturing with a sweep of his hand as though unveiling a grand exhibit. So up we go, toward the studio, toward another encounter where I have to play a part.

Heels echo sharply against the shiny floor. Each step up the staircase feels like a note in a prelude to something monumental. I ascend, aware of the hushed reverence that follows me, an invisible train of whispers and sideways glances. Do some of the show runners know what I'm here to talk about?

At the top, a door swings open to a room bathed in warm light and the faint scent of foundation and hairspray. The makeup room, a vestibule to transformation, yet I need no metamorphosis. A woman, her face a canvas of subtle contours, stands ready with powder and brushes, instruments to enhance and conceal.

"Mrs. Kane, would you like to touch up before going on?" Her offer, well-intentioned, is laced with the unspoken assertion that perfection can be bought in shades and palettes.

"No, thank you," I reply confidently. I have put on my own armor of makeup, and done so to perfection. I don't need hers.

She hesitates, then nods.

The tense silence in the room is broken by the sound of the door opening, and I turn to see a familiar figure standing in the doorway. Seeing her beaming smile, one that I haven't seen in a while, immediately softens my guarded stance.

"Charlotte," she greets me with sincerity in her voice, and her presence offers some solace amidst the coldness of my emotions. "I'm so glad you're here."

"Alice."

I nod, struggling to find words to respond as she comes closer and embraces me tightly.

"I'm sorry for canceling on you yesterday," I say. "Something came up."

"It's all right, just make it up to me some time," she tells me with a smile. "I've been missing our hangouts like we used to do all the time, bar hopping. You've been distant for months now. Not that I don't understand; and now, with what happened to Edward recently... how are you coping?"

"I'm managing. Or at least I think I am."

"Well, you look amazing," Alice continues, circling me like a shark to its prey. She never liked Edward. It's exactly why she's been the perfect person to bar hop with for years. She keeps my secrets, and I do hers. She appraises me, her eyes tracing the contours of my posture, my dress, the very essence of what I project to the world. "You always did have a way of commanding a room, even without saying a word."

"Thank you," I say.

"Coming on here, telling your story... it's... you're very brave. Are you ready for your big moment?" she asks, her tone shifting to something akin to concern, or perhaps it's curiosity masquerading as care.

Alice's presence brings back bittersweet memories of late

nights studying and laughing together. She still radiates the same warmth and kindness that drew me to her in college. We didn't speak for years since right after college, when we both got married, we drifted apart. But we bumped into each other two years ago at a mutual friend's party and decided to see one another again. It led to many nights out together, while Edward was traveling. As we chat and reminisce about old times, Alice casually mentions that the police haven't questioned her yet about my husband's death. I am not surprised—I have been very adamant about keeping our friendship hidden, so I could be with her without worrying what would come back to Edward. She is the only friend I truly trust that her loyalty lies with me and no one else.

"I'm ready," I reply, brushing off the question like a speck of dust on my sleeve. I am keeping my guard up, pretending like this is just another performance, another stage where I must play my part with care.

"Can I get you anything? Coffee, water?" Alice gestures toward the array of refreshments set up along the wall.

The scent of freshly brewed coffee lingers in the air, a temptation I dismiss with a wave of my hand. "I've had enough coffee," I confide, pulling back the edge of a smile. "I just want to get this over with, in a way."

"Of course," Alice replies, her voice tinged with a feigned respect that grates on my nerves. She turns on her heel, leading the way out of the makeup room. "If there's anything you need, Charlotte."

I nod, she doesn't need to say more.

As we approach the studio, a shiver courses through me. It's not fear, I tell myself—it's just the chill of the air conditioning brushing against my skin. But deep down, I know it's more than that. There's a thrill that comes with treading so close to the edge, where every word and gesture can tip the scales.

We step into the studio, and it's like walking onto the

surface of the sun. Bright lights blaze down from above, harsh and unforgiving, carving sharp lines of shadow across the floor. They don't just illuminate—they expose. And in their glare, I feel seen, stripped bare despite the armor of my confidence.

"Quite the setup," I say, allowing myself a moment to take it all in.

Alice gestures toward the spotlight at the center of it all. "After you," she says.

"Thank you." My reply is smooth, practiced. I glide forward, letting the light envelop me as I take my place. Here, in the blinding brilliance of the studio, I'm not just Charlotte Kane —I'm whoever I need to be. And I'm ready to captivate, to take back control of my life.

"Are you comfortable?" Alice asks, reaching to put her hand on my knee.

"Perfectly," I answer, settling into the role I was born to play, and Alice pulls back. With each breath, I let the anxiety morph into excitement, the fears into fuel. I may be anxious, but they'll never see it—the audience, the viewers at home, and least of all, Darcey. They'll only see what I want them to see: Charlotte Kane, enigma, poised for her next act.

"We start filming in five minutes."

Five minutes echoes in my head, a countdown to a moment that will either make or break everything I've worked for. With each ticking second, the anticipation builds. I adjust the hem of my dress, a slight tremor betraying the calm I've sworn to uphold. The fabric feels cool against my skin, soothing in an otherwise heated moment. Alice watches me, and I can see she's worried about me.

"Alice," I begin, my voice a purr of assurance, "a scoop is what you're after, and a scoop is precisely what you'll get." My words, a velvet hammer, are designed to crush doubt. "The viewers won't know what hit them."

Her eyebrow arches, and for a fleeting second, I wonder if

she can hear the faint crack in my resolve. But then Georgina's sweet face flashes before my eyes. I'm doing this for her.

"Very well," she says, nodding in agreement, yet her eyes linger on me like an uncomfortable afterthought.

With a practiced motion, I smooth the skirt of my dress, and cross my legs with a precision that feels almost surgical. I flash a smile, wide and wealthy, an offering to the cameras and unseen spectators who will soon hang on my every word.

"Ready when you are," I say, and it's not just a confirmation for the crew—it's a mantra for myself. Because readiness is more than preparation; it's a testament to my resilience, to the countless battles fought in silence.

The red light on the camera blinks to life. I focus on the lens, finding solace in its unblinking gaze. Poised and enigmatic, I am the mystery they yearn to solve, the story they ache to hear.

"Let's take back control," I whisper, mostly to myself, before the countdown begins.

NINETEEN

DARCEY

I wake up with my usual companion, a splitting headache. The throb in my skull is a drumline, pounding out a rhythm that has me wincing with every beat. My eyelids are heavy, reluctantly parting to let in the intrusive morning light. I prop myself up on one elbow, the room swaying like I'm still on a boat rocked by waves, not in my own bed. God, why did I think it was a good idea to drown my sorrows in wine? Charlotte and I really are alike.

I swing my legs over the side, my feet searching for the cold reassurance of the floor. The tiles feel like ice against my soles as I shuffle toward the door, steadying myself against the wall which suddenly feels like it's tilting.

The scent of something burning invades my nostrils—the acrid smell mingling with the sickly sweet aroma of maple syrup. Breakfast, the normalcy of it jarring against the chaos of my thoughts. Each step down the staircase is a careful negotiation, muscles protesting, begging me to crawl back under the covers and forget the world exists.

"Detective White might handle homicides," I mutter to myself, a sardonic edge to my whispers, "but she sure as hell can't handle her liquor." My attempt at humor does little to lift the fog that's taken residence in my head. I only remember drinking that first glass, the rest is a complete blur.

Hand on the banister, I make it to the bottom. The kitchen looms ahead, its familiar contours blurred at the edges. Bradley's there—I can hear the clink of a spatula on the pan. I pause, collecting myself, trying to push past the haze of last night.

I edge into the kitchen, where Bradley is a study in domestic normalcy, his back to me as he flips pancakes. The sizzle of batter on the hot pan fills the room with homely sounds that seem so out of place in the chaos of my mind. I manage a half-hearted smile, though it feels more like a grimace.

"Morning," I say, the roughness of a night spent overindulging obvious in my voice.

"Hey." Bradley doesn't turn around, his focus locked on the golden-brown discs he's crafting. There's something unsettling about the casualness of it all, the way he can stand there and create the pretense of a family man while secrets fester just beneath the surface.

The twins are perched on stools at the breakfast counter, their small forms swathed in the uniforms that mark them ready for the day ahead. They're a whirlwind of youthful energy, chattering away about spelling tests and recess games as if they don't have a care in the world. I envy them that innocence.

"Mommy! Did you see my drawing from yesterday?" Emma waves a crayon masterpiece in the air, her face lighting up with expectation.

"Of course, sweetheart, it was beautiful," I reply, even though the image is just a blur in my memory. Guilt pricks at me, but I push it aside. "The best treehouse I've ever seen."

"Are we going to build it for real?" Jacob asks, his eyes wide with hope.

"Maybe this summer," I hedge, swallowing down the lump of promises that might be too heavy to keep.

Bradley slides a pancake onto each of their plates, a dollop of butter melting into sweet, sticky pools. He's playing the role today, the devoted father and husband, but I know better than to trust the act. It's all part of the show, and I'm no longer sure where the performance ends and reality begins.

The smell of pancakes lingers, sweet and cloying, as Bradley turns from the stove, his blue eyes locking onto mine. His practiced smile stretches across his face, the one that used to melt my defenses like snow in the sun. Not anymore.

"Morning," he says softly, his voice tinged with a warmth that seems out of place.

I nod, trying to muster a smile that doesn't reach my eyes. "Morning."

He closes the distance between us with a few sure steps, leans in, aiming for my lips. Instinctively, I recoil, the motion sharp, almost reflexive. My skin crawls with an unease that's become all too familiar.

"What's wrong?" he asks, confusion flickering in his eyes.

I hesitate, the memory of last night rushing back like a tidal wave. Him not coming home till late, the feeling that he was lying to me, that maybe he was with another woman, the realization that the love I once felt has been slowly eroding away, leaving nothing but a hollow shell. I know he wanted us to have a great night together, to dance, just like the old days. And I guess we did. I know I have the headache to prove it. I don't remember much to be honest. But it takes more than that for me to forget his betrayal.

"I just... I am a little hungover, Bradley."

He stands still, absorbing my words. The silence stretches between us, heavy and unavoidable.

"Darce?" His voice is tinged with hurt, or maybe it's just irritation masquerading as concern. "What's wrong with you?"

"Nothing," I say, but even to my own ears, it sounds like a lie.

He tries again, this time his hand reaching out, fingers nearly brushing the ponytail that keeps my hair off my neck. I step back, out of reach, my breath catching in my throat. The air between us crackles with unsaid words, heavy with accusation.

"Your head still swimming from last night, huh?" Bradley's voice cuts through the tension, sharp and unforgiving. His disappointment morphs into something colder, something that makes me feel small and foolish. "You did hit that wine pretty hard. Now you pay the price."

I can't meet his gaze, so I turn away, focusing on the mundane task of pouring coffee. The dark liquid hits the bottom of the cup with a hollow sound, echoing in the silent kitchen. Bradley's hurt expression lingers in my periphery, but I ignore it, along with the guilt that threatens to rise.

Bradley killed Edward.

The sentence pulses at the back of my mind, insistent and terrifying. Charlotte's words slither through my consciousness, wrapping around my thoughts like poison ivy. I raise my cup to my lips and take a small sip of the bitter beverage. The hot liquid scorches my tongue, which is oddly satisfying as I try to drown out all my doubts. Bradley remains oblivious to the fact that I know his mistress very well, which brings me great pleasure. It's almost amusing how naïve he is about our connection. I realize I don't hate her any more. Not like I used to, not like I felt when I first saw her kiss my husband. My initial impression of Charlotte was incorrect; she isn't such a terrible person after all. I feel more sorry for her now. She's a troubled soul.

My gaze drifts back to Bradley, taking in the set of his jaw, the way his hands move with calculated grace. Would anyone believe he could do it? That the man who flips pancakes for our children would also be capable of something so sinister? A shiver runs down my spine, chasing the warmth from the coffee right out of me.

Would they believe he did it for her?

I might feel sorry for her, but I can't escape my jealousy at the same time. The name Charlotte still tastes like ash in my mouth, even unspoken. Her image, poised and polished, looms behind my closed eyelids, a reminder of what I am not. That I'm not as beautiful as her.

Is Bradley going to leave us?

The twins' laughter trickles in the air as they storm into the living room, innocent and carefree. It's a stark contrast to the cold calculation that might be festering in their father's heart. Would he abandon them, chase after a fantasy wrapped in designer clothes and smug smiles?

Stop it. But once the seed of suspicion has been planted, it grows wild, untamed. And I'm left sipping coffee that's gone cold, wondering if my husband is a murderer and how to prove it.

I shuffle over into the living room, where the twins are playing on the floor, giggling. Their school uniforms are pristine, not a crease out of place—Bradley's doing, no doubt. I force a smile and lean against the door frame, trying to anchor myself in their chatter.

"Hey munchkins, what's the big plan for today?" My voice comes out lighter than I feel, but they don't seem to notice.

"Spelling test." Jacob beams, his eyes bright with the sort of confidence I can barely remember.

"Art class," Emma chimes in, twirling a strand of her blonde hair around her finger. "We're painting with finger paint."

"Sounds beautiful, Em." I nod, my gaze drifting toward Bradley at the stove. His back is to us, shoulders tense. "Make sure you show me after school, okay?"

"Okay, Mommy!" she sings out, already lost in a daydream of colors and brushes.

"I'll ace the spelling test," Jacob says. "I always do."

Spell "murderer," I almost whisper to myself, the word sticky and vile in my mind. But then Jacob recounts his spelling words, innocent and ordinary, and I turn from the darkness.

"Mom, you okay?" Jacob catches my eye, a furrowed brow belying his young age.

"Of course, honey." I muster another smile, though it feels like lifting weights.

"Your smile looks tired," Emma observes with a frown.

"Darcey, you should try getting some sleep instead of creeping around the house at night like some..." Bradley's voice is sharp and cold. He doesn't finish the sentence, but he doesn't need to. The implication hangs heavy.

"Like some what, Bradley?" I hold his gaze, challenging him to continue.

A muscle twitches in his jaw, and he turns away, flipping a pancake with more force than necessary.

"Never mind." He tosses the words over his shoulder like scraps to a dog. "It's nothing a bottle of wine can't fix, right?"

"Wow, Bradley, not even eight in the morning and we're already judging lifestyles?" I shoot back, my tone laced with sarcasm. This isn't new territory for us. It's a well-worn path littered with accusations and regrets. "Hurry up and grab your lunches, kiddos, the bus will be here soon."

They nod, picking up their backpacks and lunchboxes, and I risk a glance at Bradley. His eyes meet mine, the blue in them like ice. There's something there—a flash of something darker than annoyance. Fear? Guilt?

But then it's gone, and he's just a father, telling his kids to have a great day, the perfect picture once more. And I'm left wondering which mask he'll wear today.

. . .

The bus disappears around the corner, and suddenly the street is too quiet. I turn, and there's Bradley, leaning against the door frame, his eyes tracking my every move. The morning sun catches on the edge of his jaw, casting half his face in a golden light that doesn't reach the coolness in his gaze.

"Quiet without the kids," he remarks, breaking the silence with casual indifference.

"Always is," I reply, but my voice doesn't sound like my own —it's hollow, echoing with the memory of Charlotte's high-pitched voice and Bradley's low growl as they clashed at the yacht club. Their argument plays on a loop in my mind, the intensity, the anger...

"Darcey?" Bradley's voice slices through the flashback, pulling me back to the now. "You're spacing out again."

"Am I?" I force a smile, pushing down the bubbling unease.

I step back inside, the cool air of the house a shroud. Bradley's still watching me, his blue eyes assessing, calculating. I can feel the weight of his stare, heavy and expectant, as if waiting for me to unravel right there on the spot.

"Where were you yesterday?" I ask, the question slipping out before I can weigh its consequences. It hangs between us, a thin wire taut with tension.

"Work," he answers, too quickly.

He takes a step toward me, closing the distance until I can see the micro expressions dancing across his face, the slight twitch in his jaw, the way his nostrils flare ever so slightly. "Why are you asking, Darcey? Trying to play detective at home now?"

"Should I not be?" I retort, but my heart's pounding, adrenaline coursing through my veins. The smell of burnt pancakes lingers in the air, mixing with the scent of his cologne, creating an olfactory dissonance much like the chaos in my head.

He turns abruptly, grabbing a dishcloth to wipe down the counter, his movements sharp and precise. "We don't have time for games," he mutters, the clatter of dishes punctuating the tension in his voice.

I reach for the coffee pot, trying to steady my shaking hands. "What do you want for lunch today?" I ask, attempting to inject some normalcy into the charged atmosphere.

"Just the usual, thanks," he replies, his tone softening slightly as he retrieves his briefcase from the chair.

"Don't forget your jacket," I remind him, folding the dish-cloth neatly.

He nods, slipping his arms into the sleeves as he glances at the clock. "Maybe you should focus a little more on what you do —your drinking, for instance—and less on me." His tone is hard, accusatory, each word a jab meant to wound, to throw me off balance.

"Is that what you think this is about?" I counter, but my voice lacks conviction, drowned out by the rush of blood in my ears. He's in my space, towering over me, and I'm caught between wanting to push him away and needing to hold my ground.

"Isn't it?" Bradley's eyes pierce into mine, searching, daring me to look away first.

However, I don't give in to my fears. Despite the doubts and the unsettling idea that my husband might be more than just an unfaithful spouse, I am still a detective. It's what I do. I will uncover the truth, no matter how painful it may be, because Charlotte and I need answers to save our families. We must come up with a new plan, a new approach, to get to the bottom of things. With her by my side, I feel like it is possible.

TWENTY
CHARLOTTE

The glint of the afternoon sun off the polished silver buckle catches my eye as Carla folds my favorite black dress and places it delicately into the suitcase.

"Be careful with that," I instruct, pointing toward the garment. "It's a Versace. And don't forget the Louboutins—the ones with the red soles." My voice echoes off the high ceilings of the bedroom. I glance at the wall-mounted TV screen, now silent, where tonight my face will be shown, poised and confident. The interviewer was practically eating out of my hand. Tonight, in prime time, the whole city will see Charlotte Kane tell her story. But they only get the glossy, edited version.

"Carla, the silk scarves too. And the jewelry box—no, not that one. The one with the sapphires," I add, watching her every move. I'll need everything if I'm going to make a new life with Georgina. Everything worth selling one day.

The suitcase is brimming with expensive tastes and memories. Jewelry Edward bought me on holiday, dresses and heels I wore at anniversary dinners. Before he had finished courting me.

Sitting on the edge of my unmade bed, I am overwhelmed

by a deluge of memories. Edward's piercing eyes used to radiate love and passion, engulfing me in a cocoon of adoration. But now, all I can recall is his distant stare and cold touch. A fleeting moment of grief for what could have been passes through me before I am reminded of how much he had changed over the years. As I reflect on our relationship, I realize that not many people seem to be mourning his death—not even my own parents who had once pushed us together. It's as if they knew it was doomed from the start.

Edward's smiles became scarce pretty fast after the wedding, his laughter a distant echo in the corridors of our grand home. The passion that once ignited between us flickered out, leaving behind cold embers of routine and indifference. His eyes no longer lingered on me with longing; instead, they darted away, seeking refuge in some far-off place I could never reach.

I watched helplessly as the man I loved transformed into a stranger, his gestures devoid of tenderness, his words lacking the sweet melody of affection. The chasm between us grew wider with each passing day, filled with unspoken words and unshared emotions.

With each morning, the routine between us became a silent battleground. The way he used to kiss my forehead before leaving for work had been replaced by a perfunctory peck on the cheek, as if he couldn't wait to escape my presence. There was a time when his gaze held warmth and familiarity, but now his eyes seemed to look right through me, focusing on some distant horizon that didn't include me.

One particular evening stands out in my memory. We were sitting at the dinner table, an ornate mahogany piece that Edward had insisted on, a symbol of his taste for extravagance. As I tried to make light conversation about our daughter's upcoming birthday, he merely grunted in response, absorbed in his phone. The air felt heavy with all the unspoken words lingering between us, suffocating me with their weight.

I reached out tentatively, my hand hovering over his, craving that connection we used to share. But he withdrew his hand abruptly, barely looking at me, and said: "You know, Charlotte, I regret the day I ever laid eyes on you. You're nothing but a burden to me now."

Edward sneered as his words were cutting through me like a scalpel. The cruelty in his tone sent a shiver down my spine, and I recoiled as if physically struck.

"Don't you have something better to do?" he went on. "Can't you get off my back for once?"

Tears welled up in my eyes, blurring my vision as I struggled to maintain my composure. The man sitting across from me was no longer the loving husband I once knew; he had morphed into a heartless stranger whose words were like venom poisoning whatever remained of our marriage.

In that moment, the realization hit me like a physical blow— our relationship had irreparably shattered, leaving behind only sharp shards of resentment and betrayal. Edward's coldness and disdain marked the death knell of what we once had, leaving me with a hollow ache in my chest and a profound sense of loneliness.

As I sat there, staring at him with a mixture of disbelief and feeling betrayed, a sudden resolve ignited within me. I couldn't continue living in this sham marriage. Despite the fear and uncertainty that gnawed at my insides, I knew I had to break free from this toxic bond that shackled me to a man who no longer saw me as anything more than an inconvenience.

In the silence of our extravagant mansion, I found myself straining to hold on to the fragments of our shattered connection, grasping at memories like fragile glass about to shatter. Edward's once gentle touch now felt foreign, his embraces empty of the passion that once consumed us. His absence in our shared moments screamed louder than any spoken words ever could.

I made countless efforts to rekindle the passion that had faded away, hoping desperately to see a glimmer of familiarity in his eyes, a hint that a trace of our past connection still existed. I tried to remind him of our shared memories by revisiting old places, sharing nostalgic stories, and playing our favorite songs, all in the hope of reigniting that lost spark. But Edward remained a ghost in our own home, haunting the halls with his apathy and detachment.

Each night, as I lay alone in our cavernous bed, I could feel the weight of his silence pressing down on me, suffocating any hope of reconciliation. The opulence that surrounded us now felt like a punishment, trapping me in a prison of isolation and longing.

I wanted out of our marriage. I wanted it so bad. But divorce wasn't an option. Not in his world, and especially not in his family. The house became my golden cage that I could rarely escape, only when Edward was away. When he was home I took the role of the perfect wife, while my insides screamed for change, for freedom.

And now? Now, I relish the newfound freedom of choosing my own clothes, no longer confined to the tailored suits Edward used to pick out for me. The vibrant hues and daring patterns of my wardrobe now reflect the newfound independence I savor. I can be sexy, and enjoy the stares of men—and glares of their wives—if I want to. Each morning, as I select my outfit, a surge of empowerment washes over me, gone is the stifling control Edward once held over every aspect of my life.

Dinners are now a celebration of choice, no longer dictated by Edward's rigid preferences. I experiment with exotic flavors and decadent dishes, savoring each bite as a symbol of my liberation. The culinary world is now my oyster, and I indulge in the freedom to explore new tastes and textures, relishing the simple joy of selecting my own meals.

Brighter lipstick adorns my lips, a bold statement of self-expression that I once suppressed under Edward's critical gaze. The vivid shades now paint a picture of defiance and confidence, a visual declaration of my emancipation from his domineering influence. As I glide the rich crimson across my lips, I feel a surge of defiance and liberation, a silent rebellion against the muted tones he preferred.

I thought Darcey would understand, that she could be my helper, my ally, but it is clear to me now that she didn't believe anything I told her. I was wrong to trust her. I have to take matters into my own hands. For my sake, for Georgina's.

"Charlotte?"

I glance up to see Carla standing by the open suitcase, her hands paused over the neat folds of designer clothes. She's waiting for me to return to reality. To be the composed figure everyone expects.

"Is everything set?" I ask, clinging to the normalcy of the question.

"Almost done," she replies with a nod.

TWENTY-ONE

DARCEY

I slice through another carrot. The twins' laugh while they build towers of blocks just a few feet away. They're at that age when simple things are still magical. Chloe is in her bedroom, on her phone. I'm happy to have her here tonight. I have missed her.

I spent a busy day at the precinct, trying to gather any leads on the case, and dodging Jim's demand for updates, and especially his questions about Charlotte. My team updated me on the interviews they did with Edward's colleagues, and among them, I heard Bradley's name being mentioned as someone Edward had often used as a lawyer to handle certain deals for him. Jim suggested we look into Charlotte's old college friend Alice Zorn, a local TV personality. I told him I would do so tomorrow, then went and picked up the twins from school, and now I've decided to make a comforting homecooked dinner for us all to share.

Pretending like everything is normal.

The front door clicks and swings open. Bradley steps in. He's been at work. At least that's what he wants me to believe. His briefcase is still in his office, he doesn't know I saw it in there, and Charlotte hasn't texted me back on my last message. I wonder if they've been together. Of course I do.

"Hey," he says, and leans in for a peck on my cheek. It's swift, perfunctory—a husbandly duty checked off his list. "What's for dinner?"

"Pot roast," I reply without looking up from the carrots. The chef's knife slides through another one, the sound sharp against the cutting board. It's almost therapeutic, this repetitive motion, a tiny escape from the tension Bradley brings home with him like a cloud of expensive cologne.

"Sounds good," he says, though I hear the detachment in his voice. He doesn't care about pot roast or carrots; he's got something on his mind.

I nod, my fingers curling around the stem of a wine glass that's been waiting for me on the counter. "Yep, pot roast." The words are flat, tasteless as I say them, just like I imagine the dinner will be.

Bradley shrugs off his jacket. He moves toward the liquor cabinet, the clink of bottles echoing in the silence that stretches between us. He pours himself a drink—bourbon, neat—his back to me. The TV chatters in the background, white noise filling the space where conversation should be. My grip tightens on my own wine glass.

Breaking news, the anchor's voice cuts through, commanding attention. Edward Kane's name slices into the room, sharp as the knife still in my hand. I freeze, the carrot half chopped, forgotten. My heart trips over itself, stutters.

I set the wine glass down a little too hard, the sound loud in my ears. Tense isn't the word for what spreads through the air— it's electric, dangerous. I'm holding my breath without meaning to, waiting for whatever comes next, because deep down, I know this is just the beginning. Jim hadn't mentioned anything about a press conference. Has he moved forward with something because I haven't progressed the case? Are we asking for witnesses? Why wouldn't he tell me?

I wipe my hands on a dishtowel, heart drumming a warning. It can't be good, whatever it is. I just know it. The twins seem oblivious, caught up in their own games, toy cars crashing and imaginations pealing louder than any newscast.

But I go. One foot in front of the other, I force myself into the living room. The TV casts flickering shadows over Bradley's face, painting him with light and darkness. He doesn't look at me—his eyes are glued to the screen.

Just as I step in, the news anchor clears his throat, and there she is. Charlotte Kane fills the screen, her raven hair cascading around her like a curtain of midnight silk. She's always had a taste for the theatrical, but today she's outdone herself, cloaked in mourning like a queen of tragedy.

...the widow is ready to tell her story of what happened on the day her husband—the wealthy real estate mogul and heir to the billion-dollar Kane family fortune, Edward Kane—was brutally murdered in their own home, the anchor intones.

My wine-fueled buzz dissipates, replaced by a sobering clarity that's worse, so much worse. There's Charlotte, stoicism etched into every line of her designer-clad figure. Her clothes scream wealth—what is she doing?

I clutch at the back of the couch, knuckles bleaching white. *Breathe, Darcey, breathe.* But it's like there's no air left in the room, all sucked away by Charlotte's presence. The twins' screams as they fight over a toy car ebbs into the distance, and all that's left is her image, and the cold dread that settles in my chest like an unwelcome guest refusing to leave.

The interviewer leans forward, the epitome of empathy etched on his face. *Charlotte, can you walk us through the events of April seventh?* he asks, voice soft, coaxing.

She nods, the light catching the sheen of her tears—or are

they just glassy reflections? Her lips part and the story unfolds, a narrative I've heard in pieces but never from her.

I had to clear my head that day, Charlotte begins, her voice steady as if rehearsed. *I went for a drive along the coast. I was gone for a couple of hours. When I returned...* She hesitates, drawing in a sharp breath that seems to suck the oxygen right out of our living room.

Go on, the interviewer prompts gently.

Her gaze drops, lashes casting long shadows down her cheeks. *I found Edward in our home. In our bedroom.* A shiver travels up my spine as she speaks the words. *His body was... it was surrounded by a pool of blood. Bludgeoned to death.*

A tear escapes, trailing down Charlotte's porcelain skin, shining like a solitary diamond against her grief.

Bradley shifts on the couch, his breath hitching almost imperceptibly, but I'm too focused on that lone tear—is it real?

The room tilts slightly, and I grip the couch harder, trying to anchor myself to something real, something solid.

"Darcey, are you okay?" Bradley murmurs, but I barely hear him over the roaring in my ears. Charlotte's image blurs, then sharpens, a high-definition mockery of my unraveling composure.

Can you give us more details, Charlotte? The interviewer's voice is a lifeline, pulling me back from the edge of panic.

Every detail is etched into my mind, she answers, voice cracking as if on cue. *But it's the blood... so much blood.* Her eyes meet the camera, and it feels like she's looking straight at me, daring me to challenge her truth.

The glint of Charlotte's tear seems to mock me from the screen, a calculated drop that slides too perfectly down her cheek. I swallow hard, the acrid taste of suspicion coating my tongue. My fingers curl into fists as I fight the urge to shout at the polished mask she presents to the world.

Charlotte, you've expressed some dissatisfaction with the

police investigation, the interviewer probes, voice all honey and concern. *Is that correct?*

Yes, she responds, her tone a masterful blend of sorrow and indignation. She dabs delicately at her eyes with a tissue, as if mopping away any trace of deceit. *I feel that the detective assigned to my husband's case has been... less than professional.*

A muscle twitches in my jaw, and I can feel my controlled exterior starting to crack like thin ice underfoot. What the hell is she doing?

The detective seems distracted, Charlotte continues, and I can hear the venom disguised as velvet in her voice. *Almost hungover, each time we speak. It's as if she's more interested in accusing me rather than finding the actual perpetrator of this heinous crime.*

Bradley's gaze is fixed on the television, but I can feel the weight of his unspoken questions pressing against me.

Accusing you? The interviewer leans forward, feigning surprise for the camera.

Constantly, she affirms, nodding her head with measured grace. *It's like she's fixated on me as the villain in this tragic story.*

My heart hammers, a relentless drumbeat echoing Charlotte's every accusation. I want to scream, to tell the world of the deceit that clings to her like the designer clothes she wears. Yet I remain silent, my voice a prisoner of the turmoil churning within me. The room spins faster now, my grip on reality as tenuous as my grip on the couch.

I know who did it, Charlotte says on screen, her voice a smooth caress that hides thorns. My heart skips, then races—a trapped bird desperate to escape its cage. *But no one's listening to me.*

My stomach drops.

What is going on? In her expensive clothes, her lipstick, her diamonds, she's not coming across as sympathetic. She's giving away her own motive. Look at everything she's keeping all to herself because of her husband's death.

She's about to accuse Bradley of murder on TV.

And I'll be thrown off the case. She's letting the whole world know that I shouldn't have been working on it in the first place. If Bradley's affair gets out, our marriage is over, and not on my terms. I could lose the kids...

TWENTY-TWO

DARCEY

Most certainly they must have a reason. They're doing their job, right? Why—in your opinion—aren't they looking at the person you believe killed your husband? The interviewer leans forward, the picture of concerned curiosity.

Because of the detective who is on the case. Charlotte's words are like a noose, tightening with every syllable.

I can't move. Can't think. But Charlotte isn't done yet.

She had an affair with my husband.

The accusation hangs in the air, a specter that chills the warmth from the room. It's ludicrous, absurd. Yet the seed of doubt, once planted, is a persistent weed, threatening to choke the trust I've clung to. I had an affair with Edward?

Bradley says, "What the hell is this?"

"Turn it off," I say, looking to see if Chloe has come down the stairs. But it's a whisper that's more plea than command. And he doesn't listen. And Charlotte continues:

Of course, there's evidence, she says, her velvet tone smothering me. *Menthol cigarette butts found at my home.*

I can't seem to look away from the screen, where Charlotte

sits poised like a dark angel of vengeance, her red dress clinging to her.

Detective Darcey White smokes those. Her lip curls ever so slightly, the disdain unmistakable. *And let's not forget the pictures.*

My heart hammers, a frantic rhythm threatening to break free from my chest. Pictures? No, that's impossible.

"That's a lie!"

Of Detective White, Charlotte continues. The interviewer's eyebrows rise, mirroring my horror. *Naked.*

Can you tell us more about these pictures? the interviewer leans in, the hunger for scandal apparent.

Charlotte's gaze shifts, a shimmering tear clinging to her lashes. *They're... explicit. I found them on my husband's computer. And I can't bring it to light because Detective Darcey White is in charge of the investigation. The police ignore me because of her influence.*

Reality skews the edges of my vision. This is a nightmare—Charlotte's conjured illusion to cast shadows on my name, to taint my reputation. Has she even attempted to speak to the rest of the team? What the hell is she doing?

"Darcey?" Bradley speaks but I barely hear him. "What the hell is going on here?"

"Give me a minute," I manage to say, my voice distant, as if someone else speaks the words.

"You had an affair?"

"Please," I choke out, my plea barely audible over the roaring in my ears. "Not now."

He hesitates, then stops talking.

"She has to be bluffing," I tell myself, but it's like trying to steady a ship in a tempest.

There are no cigarettes, no video. These are the desperate machinations of a woman scorned, a widow cloaked in suspicion. It's all part of the games she plays.

I remain rooted to the spot, the plush carpet fibers beneath my feet feeling like quicksand. Charlotte's image stays on the screen, her composed mask slipping just enough to reveal a crackling fury underneath.

Look at me, she demands, her voice steel. *You must understand my frustration in this. All I want is justice for my husband, and they refuse to give it to me.*

Who's "they"? The interviewer's question is gentle, nudging, but Charlotte's reaction is a volcanic eruption of pent-up rage.

The police! she spits out, her composure breaking. *My husband lies cold at the morgue, and the detective in charge... She's a murderer!*

Her words hit me like a physical blow, doubling me over as if I've been punched in the gut. Bradley's shadow looms behind me, silent now, his presence hovering like a ghost. He's watching; we're both caught in her web, prey to her accusations.

"Charlotte," I hiss below her televised indictment. "What are you playing at?"

She's got the motive, means, opportunity—

"Stop," I plead, pressing a hand to my mouth. "Please, stop."

But she doesn't hear me, can't hear me. She's a woman on a mission, hurtling toward an uncertain endgame, dragging us all along for the ride. Bradley stands there, frozen.

Justice, Charlotte says again, the word a talisman against the injustice she feels. Her eyes flash with resolve.

"Justice," I echo, finding my footing at last. "That's all any of us want." But as Charlotte's segment ends and the screen fades to black, I'm left wondering whose version of justice will prevail.

Tears threaten, anger bubbling up like lava through the fissures of my fear. What am I going to do now?

TWENTY-THREE

CHARLOTTE

The screen flickers with my image, and I can't help but lean closer, inspecting myself. I look tired, worn out. Sometimes when I look at myself these days, I have a difficult time recognizing myself. But I know I've done the right thing.

My mother's voice, ever the critic, echoes in my head, probably bemoaning the neckline of my dress or the hem. But her voice is just a ghost tonight; I'm so close to getting away from it.

I savor the clip of me speaking, each word measured, potent. They're more than mere syllables; they're weapons, and I wield them with precision. I wrap my arms around myself, imagining their shock, the sweet disarray of their perfect little world.

I remember the exact moment I saw that photo of Darcey, hidden in a folder on Edward's computer, like it was yesterday. It wasn't, it was two years ago. I didn't know who she was, till she stood in front of me on the day my husband died, accusing me of murder. I couldn't get the image out of my mind for days. She was lying there, on a bed, naked. Her auburn hair splayed out like a fiery halo. The image burned into my mind, etching a searing betrayal that cut deeper than I could have imagined.

As I stood in our dimly lit study, the soft glow of the screen casting eerie shadows around me, I felt a surge of conflicting emotions. Anger warred with hurt, disbelief clashed with a sense of grim revelation. How long had Edward been deceiving me? How many other secrets lay buried beneath the façade of our marriage? For all his issues, I never imagined Edward cheating on me. He was obsessed with me, his perfect wife to control. That was all he wanted, not sex or intimacy, not romance or love. So what was he doing with Darcey?

My fingers trembled as I scrolled through the other pictures, each one a dagger aimed at my heart.

I wanted to look away, to erase the sight from my memory, but I couldn't tear my eyes from the screen. Each pixel etched a deeper wound in my already shattered heart. How many times had he looked at this photo? How many lies had he spun to keep this hidden from me? How many others had there been? Was this why he never wanted me, why he was never affectionate with me?

A wave of anger surged through me, mingling with the crushing sense of disbelief. My hands trembled as I reached for the mouse, closing the folder with a shaky click. The silence in the room was deafening, broken only by the sound of my own ragged breaths.

Darcey. A name that now carried a weight I never knew it could bear. Back then I decided to not confront Edward about it, as I knew it might come in handy later on. I knew we were over, that I wanted out. I began planning my escape from our marriage and the chains of my childhood. Seeing these pictures made me crave freedom like never before. I hated Darcey, for the longest time. During every interview at the police station about the murder of my husband, I watched her. She seemed unbothered by the death of her lover. Had it been a one-time thing? Had he tried to control her too?

I didn't know if I could trust her. Was she on my side or against me? But then I found the cigarette butt outside. She had something to do with Edward's death. She was my way out. Now I must wait to see if my accusations save me.

I reach for the remote, my fingers grazing the cool plastic. I press the power button. The screen goes dark, my reflected grin the last thing to fade. Goodbye, Charlotte-on-the-TV.

I imagine Darcey watching me on the screen with her expressive green eyes narrowing and disbelief etched across her face. It's almost satisfying, this moment before the inevitable confrontation, knowing that I am the storm she never saw coming. She never fully trusted me. In a moment of vulnerability, I find myself feeling sorry for her.

Did I betray her?

Was it wrong of me?

My fingers glide effortlessly over the keyboard as I open my laptop with a quick flick of my wrist. With ease, I locate the file containing the evidence—a digital Pandora's box of sorts, hidden among mundane documents. There it is: the picture that proves what Darcey did to me, that I was in fact right to do what I did. I stare at it, anger boiling within me.

A knock on the door startles me out of my thoughts.

Carla enters. "Do you want me to grab your bags?" she asks.

"Yes, please," I reply.

I push aside my laptop, leaving it open and forgotten while Carla gathers my belongings. She is always so efficient, a stable presence in my unpredictable life.

My gaze sweeps over the luggage neatly arrayed by the front door—each case a sleek shell encapsulating fragments of my life. I can't help but admire my own packing skills; everything I need is there, nothing more. There's an art to leaving things behind, knowing what to take and what to let go.

"Be careful with the Louis Vuitton suitcase," I caution, lifting the champagne to my lips. The bubbles caress my throat, a liquid lullaby soothing the thrum of anticipation beneath my skin.

"Understood," Carla responds.

As the sound of wheels rolling against polished wood reaches my ears, I take a moment—a luxurious, self-indulgent moment—to look around the expansive room. This place, a gilded cage of memories and pretenses, will soon be another ghost in my past. And ghosts, as I've learned, are best left undisturbed.

"Will that be all, Miss Kane?" Carla's inquiry tethers me back from the edge of reverie.

"Yes, thank you," I affirm, setting down the empty flute with finality. "Let's go."

Stepping into the dimly lit wine closet, my hand reaches for the switch but hesitates—a part of me prefers the shadows. They're fitting, somehow, an appropriate shroud for the deed that's about to bind itself to me forever. I let out a breath I didn't realize I was holding and push past rows of dusty bottles until I'm standing before the mahogany shelf where it lies.

I see the meat mallet, just where I left it. Its metal surface is stained with a dark red hue, an eerie reminder of what transpired that day. As I reach out to touch it, my fingers tremble and I feel its weight bearing down on me. Is it the burden of consequences or the weight of guilt? Perhaps both. As I pick it up carefully, a chill runs through my body, unconnected to the temperature of the wine cellar. This object holds so much power over me, as it is not just a mere tool but also a key piece of evidence against me. It has my fingerprints on it. That's why I hid it away, knowing that if the police ever found it, it could be used to accuse me of murder. It's a constant worry in the back of my mind whenever Darcey mentions wanting to find new evidence for Edward's death. The thought makes me wonder if she knows this is here, and that's why she wanted it. Did she play me all along?

Well, who's playing who now?

Wrapping the meat mallet in a plastic bag, I make sure

every inch is covered; no sense in leaving traces, not now when I'm so close to being free. The plastic crinkles under my touch in the thick silence.

The Valentino duffel waits by the door, its gaping maw ready to swallow this last piece of my old life. I slide the wrapped mallet inside, tucking it between a cashmere sweater and a pair of stiletto heels. A perfect disguise, really—softness hiding lethality. Zipping it up, I feel the fabric stretch over the irregular shape, concealing it from unsuspecting eyes.

I hoist the bag onto my shoulder, its weight grounding me. This is real. I'm doing this. Protecting what's mine by any means necessary.

And with that, I step out of the wine closet, leaving the lingering scent of aged grapes and forgotten celebrations behind me.

I hustle out the front door. The sky is still a sleepy blue-gray, the kind of quiet you can't trust. The chauffeur nods without a word and pops the trunk of the sleek black limo.

"Make it quick," I add, though I know he's already on top of his game. I slide into the backseat, the leather cool against my skin. My heart is racing, the thump-thump-thump louder than the click of the door closing behind me.

As we slowly drive away, I can't resist the urge to twist my body around and steal one last glance at the magnificent mansion. My heart aches with bittersweet memories of a few good times spent with Edward, moments tinged with both love and pain. I remember the night we returned from our honeymoon, full of bliss and hope for our future together. And then the night we brought home our precious baby girl, Georgina, and how her cries echoed through the halls of this very house. But among these fond recollections, there is also the memory of every moment Edward slammed the door in anger, forbidding me to leave while he was away at work. As the sun sets on this grand but treacherous building, a victorious smile tugs at my lips. Goodbye, you beautiful and tumultuous abode.

"Everything to your satisfaction, Mrs. Kane?" the chauffeur asks through the rearview mirror. His eyes meet mine for just a second, but they're enough to remind me of the stakes.

"Everything's perfect," I lie smoothly. I focus on the road ahead, letting the hum of the engine mix with my thoughts. In my mind, I'm already rehearsing every move, every counter-move.

"Good," he says, the word hanging between us as we drive toward a future that's uncertain, but unmistakably mine.

"We need to make a stop on our way to the airport hotel," I say, breaking the silence that eventually settles in the car.

"Where to, Mrs. Kane?" The chauffeur's voice is steady, unbothered by my detour from our planned route.

"My parents' place," I tell him. "We're picking up my daughter."

"Very well." His acknowledgment is crisp, formal, as if we're discussing the weather.

The city of St. Augustine whizzes past us, buildings blurring into indistinct shapes, but my world narrows down to the tiny figure who will soon be sitting beside me. My heart tightens at the thought, a knot of love and fear. The airport hotel looms on the horizon of my plans, an impersonal sanctuary where I'll hold my daughter close and whisper promises of safety into her hair.

Traffic hums outside, tires on asphalt playing the bassline to my racing thoughts. I draw in a deep breath, trying to steady the flutter of anticipation that threatens to become panic. It's not just about running any more; it's about shielding the one person who means more to me than my own life.

The sleek black car rolls to a gentle stop before the iron gates, their ornate swirls a silent testament to the opulence on the other side. My heart is a mix of anxious beats and steely resolve as the driver presses the button, summoning the entrance to life. With a slow creak, it parts, revealing the manicured lawns I know so well—the façade of familial perfection.

"Wait here," I instruct the chauffeur.

I slip out of the car, heels clicking against the cobblestone driveway. As I reach for the door to my childhood home, it swings open unexpectedly. Standing there with her nanny is my daughter, her hazel eyes wide and mirroring my own. "Mommy!" she cries out in delight, arms wrapping tightly around my neck as I lift her up. Her innocent presence comforts me more than any plan ever could.

"Are you ready for our little adventure, sweetheart?" I whisper into her hair, taking in the familiar scent of innocence and strawberry shampoo. Suddenly, my mother appears at the top of the grand staircase, her piercing gaze locking on to me.

"Well, well, look who's back," she sneers, eyeing me disapprovingly. "Charlotte, dear," Mother's voice drips with condescension as she descends the staircase, her designer heels clicking against the marble floor. Her gaze sweeps over me from head to toe, lingering on my figure-hugging black dress with thinly veiled distaste. "Still parading around in these... provocative outfits, I see. When will you learn to dress like a lady of your standing?"

I tighten my grip on my daughter, shielding her from the judgmental scrutiny of her grandmother. "Mother, please," I interject, trying to divert her attention. "I'm just here to pick up Georgina."

Mother's perfectly manicured nails tap impatiently against her diamond bracelet as she scoffs at my words. "You always were one for fleeting moments and irresponsibility. No wonder your life is in shambles." The venom in her words leaves a bitter taste in my mouth. I swallow the retort that threatens to spill out, reminding myself of the delicate balance I must maintain.

Taking a deep breath, I muster all the composure I can and meet her icy gaze head on. "If you'll excuse us, Mother, Georgina and I have plans," I say firmly, stepping toward the front door.

"You will never amount to anything, Charlotte, if you keep running from your problems."

As I walk away, my mother descends to the foot of the staircase.

"Is Grandma coming too?" Georgina asks and peers at me with a curiosity that tugs at my heartstrings.

"Not this time." I brush a kiss on her forehead, the weight of our solitude settling in. "Just you and me."

"Okay, Mommy." She trusts, unequivocally, and it's that trust I'll guard with every fiber of my being.

"Thank you for your help, Lucy," I say to the nanny. "We won't be needing your services any more."

"Yes, Ms. Kane."

We move toward the car, Georgina's hand clasped in mine, a lifeline in a sea of uncertainty. As we settle into the plush leather seats, her small body close to mine, the mansion recedes into the distance—a chapter closing, another beginning.

"Where are we going, Mommy?"

"Somewhere safe. Somewhere new." It's all I can promise her.

"Will there be ice cream?" Her innocent question pulls a laugh from my throat, a sound foreign yet welcome amid the chaos.

"Absolutely," I assure her, brushing a stray lock behind her ear. "And you, my love, get to pick the flavor."

Her giggle fills the space between us, weaving a thread of normalcy through the tapestry of our escape. And as the city looms closer, with each mile putting distance between us and the past, I feel it—the resurgence of hope, the strength that comes from being her protector, her guide.

"Chocolate chip," she declares with the conviction only a child can muster.

"Chocolate chip it is," I echo, a silent vow to move mountains if that's what it takes to see her smile.

The car speeds on, and with my daughter by my side, the road ahead doesn't seem quite so daunting. I allow myself this moment, a pause in the eye of the hurricane. My little girl, my world, clings to me. With her by my side, the path ahead seems laden with possibility rather than peril.

"Mommy loves you," I say, the words catching on a sob.

She stirs, nestling closer, and I feel it—the weight of love and the heft of responsibility. A tear escapes, tracing a warm path down my cheek. I just hope I've done the right thing.

TWENTY-FOUR

DARCEY

I can't believe it. My world has completely fallen apart.

I'm gasping for air, the kind you gulp after surfacing from too long underwater. My fingers claw into the fabric of the couch as if I might fall off the edge of the world. The screen is still glaring, the image it held seared into my retinas.

Chloe's beside me now, her young face etched with concern that's too heavy for sixteen. "Are you okay, Mom?" she asks, reaching out like she might steady a ship that's already capsizing. She must have come down the stairs. I didn't even hear her.

"No. No, I'm not," I manage to say, voice breaking over the words like waves against a crumbling cliff.

I whirl on Bradley, who's sitting there with this dumbstruck look, as if he's an innocent bystander and not the architect of my misery. "What was that?" I demand, my voice shaking with a cocktail of anger and disbelief.

He blinks, slow and deliberate. "What do you mean? How am I supposed to know?"

A muscle ticks in his jaw. He's always been able to keep his cool, but I see the mask crack, just a little. I'm onto him, and we both know it. Outside, the frenzy begins. The hum of engines, doors slamming, voices merging into an indistinct cacophony that heralds an invasion. I can almost feel the ground tremble beneath the siege of footsteps.

"Damn it." Bradley's head jerks toward the window, confirming my worst fears.

I rush over and peek through the blinds. A news reporter van buzzes outside, their cameras pointed at our home like weapons. Vulture-like, they circle, awaiting the carcass of our lives to feast upon. My stomach drops as I recognize a particularly tall man from outside of Edward Kane's house the day we found him murdered.

"Bradley!" I bark, needing him to be the partner he never truly was. "Do something!"

He stands there, momentarily frozen, before his survival instincts kick in. I stare at him, my heart sinking as his words hit me like a slap in the face. The man I once thought I loved stands before me, cold and calculating. His eyes, usually warm and inviting, now pierce through me with an icy resolve.

"Darcey," he starts, his tone firm and unyielding, "you need to leave. You're the reason all of this is happening. The press, the chaos... it's all because of you." Each syllable he speaks is a harsh reminder of how alone I truly am in this marriage.

"But Bradley," I stammer, my voice trembling with fear and disbelief, "this is my home. Our children—"

"They'll be taken care of," he interrupts, his voice devoid of any warmth or concern. "Chloe can stay here to help with them or I'll call my mother if necessary. You need to go, Darcey. Go to a hotel, disappear for a while. Let things cool down."

His callous words hang in the air, suffocating me with their finality. The man I thought I knew so well reveals himself to be a stranger, indifferent to my shattered world collapsing around me. As I stand there, paralyzed by his betrayal, a surge of anger and defiance rises within me.

"You can't just make me disappear," I challenge, desperation seeping into my voice. "This is my life too, Bradley. Our children need me."

"They'll have what they need," he retorts, his gaze unwavering. "But right now, you're a liability. The press will eat this up if you stay. You'll ruin everything we've built."

Everything we've built... the words echo hollowly in my mind. I want to argue with him, but he's right; I have no choice but to comply. I want him to ask me about the affair, ask me details, so I can deny it all, but he doesn't. Bradley's mask has slipped, and I can see Chloe's brow furrowing at him as she watches my normally quiet husband tell me what to do. As I turn to gather a few belongings, the once familiar rooms of our home now feel foreign, tainted by his deception. As I reach for my coat, a sudden clarity washes over me. This isn't just about protecting our children. Bradley is pushing me out because staying at home gives him the upper hand. He's enjoying Charlotte villainizing me. But what can I do? The twins are still playing on the rug in front of the fire, and Bradley's right that the reporter outside won't leave unless I do. More will arrive.

I meet his gaze, steeling myself against the torrent of emotions raging within me. "Fine," I say, my voice steady despite the tremors in my hands. "I'll go. But remember this, Bradley: I may be leaving now, but I won't rest until every lie you've woven unravels before you."

With those words hanging between us like an unbreakable vow, I grab my purse and stride toward the door, leaving behind the broken remnants of a life built on deceit.

Bradley's eyes follow me, a flicker of unease beneath the mask of composure he wears so effortlessly.

As I step out into the harsh glare of the waiting press, their cameras flashing like accusing eyes, a surge of defiance propels me forward. They bombard me with questions about my relationship with Edward, but I refuse to back down. I stand tall and firm, ready to face whatever comes my way.

They're still yelling as my Uber arrives, the cool leather of the seat offering calm to the searing turmoil within me. I have been drinking wine. I can't drive at this point, it wouldn't be smart. I get in and the press are knocking on the window.

"Just go, please," I say, looking down and not up at their many faces next to me.

The driver shoots me a curious glance in the rearview mirror, but I deflect his unspoken questions with a steely gaze. This is not the time for explanations or vulnerability; this is a battle for survival, a fight to reclaim the last fragments of my identity.

As the Uber comes to a stop in front of the hotel's grand entrance, I step out into the night, the chill in the air mirroring the cold reality of my situation. Inside the opulent lobby, with its plush furnishings and sparkling chandeliers, the hushed whispers of other guests mingle with the clinking of glasses from the nearby bar. I check in with a forced smile that masks the storm brewing beneath the surface.

Alone in the confines of my temporary sanctuary, I pace the room, each step a drumbeat of defiance. The view from the window offers a glimpse of a city alive with its own stories, its inhabitants unaware of the battles fought behind closed doors.

As I settle onto the edge of the luxurious bed, exhaustion weighs heavily on me, both physical and emotional. The events of tonight have unraveled a thread of truth amidst the intricate web of lies that Bradley has woven around us. Charlotte's accusations shocked me. But the photo she claims to have found in Edward's belongings shocks me even more.

Is this true? It can't be. Can it?

With a surge of determination, I reach for my phone, the device that holds the key to unlocking the secrets Bradley so desperately wants to keep hidden.

As I scroll through the screenshots of messages exchanged between Bradley and Charlotte, that I sent from Charlotte's phone to mine, a sickening realization takes hold.

My fingers tremble as I type out a message to Charlotte. Each letter I press is a step further into the darkness that Bradley had led us all into, a darkness that now threatens to consume him.

Charlotte, it's Darcey I begin, my words measured and deliberate. *I need to see you. There's something you need to know.*

TWENTY-FIVE

DARCEY

The road blurs beneath my tires, each white line a dash in the letter I'm writing to Charlotte in my head—a letter full of accusations, questions, and curses. She hasn't answered my texts, so I have decided to go to her house. I picked up my car at the house along with some clothes. Bradley is at work and the kids in school. He had the decency to confirm that to me this morning, if nothing else.

My hands grip the steering wheel tighter with every thought of Charlotte and Bradley; their treachery has put me and my children in danger and the anger I feel is beginning to take hold. A tear escapes, hot against my cold cheek, but I wipe it away, furious with myself for showing even this small weakness.

Gravel crunches under my car as I pull up to the mansion that might as well be a damned fortress with its high walls and iron gates. I kill the engine, my breath coming fast and uneven. My adrenaline is pumping. I have to do this. My phone was ringing off the hook all evening and this morning with calls from Denton and Brittney, texts from Jim, and even Facebook messages from old school friends. They've heard what I've been accused of. I know I will have lost my job, though it's the last thing I'm worried about. All I can think about is making sure I get back inside my house and force Bradley out and away from my kids.

"Charlotte!" My voice is muffled by the heavy oak door that stands between us—or so I think. "Open up! We're not done here!"

I pound harder, the echo of my knocks a pathetic plea in the grand scheme of things. The door swings open abruptly, and there stands Carla, in her familiar maid's uniform.

"Miss. Kane is not here," she says, her face the picture of practiced neutrality.

"Where is she?" I demand, the words like poison on my tongue. I can feel the edges of my restraint fraying, ready to snap.

Carla shrugs, her expression unchanging. "She packed things and left. Last night. Didn't tell me where."

Left? Just like that? No smug smile, no gloating goodbye? Why would she need to leave if she's got everything she wanted?

"Let me see," I demand, pushing past Carla with a determination that borders on reckless. The polished floors of Charlotte's mansion echo under my unsteady steps as I storm up the grand staircase.

I reach the top of the stairs and head straight for her bedroom. My hands are trembling from the cold realization that this charade is unraveling faster than I anticipated.

The door to her closet—a room as large as my entire bedroom—is ajar. I push it open, stepping into the cavernous space that smells faintly of her perfume. A scent that used to make me gag, now it just fuels my anger. Racks upon racks of designer clothes line the walls, but there's something off. It's too... spacious. Too many gaps where dresses and coats should be. My heart sinks like a stone in water. Empty hangers dangle mockingly, swaying slightly as if waving goodbye.

"She is really gone," I whisper to no one. She left without a confrontation, without giving me the chance to explain.

Without Bradley?

What's going on?

I spin around, about to leave, when a flicker of light catches my eye. An open laptop sits on Charlotte's meticulously made bed, the screen glowing ominously in the dimly lit room. Something is shown on it. Put on display.

A photo of me.

My pulse hammers in my ears as I walk toward it, each step heavier than the last. It feels like walking toward the edge of a cliff, knowing full well the fall could kill you. But I can't stop, can't look away. The need to know, to see, to confront this head on, pushes me forward.

It's me on the screen. There's no mistaking the curve of my back, the color of my hair splayed across the pillow.

I can't breathe. My hands shake, my fingers brushing against the cold metal of the laptop as I draw closer. It's like watching a car wreck—horrifying, yet you can't tear your eyes away. There, on the screen, is the most private moment of my life turned into a spectacle for her amusement.

Panic claws at my chest, a wild animal desperate to escape its cage. This photo—I thought she was lying about it.

I snatch the laptop up, the device suddenly feeling like the embodiment of all my anger, all my pain. With a guttural cry, I hurl it against the wall. It crashes with a satisfying shatter, pieces flying, echoing my fractured world.

"Is this what you wanted?" I scream at the empty room, tears burning my eyes. "To see me break?"

But there's no answer, just the echo of my own voice, mocking me with its broken edges.

I storm out of the house, each step away from the wreckage

a step toward an uncertain future, my mind reeling with the implications of what I've just seen—and destroyed.

Rain. It pelts me like accusations from the heavens, each drop a question, a doubt, a betrayal. I'm running now, my feet slipping on the slick stairs that lead away from Charlotte's grand mansion.

The fabric of my blouse clings to my skin, rain soaked and heavy, as if trying to drag me down, to smother the fire inside me. But it can't. Nothing can. My breath comes out in ragged sobs, punctuating the storm's howl. The air is thick, tasting of salt and sorrow, filled with the scent of broken dreams.

"God, what have I done?" I choke out between gasps, my voice barely rising above the tumult. There's no answer, just the relentless drumming of water against earth, against flesh. It's cold, but not as cold as the realization that has iced its way into my very bones—my life as I know it is unraveling before my eyes.

I stumble, catching myself on a statue—a stone angel with sightless eyes that seem to pierce right through me. They see nothing, and yet, I feel exposed, vulnerable under its gaze. "I didn't mean for any of this," I whisper to it, to anyone who might be listening. The words are torn away by the wind, unheard, unheeded.

Finally, I reach the car, fumbling with the keys, hands shaking violently. I manage to yank the door open and practically throw myself inside, seeking refuge from the deluge. But there's no escape—not from the rain, not from the truth, not from myself.

For a moment, I just sit there, the sound of the rain beating down on the roof of the car like a thousand tiny fists. It's a cocoon of noise, drowning out everything else, even the chaos within. And yet, the silence inside me is deafening, terrifying.

"Keep it together," I mutter, but the words sound hollow, empty. Keep it together for whom? For the kids? For the job? For the mirage of a life that's been shattered by one damning photo?

Tears mix with rain, indistinguishable, both just as bitter. With trembling hands, I turn the key in the ignition, the engine sputtering to life beneath me. It's time to face whatever comes next, but God, I've never felt more alone.

The rain blurs the world beyond my windshield into a watercolor smear. My hands clutch the steering wheel, knuckles bone-white. Each sweep of the wipers feels like it's dragging across my raw nerves, clearing a view only to have it obscured again in seconds.

"You can do this," I tell myself, breath hitching as the image of me in that photo plays on a loop behind my eyes—my body on display, every detail now a weapon that could dismantle my life.

I can't shake the feeling of being watched, of being judged. The intimate moments I believed were private, now potential ammunition for Charlotte and Bradley. My stomach churns.

Suddenly, my phone vibrates against the console. The screen lights up, casting sharp shadows across the car's interior —the name "Jim" glaring back at me.

I breathe out, thumb swiping to answer as I press the phone to my ear, trying to steady my voice. "Detective White."

"Darcey," Jim's gravelly voice comes through, laced with a seriousness that sends shivers down my spine. "You need to be in my office tomorrow at eight a.m."

My pulse quickens, the city lights outside smearing further as my vision tunnels.

"We need to have a serious talk." He pauses, and I can almost hear the weight of his next words before he says them. "I received some photos, and some accusations have been made."

A coldness spreads through my body, seeping into my

bones. Is he questioning my integrity, my decisions, my entire career, the support he's given me for all these years?

"Jim—" I begin, but suddenly stop. What can I say? That it's not what it looks like? That I'm not who he thinks I am? The words die in my throat, strangled by the undeniable truth of what he's seen. "Please, you have to listen to my side of this. Jim, you know me better than that."

"Tomorrow, Darcey. Eight sharp." The line goes dead, leaving me with nothing but the sound of the storm and my ragged breathing.

"Get it together," I whisper to myself once more, but I have no idea what to do next.

The windshield wipers are frantic, trying to keep pace with my spiraling thoughts. How did Jim get those photos? How did Charlotte? Did she send them to Jim? To expose me? To ruin me? I grip the steering wheel tighter, as if I could strangle the truth from my own suspicions. There's a sick taste of betrayal on my tongue, metallic and sharp.

A stop light turns red, but it might as well be the flashing of emergency sirens, warning me of the disaster I'm careening toward. An affair is one thing—a career-ending scandal is quite another. I'm done. I'm ruined. The words echo in the hollow of my mind, a relentless gong signaling the end of everything I've built. I have a better motive to have killed Edward than either Charlotte or Bradley. I'm the scorned lover. Why else would my cigarette butts be hidden in the bushes of the Kanes' home? Jim will have sent Denton to collect that evidence. Clara will testify that I turned up this morning to destroy the computer with my photo on it.

"Damn you, Charlotte," I whisper, as the light turns green. I press the gas pedal, propelling myself forward, not just toward the hotel, but toward an abyss I can't seem to avoid. The photos, those damning pieces of digital poison, they're out there now— my downfall wrapped in pixels and data.

Chloe, the twins... Their faces flash before me, innocent casualties in a war they didn't even know was being waged. What will they think of their mother, the detective, the protector, now shown to be fallible, human... corrupted? Bradley can use this against me in court. Even if I don't go to prison. His wife has been accused of murder. I'm a mess. How can I raise children? What kind of influence will I have on them? They're better off with him. The stable father, the esteemed lawyer with the highly respected family name.

"Please, let this be some sick joke," I pray to no one in particular, because I can't afford to lose them—not to this, not to anything. But in the pit of my stomach, where fear and dread have made their home, I know hope is as fleeting as the shadows fleeing from my headlights.

I return to my dimly lit hotel room, the weight of my problems pressing down on me like a suffocating blanket. The soft glow of the lamp offers little solace as I slump onto the edge of the bed, my weary eyes fixated on the half-empty bottle of wine resting on the nightstand.

With trembling hands, I reach for the cool glass, the crimson liquid within calling out to me like a siren's song. It promises temporary relief, a fleeting escape. As the bitter taste dances on my tongue, I feel a familiar numbness wash over me, dulling the sharp edges of reality.

The room spins slightly as I take another gulp, each swallow drowning out the relentless chatter in my mind. The wine offers a temporary reprieve from the ache that festers in my chest, the ache of betrayal and uncertainty that lingers like a stubborn shadow. I close my eyes, letting the alcohol's warmth seep into my veins, dulling the sharpness of my thoughts.

TWENTY-SIX

DARCEY

The moment I step into the precinct the following morning, my heart's a jackrabbit in a snare—wild, erratic. I'm here but not present, my mind a cyclone of what-ifs that could fill an ocean with worry. The air is thick with the scent of cheap disinfectant and stale coffee, a smell that normally brings me back to reality.

Not today.

Turning left past the front desk, I make a beeline for the coffee machine, its familiar hum a weird comfort. My hand trembles as I press the button, the machine wheezing like it's on its last legs, struggling to spit out the dark liquid that's supposed to pass for coffee. It's hot, at least. I wrap my fingers around the paper cup, let the warmth seep into my skin, anything to distract from the gnawing in my belly.

"White! Get in here now."

The voice booms from Jim's open door, jolting me out of my caffeinated reverie. A pit forms in my stomach, the kind that lets you know nothing good waits on the other side of that threshold. I take one long sip, hoping the heat will thaw the ice creeping up my spine.

You can do this. It's a mantra, a plea.

I weave through rows of cluttered desks, where detectives pore over endless stacks of paperwork or stare intently at their computer screens. Some of them glance up momentarily, but quickly return to their work. They are consumed by their own cases, their own struggles. I envy their single-mindedness.

I notice two of my colleagues, Denton and Durrant, huddled together in a corner whispering. As soon as they see me, Denton makes brief eye contact before quickly averting his gaze. I don't have time to dwell on it as I continue toward my destination—Jim's office.

Come on. He's waiting. I scold myself, the irony of my own impatience not lost on me. But my feet drag, like they're suddenly made of lead. Maybe they know something I don't.

"White, now!" There's an edge in Jim's tone that halts my dallying. I toss the half-empty coffee cup into the nearest trash bin and square my shoulders. My ponytail feels tight, auburn hair pulled back, no strand out of place.

"Jim." I step inside his office, mustering every ounce of professionalism I have left. The door swings shut behind me with a click that echoes too loudly in the small space.

Jim's eyes hold mine, steady and searching. His face is all hard lines, etched with concern or suspicion—I can't tell. With Jim, it's never easy to read between the creases. He's known me for more than ten years. He has always been there for me, protected me when needed. He believed in me when no one else did. And I have always vindicated his trust in me.

Until now.

The room shrinks. Jim's office, once a sanctuary of order in a world of chaos, is now a cell. I feel the walls closing in. He runs a hand down his face, the stubble there making a sound like distant thunder. "I might as well say it right here and now," he begins, and something in his tone makes my heart plummet. "You're suspended."

"Suspended?" The word is a gasp, a cold slap to my already

pale cheeks. "But why? Because someone said some lies about me on TV?" My voice rises in pitch, the panic that's been simmering beneath the surface boiling over.

Jim's eyes don't waver from mine, but I see something shift behind them—a flicker of regret, perhaps. "We're treating you and Bradley as suspects. Given your affair you both have a motive for the murder of Edward Kane. So please don't leave town, any of you. You will be called in soon."

The room spins, the walls closing in. Suspended. Suspect. The titles brand themselves into my brain, hot and searing. I'm a detective, for God's sake. A seeker of truth. And now the truth has turned its back on me, leaving me alone in the dark with my fear circling like a hungry shark.

"Come on, Jim," I plead, my voice barely above a whisper. "Me having an affair with Edward Kane? That's nonsense. And killing him? You must know I had nothing to do with it." My hands are clasped tight and my knuckles blanch, the blood driven away by the force of my desperation. "I can't be what you're making me out to be."

He shifts in his chair, the leather creaking under his weight like a cry for help that mirrors my own. "Darcey," he starts, and there's a heavy sigh that follows—a weary sound from a man who's seen too much. "It's out of my hands now. If only we had found that murder weapon, we probably wouldn't be having this conversation. But we have nothing, no evidence so far."

My eyes search his, looking for some sliver of doubt, something to tell me he doesn't believe I'm capable of murder. But all I see is the reflection of a seasoned detective bound by the rules he lives by.

My words are coming out at a frantic pace, each one laced with panic. "I agree with you. You need to look closer at Bradley. He's the real suspect here, not me." The room seems to be getting colder and the air thinner, almost as if reality is slipping away from me. "I can prove it too—Charlotte has a phone with thousands of text messages between her and Bradley, and they met up at the yacht club just a few days ago. They had an affair. He has the best motive. You have to believe me, Jim."

Jim leans forward, elbows resting on his desk, his fingers steepled as if in prayer—or maybe it's just contemplation. "I told you, Darcey. This investigation... it's bigger than any one of us now. You know how this works."

The words hang between us, a verdict I can't accept. "But I can't leave town?" My question is rhetorical; I already know the answer.

"No, you can't," he confirms, his voice steady like the hand of a good cop reaching for his gun—calm, assured, inevitable.

"I need to make sure you understand that you and Bradley are both suspects in the murder of Edward Kane. Until we clear this up, you need to stay put. We will call you in soon for further questioning."

"Further questioning," I repeat, tasting the bitter flavor of those words. It's funny how life can pivot on such small phrases, how a few syllables can upend everything you thought you knew about your world.

"Understood?"

"Understood."

I reach into my holster, fingers brushing against the cool metal of my gun, a weight I've grown accustomed to over the years. It feels alien now, like it knows it doesn't belong to me any more. My badge, once a symbol of honor and a beacon of justice, is just a piece of tin on trembling hands.

"Here," I say, placing them on the desk with a clatter that seems to echo off the walls.

The walk back through the bullpen is longer than I remember. Heads turn, whispers cut through the air, sharp as knives. Every pair of eyes feels like an accusation, burning into me with silent questions and loud judgments. I can hear their thoughts, or at least I imagine I can: the dedicated detective, now a possible murderer, and most definitely an adulteress. How quickly tides turn.

My cheeks flame with shame, yet I force one foot in front of the other. I'm a spectacle, the center of their curiosity, stripped of my shield, stripped of my dignity. They don't know the truth, yet their stares carve out my guilt, shape it into something tangible, something heavy that I carry with me as I push through the glass doors.

"This isn't me," I mutter under my breath, trying to stitch together the remnants of my pride. But the needle's too blunt, the thread too frayed. It's no use.

The sun blazes down, unforgiving, as I step outside the police station. How do I clear my name? Where do I even start? The photo... God, that damn photo. My intuition, usually sharp as a scalpel, feels blunted by panic.

"You can do this," I whisper to myself, voice barely audible above the bustle of St. Augustine's streets. I slide sunglasses over my eyes, not just to shield them from the glare but to hide their fear. A detective's eyes should never show fear. My ponytail, once tight and orderly, now feels like a noose at the nape of my neck.

I start walking, the concrete beneath my feet suddenly unfamiliar territory. I'm no longer Detective White; I'm just Darcey, suspect, pariah. It dawns on me how much I relied on that title, how it was my armor against the world. Without it, I feel exposed, vulnerable.

A mother herding her children gives me a wide berth, her eyes skimming over me before she ushers her brood away. No doubt she recognizes me—the detective always around during school talks about safety, now reduced to whispers and wary glances. I can practically hear the murmur of gossip that will follow in my wake. Is that the woman from the news? Killed her lover, they say.

The further I get from the precinct, the heavier my steps become. Every fiber in my body screams to run, to chase down leads, to do something. But where would I go? Who would I trust? Bradley? Hardly. Charlotte? Even less. The truth is a splintered thing, and I'm without the tools to piece it together.

"Think, dammit," I tell myself, gripping the strap of my purse. "You've solved cases with less to go on."

But doubts swarm me like gnats. What if I can't prove my innocence? What then? The thought is suffocating. I can't breathe. Can't think. Not with the possibility of losing my kids, of being branded a murderer...

Focus on what you can control, I remind myself, trying to push back the rising tide of panic. *Clear your name. Find the truth.*

As I reach my car, parked in its usual spot, I lean against it for a moment, allowing myself a second of weakness. I feel every judgmental stare from the precinct, every whispered accusation—it's a cloak of lead upon my shoulders. The uncertainty of what lies ahead is a labyrinth with no clear exit.

Whatever it takes, I vow, my reflection in the car window hardening with resolve. I'll navigate this nightmare. I'll dig up every dirty secret, turn over every stone. Because I am Darcey White. And if there's one thing I know, it's how to uncover the truth.

I grab my phone and make a call to Brittney. I didn't see her when I walked in so it must be her day off. She was concerned about me after seeing Charlotte on the news and immediately texted me and asked if I was okay. I know I can trust her.

"Darcey, is everything all right? What happened?" Brittney asks with genuine concern in her voice.

"I'm still trying to figure that out myself," I reply. "I've just been suspended. I'll be okay, though."

"Are you sure? Do you need someone to talk to? What did Jim say?" She persists.

"I'll be fine, thanks for asking. But listen, can you do me a favor and let me know if there are any updates on the Kane case?" I ask. "If you hear of any leads or developments?"

"Of course," she reassures me. "Anything. You saved my life once and I owe you for that."

"Thanks, Brittney, I really appreciate it," I say gratefully before ending the call.

I slide into the driver's seat. Charlotte can try to hide, but I will find her, if it's the last thing I do.

TWENTY-SEVEN

CHARLOTTE

As I confidently stride into the lavish hotel lobby, my eyes are immediately drawn to the sparkling crystal chandeliers hanging from the high ceiling. I left Georgina with a close friend from her school and hope she's going to be okay. For a second I worry she won't and want to turn around and go back.

But I can't. It's too late now. I have to do this.

The well-dressed staff scurry around, attending to the needs of the guests. Men in sharp suits and women in elegant dresses mingle, their voices blending with the soft jazz music playing in the background. The bustling lobby is filled with a mix of busy business people and relaxed vacationers, creating a lively yet sophisticated atmosphere.

The bar beckons, a stretch of polished wood and low lights, the murmurs of its occupants a distant hum that grows louder with every step. I would normally perch on a barstool, crossing my legs, my fingers tracing the stem of an empty glass.

From the corner of my eye, I catch them—the stolen glances, the lingering looks. Men sit ensconced in their leather chairs, drinks momentarily forgotten, as they rake their gazes over me. Is it because they've just seen me on the news? Or is it the dress? I let the weight of their gaze settle over me, and try to relax. I've been here before; I know the drill. But tonight, I'm not looking to be anyone's conquest. Tonight, I have a purpose, a rendezvous with destiny—or at least, with Bradley. I have our usual hotel room key, and the elevator is over to the right. I take it and ride up to the eighth floor and find him there inside the room already.

He's exactly where I want him.

Bradley Cavendish.

His gaze locks onto mine.

"Charlotte," he greets me, warmth radiating from a smile that doesn't quite seem genuine. There's a sense of ritual in his approach, a dance we've silently agreed to—one full of secrets and unspoken truths. Neither of us is going to mention Edward. Or what I've just done to his wife. Nevertheless, he looks relieved. As if what I've done has lifted a weight from his shoulders.

"Bradley," I reply, the sound of his name threading through the air like silk. He stands before me now, the embodiment of tailored perfection.

He reaches for my hand, his touch light yet possessive. His lips brush my skin, leaving a whisper of a kiss on the back of my hand. "You look ravishing, as always."

"Flattery will get you everywhere," I quip, though the flutter in my chest is at odds with my cool exterior. It's a dangerous game we play, one that keeps me on edge—a thrill I can't seem to resist. The anger he had toward me when I last saw him at the club has dissipated. In his eyes, have I made it up to him with my accusations?

Even though he's shown me another side of him, in this lingering moment, as his fingers intertwine with mine, the rest of the world blurs at the edges. The hotel, the very air we breathe—feels charged with electricity. Despite everything, I can't help but flutter a little as I look into his eyes.

I allow myself a small smile, my gaze sweeping over Bradley's sharp suit, the one that seems to mold to his frame with a precision that hints at both expense and taste. "You clean up well despite the last few days' events," I say, ensuring my tone skirts the border of playful and indifferent.

"Only the best when I'm meeting you," he responds, his voice smooth like dark velvet, yet always tinged with something darker, something hidden beneath the surface.

A pause lingers between us. Is he going to mention Edward or am I? He leans in, his piercing blue eyes scanning me as though he's looking for a truth I'm not willing to give.

He's already ordered us two espresso martinis, which sit untouched on the coffee table in front of the bed. I take a sip, the sweet bitterness of coffee and vodka hitting my tongue in a familiar caress.

I know what he's thinking.

"Charlotte?" His voice swims through the haze, but it's like trying to reach me through water. "You okay?"

"Fine," I reply, though the word feels thick and clumsy in my mouth. My head swims, my grip on the stem of the martini glass not as steady as before. I try to smile.

"Your cheeks are flushed," Bradley observes, the concern in his tone skillfully threaded with a hint of something else—anticipation, perhaps? I wonder, does he think I did this all for him, so we could be together?

Did I?

I take another sip. We both sit down on stools by the room's decadent bar.

"Must be the heat," I manage to say, though the room suddenly feels cold, the earlier warmth leeched away by this unexpected dizziness. I want to shake it off, to regain the composure that's slipping from me like sand through fingers. I need to stay sharp, especially around him.

"Let's slow down on these," Bradley suggests, his hand

gently covering my martini glass, stilling the motion of me bringing the drink to my lips again. It's a tender gesture, but there's iron beneath his touch, control disguised as care.

"Right," I murmur, although everything inside me screams to push back, to reclaim the ground I'm losing. But the world tilts precariously, and for a moment, I wonder if this is part of his game—or if I'm simply succumbing to the potent mix of alcohol and the gravitational pull of Bradley Cavendish.

The room suddenly lurches, a carousel spinning off its axis. My hand slips, and the chill of freefall grips my stomach. It's happening too fast, the descent from poised to powerless.

"Charlotte!"

Bradley's arms are around me before I can even register the fall, his embrace solid, grounding. The warmth of his body is a stark contrast to the cold sweat breaking across my brow. His scent—crisp, like freshly laundered linen—fills my senses, a strange comfort amidst the vertigo.

"Easy now." His voice is a velvet whisper in my ear. "I've got you."

I blink up at him, my vision doubling then snapping back into focus. The barstool feels miles away, but his grip is unyielding. I hate this, the way my body betrays me, swaying like a reed in the wind when all I want is to stand tall and unshakable.

"Sorry," I force out, pride like a lump in my throat. "Drinks must be stronger than I thought."

"Nothing to apologize for." Bradley's blue eyes lock onto mine, searching, always searching.

"Shh," he soothes, as if he understands the jumbled thoughts tumbling through my mind. "I'm here."

The world tilts again, and I'm tipping with it, but Bradley's grip is iron, unyielding. "Bradley..." His name escapes my lips, a lifeline thrown into the swirling sea of my thoughts. There's longing in that single word, a plea tangled with the intoxicating fog clouding my mind.

His face swims into focus above me, his blue eyes now pools of concern. "Charlotte, stay with me."

I want to nod, to assure him that I'm still here, still fighting the dizziness that threatens to pull me under. But my head feels like it's packed with cotton wool, and my eyelids are heavy curtains refusing to stay open. Somewhere beneath the surface, I sense the danger, the precarious edge upon which we're balanced. But the fight drains out of me, seeping away until all that's left is the warmth of his embrace, a deceptive sanctuary.

"Let's get you to the bed," he murmurs, his voice a velvet command that carries me forward, even as my consciousness retreats.

He sweeps me up with ease, my head resting against his chest. The steady thump of his heartbeat becomes the last thing I cling to. We move together, a choreography perfected by his guiding hand, my body now just a weight leaning into his.

The mirror on the wall is capturing our entwined figures.

"Almost there," Bradley whispers, his breath warm on my forehead. And though I can no longer respond, I hear him, feel the promise—or is it a threat?—in his words.

"Charlotte," he says, my name a vow upon his lips. It's the last thing I hear before silence claims me.

TWENTY-EIGHT

DARCEY

I'm tapping my foot under the table, brushing the plush carpet of the restaurant. The entrance looms like a stage, and I'm the reluctant audience in this twisted play. Bradley thinks he's slick, but he's as transparent as the watered-down drinks they serve here. And Charlotte, well, she's about to make her grand entrance.

As if on cue, the doors swing open, spilling in the humid air from the Floridian evening outside. She glides in, a vision designed to captivate, and damn it, she does just that. There's a collective pause in the room, silverware clinking subsides, conversations stutter. Even I can't deny the way her black dress clings to every curve. Designer, no doubt. It's meant to look tasteful, expensive, but all I see is the intent behind it: to entice, to claim, to scream that she's here and she's not to be ignored.

I knew they'd be here.

This is why she accused me of murder. He's here because he thinks they're going to get their happy ever after.

Men crane their necks, and I catch the smirks, the appreciative nods. I guess everyone's an actor in Charlotte's audience. A part of me wants to laugh, to point out how utterly predictable this all is. But there's this gnawing feeling in my gut, like I've swallowed bitter pills with no water. This isn't just a woman making an entrance; this is Charlotte Kane, the other half of my husband's secret life, parading around as if she owns every inch of the place—and perhaps every man's gaze too. Memories of that day in the French café resurface, the day I saw her for the first time, kissing my husband, and I feel the anger and desire for revenge bubbling up inside me once again.

I clench the fork in my hand, metal biting into palm, and I force myself to set it down. Here I am, front row, watching the woman who thinks she can have anything—because maybe she can. But not for long. Not if I have any say in it.

Slutty isn't a word I use lightly. It's cheap, reductive. But as Charlotte sways past the tables, leaving a trail of whispers in her wake, I can't help but think it fits. Maybe it's the cut of this particular dress, or the way she tosses her hair, raven locks shimmering under the chandeliers. Or maybe it's just the fact that I know exactly what—or rather, who—she's here for. It doesn't matter that it's designer; it doesn't matter that every man in here is suddenly picturing her on his arm. To me, she's just another piece in a game that's gone on far too long.

I remind myself to stay calm.

So I sit, my eyes fixed, waiting for the moment when I can wipe that confident smirk off her face. For now, though, I watch and I wait. Because that's what predators do best, and tonight, I'm on the hunt.

Bradley has already been here. Ordering martinis up to the room.

Just watch and wait, I tell myself.

But my stomach churns with a cocktail of anger and disgust, thick and sour. It creeps up my throat, and I swallow hard to force it down.

How long does it take to drink a cocktail? Would a woman

like Charlotte drink it all in one go? Or would she savor it today?

Almost time. Against my chest, I feel the weight of the old gun that my late father gave to me. It's not just about catching them any more. It's personal. It's retribution for every quiet moment poisoned by doubt, for every forced smile at dinner parties while he paraded our sham marriage.

"Gotcha," I say under my breath, though they're still blissfully unaware. Soon, Bradley will know exactly what it means to cross Darcey White. And I can't wait to see his face.

I slip through the crowd. The stairs loom ahead, an ascent shrouded in shadows and uncertainty, but I don't hesitate. My hand grips the railing with purpose, my ponytail swinging like a pendulum keeping time with my swift steps. Up, up, two at a time—my legs burn, but I push through it.

"Steady," I whisper, my breaths short and sharp in the hush of the stairwell. "You've got this."

The eighth floor greets me with a dingy light and the hum of silence. I pause, listening for a clue, any sign of life behind these numbered doors. And there it is—a muffled giggle, the clumsy thud of a heel against the hallway carpet. I inch closer, my detective's senses tingling with every step.

Room 809. The gold numbers glint under the sallow light. There is a smear of red lipstick on the door outside.

Almost time. I plant myself firmly against the wall, just out of view. It's not over yet. Not by a long shot.

My breath is shallow, each inhale sharp as I press myself against the cool wall. My heart slams against my ribs—the countdown to confrontation. Every second stretches, taut as a wire ready to snap.

I slide a glance around the corner. The corridor's empty. Just me and the muffled sounds of betrayal seeping through the door of room 809. It's now or never.

"Bradley Cavendish and Charlotte Kane," I declare, the

weight of my gun behind every syllable as I ready it between my hands.

Should I leave Charlotte to have the man I married? Or protect her from the man I should never have loved?

TWENTY-NINE
CHARLOTTE

My eyelids flutter. I'm awake but not quite present, consciousness clawing its way through the fog that's settled over my mind. What happened? The room feels familiar. I strain to focus, to remember, but the details slither away. A heavy blanket presses down on me, and I fight against the suffocating weight.

Then there's movement—a shadow flitting across my peripheral vision.

"Bradley," I manage to say, my voice steadier than I feel. "What are you doing?"

He doesn't answer.

The room sways as I try to focus. Bradley's shadow looms over me.

He's watching me. Reveling in my silence, in my stillness.

"Really, Charlotte?" His tone drips with disdain, as if I've just spilled red wine on his pristine white rug.

My heart races, the thudding loud in my ears, a drumbeat to the chaos unfurling in this room that once felt safe. Bradley stands over me, the embodiment of control regained, sharp suited and sharply dangerous.

"Let's not play these silly games," he says, the false warmth of his public persona now peeled back to reveal the ice beneath. "I know what you did."

I'm about to retort, defiance still bristling despite the fear, but his hand moves too quickly—a swift motion that carries the weight of his authority, his dominance. The slap is a thunderclap, echoing off the walls, off the confines of my skull. Pain flares hot and bright across my cheek, radiating through my entire body.

I stumble backward, the world tilting, my legs betraying me. The bed halts my retreat, and I fall onto it, the soft duvet a stark contrast to the hard sting lingering on my face. My cheek burns, both from the physical assault and the humiliation that washes over me like a tide.

"Bradley," I manage to choke out, my voice sounding small, battered—everything he wants me to be. He looms closer, confidence restored, no doubt enjoying the sight of me diminished, disheveled. But even as tears threaten to blur my vision, my mind races, plotting, searching for another lifeline in the treacherous waters he's thrown me into.

My vision swims, the room's edges blurring into a watercolor of fear and confusion. Bradley's shadow looms over me, the chilling satisfaction in his eyes a clear signal that he relishes this power, this moment when he believes he has broken me. But something inside refuses to shatter, a stubborn ember of defiance that won't be snuffed out.

"Bradley," I rasp again, the name leaving my mouth like a curse. Before another word can claw its way out, before he can assert his next move in this twisted game, the solid thump of impact jolts us both.

The door—my supposed barrier from the world—buckles with ferocity, and the frame splinters as if it's made of matchsticks. Bradley whirls around, his shock mirrored on my own face. Time fractures, shards of moments hanging suspended in disbelief.

"Who the—" Bradley starts, but his words are cut short by the figure striding through the wreckage.

My pulse hammers in my ears. Darcey stands there, her green eyes scanning the room, calculating.

And I've never been so happy to see someone in my whole entire life.

"Darcey, this isn't—" Bradley starts, his charm a dull blade here, trying to mask his unease with innocence. "Come on, Darcey, you know I would never—"

"Shut it, Bradley." Her voice cuts him off, sharp, no trace of irony now. Each word is a dagger, and I can see the impact on his usually unflappable demeanor.

"Darcey, you've got it all wrong," he insists, desperation creeping into his tone. "I swear, I didn't mean for any of this to happen. You have to believe me."

My cheek throbs where his hand left its mark, but it's nothing compared to the whirlwind inside my head. My heart races, and I force myself to breathe.

"Didn't think I'd find out?" Darcey steps closer, her shadow falling over me.

"Find out what?" Bradley pleads, his eyes wide with feigned innocence. "Please, just hear me out. There's more to this than you think."

I sit up, ignoring the spinning room, fighting to keep focus. Bradley looks from me to Darcey, searching for an out that isn't there. He's slipping, and I can almost taste the shift in power.

"Shut it, Bradley." Darcey's voice cuts through the tense air, her eyes blazing with anger. I can practically feel the heat emanating from her as she steps closer to him.

He stutters, taken aback by her sudden change in tone. "What are you talking about?" he asks, trying to play dumb.

"Don't play innocent with me," she snaps back. "I know

about your affair that never ended when you promised it would, your lies, the way you've been treating me."

Bradley's face pales and he looks around nervously, searching for an escape route. But he knows there isn't one.

"And don't think I don't know about Edward," Darcey continues, her voice filled with venom. "You really thought you could hide that from me?"

Bradley's eyes widen in disbelief. "What are you talking about? Edward? That's ridiculous," he protests weakly.

"Oh please, spare me the act," she scoffs.

Bradley's charm starts to falter as he realizes he's been caught. He tries to reach out and touch Darcey's arm, but she pulls away.

"Don't touch me," she hisses, her fists clenched at her sides.

"But I love you, Darcey," Bradley pleads, desperation creeping into his voice. "Don't you see? I love us, our family. This thing with Charlotte... it's nothing. It's just... fun and games, you know? I know I said I ended things. I shouldn't have kept seeing her. I know I shouldn't. And I'm sorry. I truly honestly am. Darcey, look at me. Look into my eyes. Don't you see that it's you I love? You and you only? Remember that time we drove up to the cabin in the mountains? It was just you and me, with no distractions or worries. We sat by the fire and talked for hours, laughing until our stomachs hurt. And then we danced outside under the stars, holding each other close. That was one of the happiest moments of my life, because it was with you. We can get that back again. We can be like that. We just got a little lost along the way. Please, Darcey, don't let this mistake ruin everything we have. I love you more than anything in this world. Charlotte is just a moment's weakness. I can change. Don't give up on me."

Tears stream down his face as he pleads with her to forgive him and remember the good times they shared. "Please, look into my eyes and see that it's you I love, and always will."

"You love yourself and your own desires," Darcey retorts. "You never loved me."

The room feels like it's spinning as their argument intensifies. I struggle to stay focused on their words, my heart beating faster and faster.

Finally, Darcey takes a step back and looks at Bradley with disgust. "I'm done with you," she says firmly. "You can keep your apologies and your charm. They mean nothing to me any more."

Bradley's face crumples, the color draining from his features as he stares at Darcey in disbelief. His mouth opens and closes a few times, but no words come out.

"You don't know me," he spits back, trying to regain control of the situation. "You have no idea what you're talking about."

I watch as Darcey crosses her arms over her chest, her posture defiant. "Oh, I know exactly who you are, Bradley," she seethes. "A liar, a cheater, a manipulator."

Bradley's attempt at a smile falters, his eyes flitting around for an escape. He's trapped, caught in the web of his own lies.

"This is all a mistake," he tries, but it falls flat against Darcey's determined gaze. "Charlotte is the one, she's the one who wanted to meet today. I tried to cut her off, but she kept texting me, wanting to see me. She's the one who is to blame here. Not me."

His desperate denial echoes off the walls, falling flat against Darcey's unwavering gaze. She scoffs at his feeble attempt to shift the blame onto someone else.

"Oh please," she laughs bitterly, her eyes betraying a mix of sadness and anger. In that moment, it is obvious to me, that he realizes that he has lost her for good. There is no going back.

Darcey's eyes meet mine.

"Charlotte, you okay?"

"Better than he'll be," I say, my voice low but steady.

There it is—the briefest flicker of surprise in Bradley's eyes. Darcey smirks.

The room goes still, so quiet I could hear a pin drop. Or a heart shatter.

Darcey breaks the silence. "Bradley Cavendish, you're under arrest. For assault on Charlotte Kane." She takes a deep breath. Finally. She may never be able to prove how many times he has drugged her, but he can go down for this one. The video of him slipping powder into my drink downstairs sits safely on her phone. "And the murder of Edward Kane."

The words hang in the air, a sentence passed down like judgment day.

I'm certain the murder weapon, covered in Bradley's prints, will already be at the station by courier.

Bradley's face pales, the color draining as if someone pulled a plug.

I guess we just did.

THIRTY

CHARLOTTE

Twenty-four hours earlier

I swipe the screen of my phone, the soft glow casting a halo on the crisp white sheets of the hotel bed. My thumb hovers, then descends to confirm my check-in—two passengers on a long-haul flight. It's done. A new life awaits, one I've conjured from the ashes of the old, and it pulses with promise and peril. Nerves prickle under my skin, an electric current that dances with the thrill of escape.

Here's to fresh starts. I raise the flute of champagne room service had left beside a chilled bucket. The bubbles tickle my nose before I take a sip, the liquid gold carrying notes of affluence that linger on my tongue. For a moment, I bask in the decadence, allowing myself this small embrace of opulence that feels like a stolen treasure. The last remnants of my life with Edward before I start afresh. The money he lost, yes, but I have my own that he didn't know about. Put aside over the years, while planning my escape.

The glass chimes softly as I set it down, the sound a delicate reminder of the fragility of this moment. I draw in a breath, feeling the weight of the diamond bracelet on my wrist, a trinket that no longer binds me to a past rife with shadows and whispers. It's just Charlotte now, and her little girl—against the world, against the tide, against all odds. We won't have as much, but we'll be safe.

I reach for the platter of chocolate-covered strawberries, my hand trembling ever so slightly. I select one, its glossy surface dimpled with seeds, and bring it to my lips. The rich dark chocolate gives way to the burst of ripe juiciness within, an indulgence that paints my palate with the taste of a future too sweet to fathom. I close my eyes, allowing myself this one moment of pure savor, where fear and excitement meld into an intoxicating concoction of what lies ahead.

The soft rustle of sheets pulls me back from my reverie. She's stirring, the little one who dreams in innocence beside me. My heart clenches—a mother's instinct—as I set aside the luxury of berries and champagne to attend to her needs. In the semi-darkness, her cherubic face is a beacon of hope, the very essence of why every risk is worth taking.

"Shh, baby," I whisper as I pull up her blanket, tucking it gently around her small shoulders. My fingers brush a stray lock of hair from her forehead, and I marvel at how peaceful she looks amidst our chaos. Her eyelids flutter but do not open, and I exhale a silent prayer that she remains cocooned in her dreams for just a while longer. Because when she wakes, we'll step together into the unknown—a world I've promised will be ours, a sanctuary from the storms we've weathered.

For now, let her sleep, I think, watching her chest rise and fall with shallow breaths. Let her be spared the clutches of anxiety that gnaw at my insides. The weight of our impending journey presses against my ribcage. But I won't let it show, not to her. For her, I am the fortress, the unfaltering smile that assures all is well.

"Everything's going to be okay," I murmur more to myself

than to her. I stand vigil by her side for a moment longer, then inch away, careful not to disturb her slumber with each step I take back to my glass of liquid courage.

My gaze drifts to the room service cart. A half-eaten burger lies abandoned on the plate, ketchup smeared. I chuckle, picturing my daughter's determined bites before sleep claimed her.

"Looks like princess and the pea chose slumber over supper," I whisper to myself, shaking my head with an indulgent smile. It's just like her, diving into everything with gusto until something shinier—or in this case, sleepier—catches her eye.

I set the dome aside and push the cart toward the door just as a soft knock raps against the wood, swift and discreet. "Room service," a voice calls from the hallway, the words muffled but polite.

"Come in!" I call back, readying my wallet from the purse that lies like a confidant on the table.

The server—a young man whose name tag reads "Liam"—enters, his eyes grazing the floor. He wheels out the old cart, replacing it with another bottle of champagne that I ordered, replacing the empty one in the ice bucket. His movements are efficient.

"Thank you, Liam," I say as he finishes, handing him a generous tip that makes his eyes widen for just a second before he schools his features back to professional gratitude.

"Ma'am, you're too kind," he replies, sincerity touching his voice despite the formality.

"Consider it a token of appreciation," I tell him, my tone lighter than I feel. "Good service is hard to find these days."

"Much obliged." He nods, slipping the bill into his pocket. "Enjoy your evening," he adds, before disappearing behind the closing door.

As the latch clicks shut, the silence settles back in, wrapping around me like an expensive shawl. The generosity wasn't just for Liam's sake; it was a reminder to myself that I'm not yet the person I dread becoming. With every act of kindness, I stitch another patch over the frayed edges of my conscience, willing the good to outweigh the bad. I still believe in good in this world.

Escape is near. It tastes like a promise or a prelude to a confession. My mind wanders to Darcey. But there's no time for doubts now. *Only forward, now, only forward.*

I pull the printed photograph closer, the one I've been staring at for weeks now, yet it never fails to ignite that spark of anticipation within me. The house looks like a slice of paradise, all sun-bleached walls and turquoise shutters, framed by palms whispering promises of tranquility. I trace the outline of the veranda, picturing us there, my daughter laughing, her hair lightened by the sun, free from the shadows we're leaving behind.

New beginnings. I allow myself this dream, if only for a moment. This house represents more than just an escape; it's the tangible form of hope, a life raft. I imagine our mornings filled with salt air and evenings bathed in the warm glow of sunsets, our lives slowly stitching together in a new tapestry of brighter days.

The knock comes uninvited, sudden—a thunderclap in my serene daydream. My breath catches in my throat, heart pounding against my ribcage as if trying to escape. Who could it be? I haven't ordered anything else, and visitors, well, they aren't exactly on the agenda. Not when secrecy is your bedfellow.

"Get a grip," I scold myself under my breath, placing the photo down as if it's evidence that needs hiding. But the damage is done; that simple sound has unraveled me, turning champagne bubbles into a churning stomach. Whoever is on the other side of that door is an unknown variable, and I can't afford any more complications. My hand hovers over the doorknob, a cold sweat forming in the room's controlled climate.

Hesitation grips me for a moment—it's probably just the pillows I asked for earlier. I didn't think they'd come so late, but then again, time has slipped from my grasp today, melting into a pool of nervous anticipation about tomorrow's flight.

"Who is it?" My voice betrays a tremor that I despise, sounding less like the confident woman I project and more like the girl I once was, afraid of shadows and whispers.

"Hotel staff," comes the muffled reply from the other side of the door. Relief floods through me, and I chastise myself for the spike in adrenaline over something so mundane. Yet, as I reach for the door handle, the unease remains, coiling in my stomach like a serpent waiting to strike.

"Okay, Charlotte, just pillows. Nothing more." The mantra does little to assuage the tightness in my chest as I twist the lock and pull open the door.

The sight that greets me seizes my breath, and for a second, I feel the world tilt. Darcey stands there, her deep-set green eyes boring into mine with an intensity that feels like it could scorch the very air between us. Her auburn hair, usually tied back in a ponytail that speaks to her practicality, now frames her face in loose waves—a deceptive softness to her otherwise rigid demeanor.

"Darcey?" I stammer, my composure slipping. This isn't the encounter I've prepared for; this is a scenario I haven't dared to even imagine.

"Carla told me," she says. "After I made her understand it was a matter of life and death." She doesn't wait for an invitation, her presence commanding the space as certainly as if she owns it. And in a way, perhaps she does; Darcey possesses the kind of authority that seems to bend reality to her will, making me feel like an intruder in my own rented room. I sense a storm brewing behind those scrutinizing eyes. There's no trace of warmth, no flicker of camaraderie. Just the cold professionalism of someone used to getting straight to the point. Her lips part, about to speak, and I brace myself for my world to come crashing down. "We need to talk," she states, her voice steady, and the door swings shut with a click behind her, sealing us in together.

"Talk about what?" My heart's pounding out a rapid tempo against my ribs. The plush carpet beneath my feet might as well be quicksand, dragging me down into an abyss of uncertainty. I expect her to be angry, to lash out. But she doesn't seem upset at me.

"Charlotte... I... I have something to tell you."

Darcey's gaze locks onto mine, unyielding and sharp. Her presence fills the room, imposing and undeniable. She's always had this way of dominating a space, making it clear that she's not one to be trifled with.

I swallow hard, my throat suddenly dry. Surely, she's here about my segment on TV and the things I said. She's got to be mad about that. But there's something else. There's something hidden in the depths of those green eyes that hints at danger.

"Is it Bradley?" I hazard, though saying his name leaves a bitter taste on my tongue. The air between us crackles with tension, each second stretching out like a tightrope I'm unprepared to walk.

"Yes," she says. "It's about Bradley... and a lot more."

"What do you mean by 'a lot more'?"

"Charlotte... I'm..." she sighs and rubs her face briefly, then continues. "I'm his wife."

"You... you're what?"

"I'm Bradley's wife. I'm the one passing out on the couch when he sends you those pictures."

"What?" I gasp, my eyes widening in disbelief. "You're his wife?" I feel like the ground is shifting beneath me, the solid foundation of my beliefs cracking and crumbling.

She takes a deep breath and nods, her expression pained as she finally reveals the truth to me. My mind races, trying to process this information. How could I have been so oblivious? So naïve? My mind reels at the revelation, unable to fathom how I have been so blind all this time.

Images flash through my mind—of him, of her, of the two of them together. The many hours in the interview room, now taking on a new meaning. How could I have missed the signs? The clues were all there, staring me in the face. But I had been too caught up in my own feelings, too focused on saving myself, to see the truth. And now it is too late. The damage is done, irreversible and devastating.

As I look at her, the woman who has been nothing but a source of pain for me, I can't help but feel a deep sense of sadness and regret. And confusion. What does this mean? My mind swims with thoughts. Darcey's presence in my peaceful hotel room is like a storm cloud rolling in, dark and unpredictable.

THIRTY-ONE

DARCEY

"Darcey? I don't understand?"

Charlotte's voice, a soft lilt of concern, barely reaches me through the fog of my misery. I sense her moving, the muted rustle of fabric, and then she's beside me, close enough that I can feel the warmth radiating from her body. The bed dips under her weight as she sits down, mirroring my posture, our shoulders almost touching.

Charlotte's voice trembles with disbelief as she speaks. Her composure, usually unbreakable, is now visibly cracked. "Darcey," she manages to say through gritted teeth. "You just walk in here and drop this bomb on me? You've known all along that you're married to the man I've been seeing? How... how did you even know who I was?"

My head bows in shame as I respond, my voice barely above a whisper. "I saw you two together a year ago at a café downtown. I couldn't believe my eyes."

Charlotte's gasp echoes through the room as she processes this shocking revelation. "You did what?"

Her hands start to tremble, her hazel eyes narrowing at me with a mix of anger and fear. "You... knew? And you've been waiting all this time, watching and pretending? How could you do that?"

Her accusation is a sharp blade, and I feel the weight of guilt pressing down on me.

"It must have been... like torture to listen to me talk about him. Who... who does that? Why would you do that to yourself?"

Taking a deep breath, I steady myself and lock eyes with Charlotte. "Because I needed your help. I needed you to point your finger at Bradley," I explain, my words tinged with urgency. "And now that we're both aware of Bradley's deceit, we have a chance to bring him down together." The tension in the room is palpable as Charlotte processes my words, her jaw clenched in frustration. "I promise you I haven't been having an affair with Edward."

"What do you want from me?" she asks, her voice laced with defiance.

"I want your cooperation," I reply firmly. "I want us to work together to gather evidence against Bradley. We need to be one step ahead of him."

She wrinkles her forehead. "But why? It doesn't make any sense. You should be angry at me. You should want me behind bars. Why do you want Bradley accused of the murder of Edward?"

"Believe me part of me wanted you to go down for it as well."

"Wait... what do you mean 'go down for it'?"

My heart stumbles over its rhythm, a heavy thud against my ribcage. My hands fall away, revealing the wet tracks of tears on my cheeks. I look up at her, my vision blurred by the saline betrayal.

"I needed to stop him," I say, my voice breaking. "Before he did it to you too."

Charlotte's sigh is a ghost of sound, and she leans into me, her distress a mirror of my own. "You're making no sense here, Darcey," she says.

"God, Charlotte." My throat tightens, words strangled by the realization of the horror she's endured. "Did you not wonder why you got so incredibly drunk the other day when having lunch with Bradley? And why you couldn't remember anything the day after? I watched him slipping something into your drink when you went to the bathroom."

Charlotte's eyes widen in disbelief, her hand instinctively moving to her stomach as if to protect an unseen danger growing within. The realization dawns on her face, contorting it with horror and anger.

"Are you saying... he drugged me?"

Her voice quivers, the pieces of a twisted puzzle falling into place before her eyes. I nod solemnly, regret weighing heavy on my shoulders. "Yes, Charlotte. It's the only way he could have orchestrated everything so meticulously." The room feels suffocating as the truth hangs between us like a heavy fog. Charlotte's breath comes in short, ragged gasps as she processes the depth of Bradley's deception.

Her hands tremble as she covers her face, her voice muffled but fierce. A shuddering breath escapes her, and she looks away, vulnerability etched into the fine lines of her face. Her gaze turns back to me, piercing in its intensity. "He did it to you too? How did you find out what was going on, what Bradley was doing to you?"

I swallow hard, my throat a barren landscape. My eyes seek hers—seeking comfort in the abyss.

"One day I went on his computer," I begin, my voice a whisper of its usual strength. The memory claws at my insides, eager to escape. "I saw the photos."

Charlotte's hand flinches, as if touching a flame.

"Darcey..." Her voice is a warning wrapped in fear.

"There were hundreds of them," I continue, the words

tumbling from me like stones down a hillside. I can't stop them now, even if I wanted to. The image is seared into my brain—the moment of realization, the unveiling of a sinister truth. "That's when I realized it. After another night waking up and not remembering anything, I took a test at the police station, from the rape kit, and it came back positive for a well-known date rape drug. That's when I knew. He's been drugging me for years."

The room seems to close in around us, the walls witness to our confessions and secrets. We sit there, two souls haunted by the same specter, the silence between us filled with the echoes of a past too painful to bear alone.

Charlotte's grip is cold and firm as she seizes my hands in hers, a lifeline thrown across the chasm of our shared nightmare. Her voice, when it reaches me, has a tremor beneath the steely composure.

"Pictures like the ones Edward had?"

The question hangs heavy in the air, a grotesque shadow looming over the space between us. I nod, the admission wrenching from me as if each word is a physical blow.

"Yes," I manage to say, my voice barely audible above the hum of the hotel room's air conditioning. "This is how he controls women. When I am out like that he can do whatever he wants."

A single tear escapes, tracing a hot path down my cheek. The dam inside crumbles bit by bit, threatening to unleash a flood I've held back for too long. So many of them haunting my every waking moment.

"Charlotte..." My voice cracks, and I'm on the brink—a precipice overlooking an abyss I've been skirting since that first click, that first picture. Me in all kinds of positions. Him and me together. And meanwhile I remember nothing. Not a single second of it all.

Charlotte's next question is a soft blow, almost tender in its delivery. "And you were passed out?" Her eyes search mine, looking for the truth that she already knows. "In all these photos?"

A shiver runs through me, and I swallow hard. "Yes."

The word is a stone dropped into the still waters of my mind, rippling out to every corner of my being. It's stark, irrefutable—a confirmation of the helplessness that marked those nights.

The vulnerability of it constricts around my chest like a vise. The memories claw at the edges of my consciousness: the taste of wine turned bitter, the heavy curtain of sleep descending without warning. The morning afters, waking up with my head pounding and the world spinning, disconnected from my own body as if I'd been unplugged from myself and set down somewhere unfamiliar.

"Charlotte," I whisper again, and there's an apology in her name—apology for my ignorance, for my weakness, for not seeing sooner the horrors that lived in the shadows of my marriage. The tears threaten to come faster now, but I fight them, blinking rapidly. This is not the time for tears; this is the time for truths, ugly and raw as they may be.

Charlotte's gaze holds mine, steady and unflinching. "And when you woke up," she begins, her voice a low murmur that seems to curl around the edges of the room, "you thought you'd just drank too much, and was hungover." She pauses, her fingers brushing against the bruise on my arm—a reminder of nights I can't remember. "But that didn't explain the bruises."

I shift uncomfortably, the fabric of the blanket on top of the bed prickling against my skin.

"He told you," Charlotte continues, the haze in her eyes reflecting my own turmoil, "you were so drunk you'd fall, or hurt yourself somehow." She mimics the disdain, the scorn that Bradley would lace his words with, making me recoil inwardly. "He made you feel like you were a drunk and a slob," she says, her voice dipping into a whisper, "made you feel guilty and inadequate."

I nod, the memories surging like bile. "Exactly." My voice is hoarse, as if the words are scraping their way out. I glance down at our intertwined hands—hers elegant and poised, mine calloused and clenched. "It wasn't until I saw the photos I realized what was really going on." The sentence hangs between us, heavy with the weight of betrayal and loathing. The screen flickering in my mind's eye, playing scenes of a life I never consented to—of a body that was mine but not under my control.

"And those were the kinds of photos that Bradley sent Edward," she says, a light gasp escaping her lips. "That's what I saw. He sent them for 'fun', right?"

"Yes, that's what I figured happened. They're old friends from Harvard," I say.

The air in the room feels thick, charged with our shared pain and the electric current of revelations yet to come.

"Darcey?" Charlotte's touch is feather light on my arm, grounding me.

I blink away the wetness threatening to spill. "I got better at avoiding it," I say, more to myself than to her. "Not drinking the entire glass when he gave it to me." My laugh is bitter, humorless. "Pathetic, right? Playing these little games just to stay one step ahead of him."

Her grip on my arm tightens.

"He saw through it," I press on, my voice quivering like a plucked string. "Started making threats." A cold laugh escapes me, more bitter than anything. "About the kids, Charlotte. He said he'd take them from me if I ever tried to leave." The room feels smaller, closing in around us, heavy with the unspoken implications of Bradley's control. "And everyone knew what a drunk I was," I echo Bradley's lies with a scorn that feels like it's scorching my insides. "He comes from a long line of lawyers and judges. His name is well known. He could easily have won. You know how that world is."

Charlotte's eyes are fierce, a silent vow passing between us.

"I couldn't leave him," I confess, the weight of isolation heavy in my chest. "No one would believe me. My colleagues had seen me time after time showing up hungover. I had spoken to my doctor about it, admitting I thought I needed help. The doctor is also Bradley's family's doctor. He would throw me under the bus in an instant. I would lose. Because they knew what I was—or what he made me out to be."

"Darcey," Charlotte whispers, her voice cracking like thin ice beneath us. "They didn't know you."

I reach for a tissue, the paper thin and inadequate against the flood threatening to escape my eyes. Charlotte's gaze doesn't waver, her own pain reflected in the depths of those dark, knowing orbs. She takes a breath, as if bracing herself against a storm only she can sense.

Her face pales, her lips parting slightly as if to speak or scream—I can't tell which. But no sound comes out, just a silent scream that echoes through the room, reverberating off the stark hotel walls. I can see it in her eyes, the same betrayal, the same shattered trust that now lies in fragments at our feet.

A tear escapes, tracing a hot line down my cheek. It's not just sadness; it's rage, too—a burning, bitter fury that twists in my gut.

"I found those photos, as you know," Charlotte says. "And that was how I figured you were having an affair with my husband. Oh dear God, Darcey, what a nightmare you have been through. I can't... I can't believe it. And you say he did it to me too?"

"He tried to. That day at the yacht club. But I assume you started to talk about Edward and ask him questions about the murder, and I believe he got so angry he gave up waiting for you to pass out. Bradley," I say, the name like acid on my tongue,

"I... I can't... he took everything from me. My rights to decide what happens to my own body. I couldn't let him do it to you. I knew he wouldn't do it at first, not right away when he met you. He would wait, at least a year or so. First, he needed to gain your trust." My voice cracks, the mask of calm I've fought to maintain crumbling into dust. "I couldn't arrest him for it. Even if we have the pictures, he'll say I consented to it. That I was a part of it all. But I wasn't."

Charlotte reaches out, her fingers brushing mine—solidarity in touch. "We were blind," she whispers, "but now we see."

In her touch, there's a promise, an unspoken pact forged in the fires of our shared hell. We are more than what he made us, more than victims in his twisted games. And together, maybe, just maybe, we can rise from the ashes of what he destroyed.

My hands shake, the memory of seeing the pictures too raw, too vivid. It's one thing to suspect, another to confirm the darkest corners of your reality. Charlotte's eyes lock onto mine, her hand still a lifeline.

"Darcey?" Her voice pulls me back from the edge. "What did you do after you found out?"

I swallow hard, the words like shards of glass in my throat. "I... I shaped my plan," I murmur, the confession heavy with the weight of what I've done. Each syllable trembles, laced with fear and determination. "And when you came into Bradley's life, I knew I needed a way out. A way that made sure I got to keep my children."

Charlotte's grip tightens; she's trying to understand, to see the world through my shattered lens. "I understand. You needed to protect yourself," she says.

"Not just me." My eyes dart away, then back to her face, searching for judgment or absolution in those hazel depths. "To protect you, Charlotte. I knew he had started to see you because he no longer was able to do it to me. I didn't pass out anymore, so he couldn't do it." The words are bitter, tinged with poison.

"So he found someone else. I wanted—no, I needed—to stop him."

She nods, a slow, somber movement that acknowledges the gravity of our shared secret. Her presence is a silent vow of solidarity, her understanding a balm to the open wounds of my soul.

"Charlotte, I..." A sob catches in my throat, choking the rest of the sentence. I'm a detective; I should have been in control, should have seen it coming.

"Shh," she soothes, her voice a whisper against the cacophony of my thoughts. "I know. I know what you meant to do."

And in that moment, I realize we're reflections of each other —two women broken by the same man, bound by the desperation to reclaim our lives. We are survivors, warriors in a battle we never chose to fight.

My fingers tremble as they weave through the air, sketching the outline of my last-ditch plan. "And framing him for murder was the way to go." The words hang between us, heavy with the weight of unspoken fears and desperate hopes. "But it had to be airtight."

The silence in the room is thick, almost tangible, as if it's another presence sitting with us. My heart races, each beat echoing like a drum in my chest. She's the one who says it. The words I haven't been able to speak yet.

"So you murdered Edward."

The words hang in the air, sharp and accusatory. It's not a question but a statement, a fact presented for me to own up to. I lift my gaze slowly, finding Charlotte's eyes fixed on mine. They're filled with a mix of hope and horror, as if she wants this to be true yet dreads the confirmation.

I stare back. My breath hitches in my throat.

"Charlotte..." My voice trails off, unsure how to navigate through the minefield of truths and lies we've laid out between us. But it's all I have—the truth in its rawest form. Our eyes remain locked, both of us searching for something in the depths of the other's gaze. Is it absolution or understanding we seek? Or perhaps it's just the comfort of knowing we are not alone in this?

"Charlotte," I repeat, stronger this time. "Yes. I did kill him." The confession doesn't offer relief but plunges me deeper into this abyss. "I've been watching you, and I could see that Edward was controlling. Everything you told me about him that morning at the precinct, I'd already seen it for myself. When I saw you with my husband the first time, I looked you up and found a police report filed years ago. He had hit you, and you had a big bruise on your face. Yet somehow, he got you to retract the charges back then, but knowing these types of relationships, I knew it wasn't over, it hadn't stopped. He was still doing this, just getting better at hiding it, and so were you. It took me a long time to get the courage to do what I was planning on. That's why I was there, smoking outside of your house. You found my cigarette butts. Bradley was prepping Sunday dinner on Saturday night. He used the meat mallet. Wearing gloves, I put it in a bag and took it with me to your house the next day. I saw you leave, while smoking outside. I got in through the sliding doors in the back that weren't locked. I heard the water running and walked up to the bedroom. Edward was in the shower. When he walked out the bathroom door, I... I hit him from behind. I left the mallet there, with Bradley's fingerprints on it. It was easy for me to erase the surveillance footage as it is the same system as mine, and going on Edward's phone, using his face to open it, it was done in a matter of minutes in the app. I had thought of everything. It was all perfect. Till you ruined it."

The words fall flat between us, their echo bouncing off the walls of the hotel room, leaving a tinge of doubt like a bitter aftertaste. My admission should bring relief, a clearing of conscience, yet it hangs heavy, muddled with ambiguity. The silence that follows is deafening—a silent scream in a void of unspoken truths.

"I knew you had taken the mallet," I say, breaking the silence. "Because it was there on the carpet when I left. When I came back later that same day, when I was called to the scene, it was gone. It was nowhere to be seen. It could only have been you. At first I believed it was because you wanted to protect Bradley, because you thought he had done it. But then you accused him of murder, so that couldn't have been why you took it."

She nods with a deepfelt sigh. "When I came home and found Edward, I accidentally picked it up. I was in shock. I was scared. I feared it was Bradley who had murdered him, yes. And now my fingerprints were all over it too. If Bradley was arrested, I knew you'd come for me too, with my fingerprints being on it. You'd think we were in it together. I needed you to believe in his guilt without the mallet. And I knew I had to get rid of it, some-how. So I hid it. In my wine cellar, and prayed they wouldn't find it. They didn't."

"So where is it now?" I ask.

She swallows hard. "I brought it with me. It's in my bag. I was going to get rid of it in the Caymans, knowing no one would look there."

Charlotte's gaze pierces through me, searching for some-thing I'm not sure exists. Her eyes, those deep pools of hazel, reflect a myriad of questions, each one a splinter pushing deeper into the raw flesh of our reality. In this moment, stripped of all pretense, we are just two women tethered to a nightmare neither of us can wake up from.

Time stretches, thin and fragile, as her breath catches in a silent gasp, a mirror to the anxiety clawing at my chest. It's as if she's looking right through me, seeing past the detective, the wife, the mother—to the core of who I am, or perhaps who I used to be before the world turned upside down.

"Darcey," she finally whispers. Her hand reaches out, hesitating in mid-air before retreating, an aborted lifeline that leaves us both stranded. "We both know what we have to do next."

Our eyes meet. For a minute I am wondering if she means to turn me in, but I can tell in her eyes, that's not what she wants. I know in that instant exactly what she wants. It's what I want too.

"I have an idea how we're going to do it," I say. "But it involves you getting back in that hotel room with him. Do you think you can do that? Could you contact him and set up a meeting? He will go because he wants to regain control. Everything is such a mess right now; he will like to feel in control again. He will try and drug you, to get that control. Can you do that? Can you go there again? I promise I will be there before anything happens. Leave a mark on the door to your room, red lipstick. I will be there. I'm not going to let anything happen to you. Do you think you can do it?"

Our eyes lock again, a silent conversation flowing between us. Hidden beneath the surface lies a labyrinth of fear, guilt, and desperate understanding. We're both prisoners of the same war, fighting battles that leave scars too deep to ever truly heal. Charlotte shivers for a second and I can tell she's thinking about being there again, facing that again, risking everything. Then she looks at her sleeping daughter in the other bed, and nods.

"If that's what it takes, then I will."

We share that look once more while making up our minds, a shared secret suspended in the charged space of the hotel room.

THIRTY-TWO

DARCEY

Present Day

I push the door open. My shoulders slump as I take in the sight of Chloe, her back to me, humming softly while she rounds up the scattered toys in the living room. It's a simple melody that softens the chaos of the day—a lullaby of normalcy.

"Hey, sweetie," I say, my voice softer than I intend, revealing the weariness I can't seem to shake.

Chloe turns, and there's this flicker in her eyes—a mix of relief and something else, something deeper. Her smile is gentle, not quite reaching those eyes that mirror my own. "Mom, you're home."

"Finally," I exhale, and I mean it in more ways than one. "Are the twins asleep?"

"Yes, they went down for the count about half an hour ago. Took forever to get them to sleep."

"I'll kiss them in the morning, then."

I can still hear the loud voices and sense the adrenaline rushing through me from when backup arrived at the hotel last night and Charlotte and I told our story, the one we had agreed to. The mallet had arrived at the station with Bradley's finger-prints on it and Edward's blood. Charlotte's fingerprints would be on it too, but it was easily explained. She told Jim she picked it up when she found Edward. There is no other reason Bradley's prints would be there... unless he killed Edward.

The relief that Bradley is behind bars is a tangible weight lifted off my chest, an exhale after holding my breath for too long. I can still feel how my colleagues gathered around me earlier today, their sympathetic glances and gentle pats on the back giving me the strength to face the truth—not only did Bradley have an affair, but he lured me and Charlotte into his sickening trap. Together, we will rebuild and move forward from this dark chapter in our lives.

But now, looking at Chloe, it's like I'm seeing her for the first time since the whole ordeal began.

I walk over, feeling the creak of the floorboards underfoot, familiar groans of the old house matching the tightness in my limbs. I reach out, brushing a stray lock of hair from her face, and plant a kiss on her cheek, the gesture carrying all the gratitude and love that's been pent up inside me.

"Are you okay?" I ask, and it's more than just a question—it's an anchor, a plea for her to be untouched by the mess that's become our lives.

She nods, her lips pressed into a thin line, and I know there's so much unsaid, so many secrets that weigh heavy between us. But for now, for this stolen moment, we let the silence speak, both of us basking in the stillness that follows a storm.

"Really, Mom, I'm fine," Chloe insists, but her voice has the tremble of vulnerability, a violin string pulled too tight.

"Good, that's good." The words are automatic, but they come from a place raw and sincere. I want to shield her from everything—from the man who was supposed to protect us, from the horrors that lurk in dark corners, from the truth that sometimes the people closest to us are the ones capable of the deepest betrayal. "Did Nanna come?"

"No, it's just been me," she confirms, and I feel relieved. Bradley's mother must be at the precinct now.

"Let's talk for a minute, yeah?" I suggest, and there's this unspoken understanding that we're not just talking about work or school. There's more to it than that.

Stepping out onto the back patio, the warm air wraps around us. I haven't slept all night, but it doesn't matter. I can sleep when I'm old or dead, or however the saying goes.

Chloe slips onto the patio swing beside me, our shoulders brushing in silent camaraderie.

"Thanks for being here, Chloe," I breathe out the words. "For looking after your siblings."

Her fingers toy with the frayed edge of her shirt. "It's what family does, right?"

"Right." I nod, though I know "family" means different things to different people. To Bradley, it was a cover—a façade. To me, it's a ship trying to navigate through a tempest without capsizing.

The silence isn't uncomfortable. It's thick with understanding, with shared experiences that neither of us asked for. We sit there, two souls seeking solace in each other's company, while the sky watches over us—indifferent yet infinitely vast.

I tilt my head, studying Chloe's profile. The soft glow from the sunlight dances across her features, casting gentle shadows that somehow make her seem older, more world-weary. I smile at her, trying to infuse as much warmth into it as I can muster. It feels like a balm, or maybe it's just wishful thinking on my part, hoping to soothe the raw edges of our reality. Her eyes tear up, and she leans on my chest.

"Mom I can't believe what Bradley did to you."

Her sobs fill the silence of the night, raw and wrenching. I put my arms around her, cradling her like I did when she was small, whispering words meant to soothe, to heal.

"Shh, it's okay, baby. It's over now," I murmur against her hair.

She clings to me, her body racked with grief, but slowly, she begins to calm, her breathing evening out. I hold her tight, offering all the comfort I've got. Because that's what mothers do, isn't it? We protect our children, no matter the cost. Just as they will do for us, if need be.

Silence settles over us, punctuated by the distant sound of waves against the shore. I feel Chloe's gaze on me, searching, perhaps, for cracks in my armor. But in this moment, I am made of steel, of motherly love forged in the fires of betrayal and vengeance. And I will do what needs to be done. For her. For all of us.

Chloe's head rests against my shoulder, her breaths steady in the stillness of the backyard. My arm wraps around her, holding her close as we sit there on the back patio, two survivors of a storm that has finally passed. The tension that's been coiling inside me unravels little by little with each shared heartbeat.

"Mom?" Chloe murmurs, breaking the silence that has settled over us like a comforting blanket.

"Hmm?" I reply, the vibration of my voice felt more than heard.

"Bradley's locked away, and we're... we're okay now, right?"

"Right," I confirm, my response immediate and certain. "We are more than okay, Chloe. We are together, and we are strong."

She nods, leaning into the assurance my words provide. I can feel the shift within her, a subtle release of the fears that have clung to her like shadows. We look out into the yard, beyond the patio, where the outline of our future waits, ready for us to step into it, and shape it with our own hands. It's a

blank canvas, and for the first time, the thought doesn't scare me
—it excites me.

"I never liked him." She smiles and I can't help but laugh.
That's true. She never did warm to Bradley, and I make a note
to ask for her opinion more often. Not that I'll likely ever date
again. "What happened to Charlotte?" she finally asks.

I smile. "No idea."

I picture Charlotte, with her raven hair boarding a plane
somewhere, clutching her daughter's hand. She needs a new
life, after everything she's been through. I'm happy she got one.

And as the chapter of our lives marked by fear and control
closes, I know that we are stepping into a new day, one filled
with promise and the certainty that no matter what comes, we
face it together. With that thought warming my heart, I reach
for the cigarettes in my pocket, with the intent to pull one out. I
stare at the package, then scoff. I look at Chloe with a wry smile,
then crumple the package up into a ball and throw it at the trash
can in the corner. Then I stand, offering Chloe my hand to join
me. Together, we walk back into the house, ready to write the
next chapter of our lives.

A LETTER FROM WILLOW

Dear reader,

I want to say a huge thank you for choosing to read *My Husband's Mistress*. If you did enjoy it, and want to keep up to date with all my latest releases, just sign up at the following link. Your email address will never be shared and you can unsubscribe at any time.

www.bookouture.com/willow-rose

As some of you might already have guessed, this story was inspired by the case from France where a woman found out that her husband had drugged her and used her to make video tapes of her with other men for over ten years. The husband was recently convicted of orchestrating the assaults over the years and was given the maximum sentence of twenty years in prison, while his co-accused—forty-nine other men!—were given sentences ranging from three to fifteen years. It's a truly gruesome story, and if you haven't heard about it, then you can read more here:

https://www.bbc.com/news/articles/cd9dwxexp770

https://www.cbsnews.com/news/gisele-pelicot-france-husband-dozens-of-men-found-guilty-rape-trial/

I hope you loved *My Husband's Mistress* and if you did I would be very grateful if you could write a review. I'd love to hear what you think, and it makes such a difference helping new readers to discover one of my books for the first time.

I want to thank my editor, Jennifer Hunt, who encouraged me to write a psychological thriller for the first time. This was brand new territory for me, and I enjoyed writing this so much.

Take care,

Willow

https://www.willow-rose.net

facebook.com/willowredrose

x.com/madamwillowrose

instagram.com/willowroseauthor

bookbub.com/authors/willow-rose

PUBLISHING TEAM

Made in United States
Orlando, FL
12 April 2025

60425581R00152